THE CORRIGAN WOMEN

The Corrigan Women

M.T. DOHANEY

Cover illustration: "Old Lobster Buoys," C. McIntyre/Photolink.
Cover design by Julie Scriver.
Book design by Ryan Astle.
Printed in Canada by Transcontinental.
10 9 8 7 6 5 4 3 2 1

Library and Archives Canada Cataloguing in Publication

Dohaney, M. T.
The Corrigan women / M.T. Dohaney.

ISBN 0-86492-321-X

I. Title.
PS8557.O257C6 2004   C813'.54   C2004-903408-1

Published with the financial support of the Canada Council for the Arts,
the Government of Canada through the Book Publishing Industry Development
Program, and the New Brunswick Culture and Sports Secretariat.

Goose Lane Editions
469 King Street
Fredericton, New Brunswick
CANADA E3B 1E5
www.gooselane.com

In memory of Alan

I wish to thank everyone at Goose Lane Editions, individually and collectively, for bringing *The Corrigan Women* back into print. I am also grateful to my agent, Leona Trainer, for the untiring efforts that made this republication possible. Although *The Corrigan Women* has been virtually unavailable for many years, its loyal admirers have never wavered, and I am grateful to them for their faith.

Prologue

Millie Morrissey and Tessie Corrigan perched at the edge of the grave like two gulls on a rock: heads tucked in out of the cold, legs stiff and unsteady from the biting wind. Powder-fine snow snaked around the gravestones and funnelled into the tops of their boots. It even curled up their coat sleeves, numbing their wrists.

Millie had anchored her hat with a scarf of some slippery material that wouldn't stay tied, and she had to worry it constantly to keep it from coming loose. Once, when she had yanked the knot so tight her jowls bulged out, she cackled with satisfaction, "There now, be God. Any tighter and I'd hang meself fer sure." Her voice squeaked from the frost. "In all of me seventy-nine years, this is the coldest divil of a day I've ever witnessed."

The pallbearers huddled a few feet away, crouched over like praying monks, their parka hoods almost obscuring their faces. Like Millie, they too grumbled from time to time about the certainty of freezing to death if Father Duffy didn't soon make his appearance.

Millie's brother-in-law, Joe Patterson, straightened up and flogged his waist to keep his circulation going, grumbling it was about time for the priest to show up. "I'd have the *Titanic* unrigged by now, much less take off a few vestments." He squinted through the drifts towards the cemetery gate.

Millie whipped around on her perch so fast her scarf fell down around her neck. "Don't be fergettin', Joe Patterson," she snapped, "he had to clear the altar too. *And by hisself*." Each word was a reprimand for Joe's grandson, who had promised to serve the Mass and then never showed up. Her tone left no doubt that if there had been an altar boy in attendance, the graveside prayers would be over and done with by this time.

Sandy Tobin tried to smooth things over. Besides Tessie, Sandy was the only one who wasn't kith or kin to Millie, and it was his station wagon that had sidled up Dickson's Hill with the casket sticking out through the tailgate. "Won't do a bit of good to harangue over Father Duffy, Joe me boy," he said. "If he don't soon get here, he might jest as well stay wherever the hell he is because we'll all be frozen harder than sheep shit." He bobbed his head in the direction of the grave. "We'll be stiffer than Carm —" He abruptly bit off Carmel's name and then shot Tessie an embarrassed look, hoping the wind had muffled his words. The others coughed and shuffled their feet.

Millie interjected quickly. "We'll be stiffer than pokers. Bloody pokers. That's what we'll be." Even as she spoke she knew it wasn't enough, and she reached over and plucked at Tessie's arm.

"See that tree up there," she said, shouting above the wind. She pointed to an alder bush sticking out of a snowdrift. "Yer mother and me, we tore it out of Martin's grave last summer. It was as big as yer wrist, girl, and growing right in the middle."

Tessie pictured the two women tugging and pulling to break the bush loose from the centre of Martin, and her stomach lurched. To discourage Millie from continuing, Tessie pretended not to have heard and pulled her face further into her coat. But Millie wouldn't be put off so easily.

"See!" she persisted, nudging Tessie's arm again. "See!" She poked her with her elbow. "See!"

Tessie hauled her face out into the wind and forced herself

to look in the direction of Millie's pointed finger. But she aimed high, focussing well above the fence and snowdrifts.

"Not there! There!" Millie directed irritably. She took a couple of quick steps into the snow bank and clutched the trunk of the bush, raising it slightly out of the snow. "See how big it is! A real brute of a thing that would have took right over if we had let it." The wind kept sucking her breath away, and she had to strain to get the words out.

Tessie dropped her gaze, and her eyes riveted on the young alder tree upended in the snow, a few whiskers of root still clinging to its frozen stump. She stared as though mesmerized, her mind absorbing every detail, her eyes lingering on every root socket she imagined had locked itself into Martin. When she managed to wrench her gaze from the tree, she was able to look into the newly blasted hole beside her and at the grey box wedged in between the splintered rocks. She not only saw the casket, she saw *inside* the casket. She saw her mother's slight frame pressed gently against the pleated ivory satin. She saw the apple green suit, the good Sunday suit that was kept for special occasions. The skirt was faded several shades lighter than the jacket because it had been worn winter and summer, but the jacket had been reserved for summer Sundays when it was warm enough to go without a coat. She saw her mother's hands, folded one over the other, clasping a silver rosary. It was Millie's rosary. She had bought it to help pay for the Redemptorist Father's last mission in the Cove. Tessie could even feel the cold of the beads where they pressed against the soft flesh of her mother's fingers. She wished she had removed the rosary before the lid had been closed. And she wished she had restyled her mother's hair from the way Millie had done it. Carmel would not have wanted the white streak showing at her temple. At fifty-two, Carmel's hair was as richly red as it had been when she was a young girl. The white streak was Martin's doing.

Martin, Martin, went to bed fartin',
Got up stinkin', went away winkin'.

As Tessie's eyes lingered on her mother's casket, she recalled how the coarse ditty had been the cause of Carmel's white streak. She let the event of that long-ago day flit across her mind — an event that had been told to her by her grandmother as they sat beside the fire on winter nights or as they worked together airing out the parlour for summer visitors. Tessie looked from her mother's grave to Martin's and from Martin's to her grandmother's, although under the snow the latter two were no longer separate and could be distinguished only by the stone markers that leaned rakishly into the wind. Tessie's thoughts, like the snowdrifts, sorted themselves into piles.

"Frost heaves, girl," Millie offered, noticing the direction of Tessie's gaze. "They lurches up every spring on their own, but the divil the bit they'll go down on their own."

But Tessie hadn't even noticed the up-flung gravestones. She had been thinking about what Millie had said to her that morning — that the Corrigan family had always been a short-tailed one, and now it had withered down to her. And she had been thinking about those others who, either in life or in death, had pulled and tugged at her very being as Millie and her mother had pulled and tugged at the alder bush. There was Ed Strominski, a man in a photograph. There was Ned Corrigan, a grandfather buried in uncon-secrated ground, his unmarked grave nudged up against the cemetery fence in an exile of his own making. And there was Carmel, the woman who had been less mother than summer visitor, and Bertha, who had been more mother than grandmother. And there was Sister Jerome and Dennis Walsh and . . .

A shout from one of the pallbearers broke her reverie.

"Be God, he's here at last. And about time."

Everyone looked towards the cemetery gate as Father Duffy pushed through the drifts, the earflaps on his Cossack-style hat blown out in full sail. The pallbearers shuffled themselves into a more respectful stance, and Millie gave one last tug to her scarf to make certain it stayed tied during the graveside prayers. Tessie let her face take the full brunt of the wind and forced her stiff legs to hold her up straighter. Her mother had always been a stickler for proper decorum, especially in matters of religion, and she would never consider a vicious northeast wind an excuse for slouching during prayers for the dead. Tessie squared her shoulders and let her arms hang loose at her sides. Standing up straight was the most she could do now for Carmel.

Bertha's Story

Bertha Ryan was three days shy of her sixteenth birthday when she left home to go to the Cove and into service for Selena Corrigan. On the morning of her departure, she got up before daylight and stuffed the last of her belongings into a cardboard suitcase, then tied it shut with a piece of fishing line. She made a lunch to eat on the way: three slices of freshly baked bread coated with molasses and a few strips of cured codfish that had been roasted the night before in the kitchen stove. Just before she walked out of the house she was unlikely to enter again, she ran upstairs to say goodbye to her two younger brothers, Matt and Brendan. Her final act was to tiptoe into the room she had shared with Bessie, a sister two years younger, who, in the wake of her own departure, would now have to become woman of the house.

The sun had just started to inch its way above the hills when she began the two-mile trudge along the gravel road to the train. After the six- or seven-hour train ride (depending on the condition of the tracks and the number of stops), another two-mile stretch of gravel road awaited her. Before her father left for his job in the lumber woods, he had written to the Corrigans saying that his daughter would be coming to work for them. Because he had neglected to say when she would be arriving, there was little prospect of anyone's being at the station to meet her.

Mr. Ryan had heard about the job from a teacher who had gone home to the Cove for the Easter holidays. She had told him that working for Selena Corrigan — or as everyone called her, Mrs. Selena — was not a job to be envied. She was a sharp-tongued old woman with chronic bronchial problems and a mind that was starting to wander. Some days she wasn't much better than her son Vince, and he often didn't know daylight from dark. The teacher told him that servant girls usually stayed only long enough to land another job, and according to rumour, the last girl got up early one morning and walked away without even so much as a farewell to anyone.

The teacher also told Mr. Ryan about Mrs. Selena's younger years. She had been widowed when her skipper husband drowned off the Grand Banks. Her two boys were young then, but there had been enough money to keep the wolf from the door and a little to spare for luxuries like servant girls. The boys were now grown men. Vince was close to thirty, and although he was bodily healthy, he had an intellect problem. She had tapped her finger against her forehead. "There's a room not finished." She said Ned, who was twenty-five or so, was the one who kept the place together, and even though he tried to leave home several times, Mrs. Selena always found some reason to pull him back.

It was Ned who was looking for the servant girl. It wasn't so much for the housework as to have someone on hand when he was in the fields ploughing or haying, just in case his mother took one of her bronchial spells and choked to death.

Bertha's father culled this information and passed only the best on to her. He couldn't afford to keep her at home any longer now that Bessie was old enough to take over the house. But he didn't want her to go just anywhere, and he thought the Corrigans would give her a good roof over her head and plenty of food for her stomach, as well as a little cash for her pocket. By way of softening her leaving, he told her that the door of his house opened from the outside as well as from the inside, so if things ever got too hard she could always turn the knob.

But Bertha understood she was not expected to return home. She knew that if she did, it would be as a visiting relative only. She thought about this as she walked from the train to the Corrigans', her arms weary from carrying the suitcase, her tongue coated with dust from the gravel road. She thought about it as she switched the suitcase from one hand to another and rebalanced the extra pair of boots she had slung around her neck. She thought about it as she entered the Cove and asked directions to the Corrigans' house.

It was the end of April, and the wind was wet and raw. The closer she came to the Cove, the colder it got. She hadn't eaten any of the lunch she had packed because her stomach had been too queasy from homesickness. Just before she entered the Cove, she tossed the bag of molasses bread and strips of codfish into the bushes by the side of the road. There was no way her mind could think about food when all she wanted to do was retrace her steps and beg her father to allow her to stay home just one more year — just until Matt was old enough to go to school.

※

That first night as she lay awake in the back bedroom of the Corrigans' house, listening to the foghorn on the beach bawl like a caged bull, she was certain she could never feel lonelier than she did at that very moment. She had gone to bed less than an hour after she arrived. She was so tired she hadn't even taken off her best petticoat — the one with the hand-crocheted edging she had sewn especially for the trip. She had been too weary even to ask for matches for the kerosene lamp in her room. When she had been shown to the room by Ned, she had barely waited for him to go downstairs before throwing herself face down on the strange quilts that smelled of the goose grease Mrs. Selena rubbed on her congested chest.

She had tried to pretend she was home in her own bed, but the goose grease kept reminding her she was in a stranger's bed, in a stranger's house, in a village that looked no bigger and no better than the one she had walked away from.

Every inch of the Corrigans' house smelled of rancid oil. The smell even hung in the air in the back porch. She knew it well, remembered it well, although she couldn't recall it ever being so rancid. Her mother had always saved a can of goose grease after the Christmas meal, and whenever the children got colds she would scoop out a fistful and put it in a dish to melt on the stove. When she rubbed the dripping liquid on their chests, she often placed a piece of red flannel inside their undershirts, next to the skin, to keep the heat on their flesh and the mess off their clothes.

Bertha remembered how she had rubbed the melted grease on her mother's lungs that winter before she died. Her mother had been carrying another baby, and as she always did when she carried a baby in the winter, she got pleurisy. The pains used to shoot up her shoulder blades, so sharp and piercing she would have to gasp to catch her breath.

"Oh my goodness, Bertha dear," she would say as soon as the spasm passed. "Nothin' seems to help very much this time. Nothin'!" She would fall back on her pillow and close her eyes, too weak even to whimper.

And Bertha remembered the conversation the doctor had with her father the night her mother gave up fighting the pleurisy pains along with the birth pains. The two men were standing in the upstairs hall outside the bedroom where her mother lay, cold and stiff, her stomach still puffed up from the dead baby her grandmother had helped Dr. Flaherty pull from her.

"The pleurisy got her, didn't it, doctor?" her father had asked, his voice pleading for the doctor's agreement. But Dr. Flaherty was too angry to soften his answer.

"Hell's flames, no!" he exploded. "It was too much birthing that killed her. She was never meant for having babies. She wasn't built right. And she was delicate besides." He had stared accusingly at her father. "I told the both of you that one of these times she wasn't going to make it."

Bertha buried her face deep into the quilts to blot out the memory of that night, and the rancid goose grease smell flowed up her nostrils. She surmised the quilts hadn't been washed in years. The servant girls no doubt had washed the flannel sheets every so often, but none of them had stayed around long enough to tackle the heavy quilts.

She felt her stomach beginning to turn, and she wondered what she could vomit in if she couldn't get the queasiness under control. It was certainly too dark to go groping around the room looking for a basin, and she was too embarrassed to go downstairs and ask for one. She turned over on her back and tried to concentrate on something other than the rising nausea. She thought about the Corrigans' house — or what she had seen of it so far. It was big, just as her father described. But it was neglected and run down, and he had said nothing about that. The paper in the kitchen was faded and soiled, and the curtains looked as though they hadn't seen water from one year to the next. The door to her bedroom was so warped it wouldn't latch. She got up and tried to open her window to let in a little fresh air. She pushed upwards on the sash, but it wouldn't budge, and the blistered paint came off on her hands. She lay back down, telling herself with wry humour that if the rest of the house was in as bad a shape as the kitchen and bedroom, she wouldn't get lonely for want of work.

The school teacher had told her father that Mrs. Selena's house was the biggest one in the village and that at one time it had been the fanciest as well. She said Skipper Ambrose Corrigan had made plenty of money in his time, and because he doted on his beautiful Selena, nothing had been too good for her. Once he had even made a special trip with his vessel to St. John's to pick up furniture.

Bertha recalled the old woman she had left downstairs sitting in the barrel chair by the stove, all hunched over, wearing a black shawl and smoking a corncob pipe, and she had difficulty imagining her ever being young and pretty enough to stir a man's heart. But she allowed she must have been. And she allowed she must have been soft-voiced as well, because if the old woman's tongue had been as sharp and biting back then as it was now, Ambrose Corrigan — or anyone else for that matter — would never have fallen in love with her.

Bertha had been hoping that Mrs. Selena would be a little like her own mother — kind, loving and giving. But in the short time she had spent with her, she was certain she was not. She hadn't been in the house more than five minutes when Mrs. Selena used her sharp tongue on one of her sons — a shocking thing to do, she thought, in front of a total stranger. She had snapped at Vince, who was gawking across the room as though he had never seen a stranger in his life. "Vince! Don't jest stand there with yer mouth hanging open like a fish catching flies. Get the girl something to eat before she famishes on us." As she tongue-lashed him, her bronchial tubes began to rattle like wind in a bottle. She started to cough and wheeze until Bertha was certain she was going to choke.

Vince had been sitting on the couch pretending to look at a seed catalogue, but all the while he had been staring at her with a foolish look on his face. He jumped to his feet as soon as his mother shouted at him and slunk off to the pantry, but he wasn't even out of hearing distance before Mrs. Selena began whining about him.

"Hope yer not too hungry, girl," she said impatiently,

waving aside clouds of smoke and looking at them with disgust as though someone else had made them. "He's as slow as molasses running up a hill in January." She jerked her pipe in the direction of the pantry.

"Jest watch now! Bet he brings out the bread he made yesterday." She pulled her shawl closer around. "Not fit fer a starlin' to eat." She took a long draw on her pipe and opened her mouth wide to let out the smoke in one huffing blow. Immediately she went into a fit of coughing even worse than the one Bertha had witnessed earlier. After the spell passed, she patted her chest sympathetically.

"Me poor chest. 'Tis filled with *assmay*." Bertha almost felt sorry for her. She searched inside her own shyness for something nice to say, but before she had time to come up with anything, Mrs. Selena barked at her.

"Don't spose ye can do any better. A youngster like ye. A starlin' probably would turn up his bill at yer baking." She pulled a face as though she had smelled a bad smell. "Don't know why I keep gettin' saddled with youngsters still wet behind the ears."

Bertha fumbled with her hands, twisting the gloves she had forgotten to put in her pocket when she had been told to hang her coat in the porch. Certainly she could make bread, probably better than anything Mrs. Selena had ever eaten. But she couldn't find her voice, so she just sat in the chair squirming under the derisive gaze of the old woman.

Mercifully, Mrs. Selena's second son, Ned, came into the kitchen at that moment carrying an armload of firewood, and the old woman turned her attention to him. Ned was so startled at finding a stranger in the kitchen that he just stood in the centre of the room holding the wood and watching her. It took him several seconds to gather enough composure to dump the wood into the box behind the stove.

While he was still brushing pieces of bark from his sweater,

Mrs. Selena said testily, "I had to hoof it from the station when I came to work in the Cove. No one came to pick me up." She looked accusingly at Ned, as though he had wasted his time picking up a servant girl.

"Ye must be Bertha," Ned said, ignoring his mother's comment. "If I'd known what time ye were comin' I would've met ye."

Bertha didn't answer, but continued wringing her gloves as though they were a pair of her father's wet socks.

"Ye never left the place, Ma," Vince said peevishly, coming back to the kitchen with the bread and jam he had been told to bring from the pantry. "I heard what ye said about hoofin' it. Ye were born right here." He pointed with the jam crock in the direction of the window. "Jest down there. Ye told me that hundreds of times."

Ned shot Vince an exasperated look. "Stop contradictin' her. I've told ye to stop doin' that." He spoke out of the side of his mouth and in a low voice so Mrs. Selena wouldn't hear. Mrs. Selena gave no indication she had heard either of them. She looked at the armload of food Vince was carrying and sniped, "Lazy man's load, as always." She went back to talking about herself. "And I could make bread as light as a feather." She looked accusingly at Bertha. "I bets ye can't make bread any better than he can. I bets ye can't." She pointed her pipe at Vince. "As sour as his, probably — like vinegar."

Vince dumped the food on the table, letting the cup and saucer clatter noisily against the jam crock. He shot his mother a surly look but said nothing. He returned to his seat on the couch, and this time he stared at Bertha without making any pretence to read.

"Of course her bread ent sour," Ned offered easily, his tone intended to make Bertha feel better, while not getting his mother riled up. He talked to Mrs. Selena as though Bertha wasn't in the room. "I could see jest by the way she wrung out those gloves that she could make bread almost as good as ye, Ma. Like ye said. Light as a feather." He turned to Bertha and gave her a quick wink. "Ent that so, Bertha? Tell her ye were the best bread maker in Salmon Head."

Bertha's mouth was as parched as the pasture meadows back home in August, but she managed a halting "yes" and a nod of her head. She wished she could shut her eyes and open them up again to find she was getting Brendan and Matt ready for bed. She wished she were helping Bessie set the table for supper. She wished she had never come to the Cove.

Mrs. Selena turned on Ned as though it had just dawned on her that he was trying to humour her. "Don't play me for the fool, me son. I knows what yer all about. Ye'd hire a sheep to look after me if ye thought it would make it easier for ye to turn tail and leg it out of the Cove. All ye wants to do is get to Grand Falls." She shook her head disgustedly. "That's all I hears around here. Grand Falls. Grand Falls. Grand Falls. Me ears are piesoned with the place. Pure piesoned."

Ned didn't appear to be embarrassed by his mother's dressing down. He took off his heavy outside shirt and laid it across a chair, saying gently as he did, "Oh, come on, Ma. I was jest tryin' to make Bertha feel at ease. She's sittin' there practically turned to stone, and her tea will be like ice if she don't get busy drinking it."

A little while later, after Bertha had eaten the bread spread with partridgeberry jam and washed it down with Vince's weak tea, Ned brought his accordion from the parlour and began to tune it up.

"Come on, Ma. Give us a step." He squeezed out a few bars of a fast tune and then coaxed with a wink, "Come on, Ma. Show Bertha yer steps." He grinned. "Come on. Show her what ye can do."

Mrs. Selena shot him a look that said she was fed up with his nonsense. "Don't take me for a fool," she snapped. "Better fer everyone if ye'd show yer stuff by puttin' more time in on the gardens. Try eatin' that accordion next winter. Besides, I'm piesoned with that tune. Seems all ye knows is 'Cat Shit in the Shavings.' Ye plays it night and day. 'Tis enough to drive a body off the head."

Ned burst out laughing. "Ma, how many times do I have to tell ye 'tis not 'Cat Shit in the Shavings.' 'Tis yer favourite, 'Fishing off the Grand Banks.'"

Mrs. Selena jerked her shawl tighter around her shoulders and snorted. "Well, 'tis 'Cat Shit in the Shavings' as far as I'm concerned."

Ned said no more and kept on playing. After a few minutes, Mrs. Selena said to no one in particular, "At least that's what 'twas called in me own day."

Her voice was almost soft. She reached on top of the oven and took down the plug of tobacco she kept there away from the dampness. She took a paring knife from under her cushion and began paring off tobacco curls to stuff into her pipe. Every few seconds she tamped the mound. When the bowl was filled to her satisfaction, she relit it and began taking long draws to get it into full throttle. Her black slippers poked out from beneath her long skirt, and as Ned kept playing, Bertha could see the old woman's feet begin to keep time with the music. In a little while her fingers began to drum on her knees.

"Dee diddle diddle, diddle dee, diddle dee." Her spidery, tuneless whisper banished the last traces of harshness from her face, and she shuffled herself into a more comfortable position and went to sleep.

Bertha's head began to nod, and Ned stopped playing and said gently, "Yer dead on yer feet, girl. Ye go to bed, and I'll look after getting Ma upstairs tonight."

When Vince heard Ned tell Bertha to go to bed, he immediately put the seed catalogue aside and started to get up to take her suitcase. Ned intercepted him. "That's all right, Vince," he said, laying the accordion on the couch beside him and quickly reaching for the suitcase himself. "Jest keep on with yer readin'. I'll take her suitcase up." He hoisted the suitcase under one arm and then reached for her boots. On the way upstairs he told Bertha how to get along with his mother.

"She can be pretty ornery at times. She's not well. And her mind ent what it used to be. Sometimes 'tis as clear as a bell, but other times she's off gathering flowers with the fairies." He gave a small laugh that had an edge to it. "I can tell ye 'tis not goin' to be easy. But jest humour her. Pretend ye don't hear her when she gits on one of her tirades. Let it go in one ear and out the other." He ended lamely, "That's how I handles her, anyway."

Bertha had been relieved when she saw Ned grabbing her suitcase. Vince gave her the creeps, the way he kept looking at her and grinning and never saying a word. Ned had left her suitcase at the head of the stairs — just outside her bedroom door. She understood what he had said about how to deal with Mrs. Selena, but right then she had been too exhausted to worry whether she could get along with the old woman or not. Or with Vince, for that matter. She had noticed that the two brothers were no more alike than if they had been born strangers. Vince was short and stocky, and the crown of his head showed through his black hair. And he sniffed all the time, as if smelling for fire. Ned was tall and slender, and his hair was the colour of cured hay. Whatever good sense there was in the family, Ned seemed to have it all.

Bertha threw herself on the bed, intending to rest awhile before getting undressed. The rancid goose grease wafted up her nostrils, and she wished she had the will to get up and get dressed in her clean nightgown so she could haul it over her face to stifle the smell. But she couldn't move a muscle. She pulled a pillow over her head to shut out the sound of the foghorn and tried to settle the sickness in her stomach. She began a prayer to her Guardian Angel but fell asleep after the first couple of words.

———⋙·◆·⋘———

The first two weeks Bertha was in the Cove, she got up every morning wishing something – anything – would happen to allow her to go back home. She even considered not eating so she would get sick and the Corrigans would have to ship her back. But she couldn't keep from eating. There was so much work to be done, both inside and outside the house, that she was always ravenous.

She hated everything about the Cove. She hated the look of it — it wasn't much more than a gouge in the side of a cliff. She hated the fog that came in every day, damp and chilling. Most of all, she hated the sea that battered against the land-wash. On stormy days, the water turned green and foamed at the mouth. Bertha was certain there would come a time when the sea would ignore the narrow strip of leaky beach that kept it at bay, and it would sweep in over the Cove and suck them all out into the mid-Atlantic. But sometimes her homesickness was so painful she felt being washed out to sea was preferable to lying in the back bedroom of Mrs. Selena's house and crying herself to sleep.

However, by the time the middle of May arrived, Bertha had become almost contented with being in the Cove. The weather had warmed, and even though the nights were as raw as ever, the days were soft and gentle. By late morning, curls of frost would begin to rise from the meadows like puffs from Mrs. Selena's corncob. The wind was no longer high, and the sea had calmed. Indeed, the sea had become so calm she had to listen to hear the waves breaking against the rocky land-wash. Outside was filled with the sounds of people working the land: ploughing, manuring, mending fences. Often when she went out to feed the hens or to hang clothes on the line, she could hear the scrape of the dories being hauled up the beach after the men had come back from fishing.

But the weather wasn't the real source of Bertha's contentment. Ned was. He always treated her with such kindness, often shielding her from Mrs. Selena's tongue, that she had fallen wildly in love with him. Of course, Ned knew nothing about those feelings. She would have died of embarrassment if she thought he had any inkling that she lay awake every night thinking about him: imagining, dreaming, yearning.

It was one of her duties to cook breakfast for Ned and Vince, but she no longer considered this a duty. It was a labour of love, and it was by far the best part of her day. She always made certain her hair was combed and her dress freshly ironed. Sometimes she pinched her cheeks to make them rosy. She wished she had a bottle of scent to dab on her wrists. She wished, too, that some morning Ned would come to breakfast without Vince in tow. Vince never wanted to get up, and Ned was the one who had to force him out of bed. Bertha wished Ned would let Vince sleep for a week, or a month would be even better. She wished Vince would go away someplace so she could have those early morning moments alone with Ned.

Always, as soon as Ned and Vince left the kitchen, she would turn out the lamp and sit in Ned's chair at the kitchen table. All the rest of the day she could feel the heat of him penetrating her loins. Sitting on his body-warmed cushion was like feeling the touch of his lips — at least it was like how she imagined Ned's lips pressed against her own would feel. She had never been kissed — not by anyone. The heat of him was like a caress, too. Or more, although she wasn't quite sure what the *more* entailed.

Even so, she ached to experience the *more*. But only with

Ned. Just the sensation of having the warmth of his buttocks trickle up through her centre was enough to take the bite out of Mrs. Selena's tongue. In fact, some days she hardly heard the old woman's carping at all.

Sometimes when Mrs. Selena couldn't get a response out of her, she would rasp, "What's gotten into ye today, girl? Goin' around in a daze." The old woman would be so riled up over having to shout at her that she always went into a wheezing spasm, and Bertha would have to rouse herself from her pleasure world and run and get the goose grease or some other mixture of medicine.

Bertha began to suspect Vince knew what had gotten into her. She often caught him watching her, his look raw and watery eyed. It was a look that made her want to pull down the sleeves of her dress and cover up every inch of exposed flesh. Every morning he returned to the house on some pretext, and he would sit and stare at her, out of range of his mother's view. Once when she was putting the morning's milk on the stove to scald and his mother was dozing in her chair, he had sidled up to her and said in his thick voice, "I knows why ye've got that moonin' look. Can't fool me, ye can't." He sniffed. "No siree, ye can't fool me." She had practically run to stand behind the old woman's chair, feeling the need for a physical barrier against his words. From that position, she forced herself to look at him and say in a low, threatening voice, "Leave me alone, or I'll wake her and tell her yer hinderin' me from gettin' me work done." He had given her a smirking look, as much as to say he knew she didn't have nerve enough to do that. Still, he went out right away, sniffing as he closed the door behind him.

On the mornings that Ned had to use a spoon or fork for breakfast, Bertha could barely wait for him to leave. As soon as the door closed behind him, she would sit on his cushion, and, with the heat of him spiralling up through her, she would put the spoon or fork in her mouth and let it loll on her tongue. It was like feeling the inside of Ned's mouth. It was as though his tongue was touching hers. It was like having his lips brush gently across her own. She shivered from the ecstasy of this make-believe kiss.

One day when she was sure both Ned and Vince had left for the day, she turned out the lamp and sat daydreaming in the early dawn light. She didn't hear the door open nor Vince's step. He stood watching her as she stared out the window thinking about Ned. She was completely unaware of his presence until she felt his hand on her bodice. For a split second she relished the touch, knowing she shouldn't but unable to resist because she was certain it was Ned's hand on her breast. Then she heard: Sniff! Sniff!

She jumped to her feet so quickly she knocked over her chair. "Get away from me, Vince," she hissed vehemently, repulsed. She threatened to tell Mrs. Selena, knowing full well she didn't have the nerve. Worse still, she knew Vince knew she didn't. In some ways Vince didn't have enough sense to know daylight from dark, but in other ways he was as cunning as a fox.

"Aw, come on," he coaxed. "Ye'll never miss a little feel."

"Get yer rotten hands off me," she ordered, her voice low so as not to wake the old woman, whose bedroom was directly over the kitchen.

"Shout a little louder," he taunted. "Then Ma will want to know what the ruckus is about." He gave a smirking laugh. "Go ahead and tell her I ran my hands over yer udders."

"I jest might do that," she answered hotly. She looked straight into his face when she spoke, and even in the half-light her determination to keep him away must have shown, because he slunk off as though whipped. For the next week he never even gave her one of his watery looks.

———＞◦＜———

Along with the spring weather and her fantasies over Ned, Bertha had found another reason to start liking the Cove. Millie Morrissey, who was only a year or so older and whose house was in the meadow next door to the Corrigans', had become her friend. If Bertha didn't bother with the lane and climbed over the fence, she could be at Millie's within a couple of seconds. Although Millie was married to Aloysius, a widower several years older than herself, she was just as delighted as Bertha to have found a woman friend close by.

Almost every afternoon when Mrs. Selena took her nap, Bertha would climb the fence and race across the meadow to have a chat and a cup of tea. Millie never came to the Corrigans' house because she said Vince gave her the heebie-jeebies almost as bad as Mrs. Selena's wheezing and complaining did.

On the day that Vince had fondled her breast, Bertha had rushed over to Millie's as soon as Mrs. Selena closed her eyes for her nap. She related what had taken place. Of course, she left out the fact that her mooning over Ned was the reason why she hadn't heard Vince come into the kitchen.

Millie gave an exaggerated shiver as Bertha recounted how Vince's hand had slithered up her midriff and pawed her breast.

"Oh God be praised, Bertha," Millie exclaimed, hauling her sweater closer around her. "I'd rather find a nest of rats in one of me boots than have him lay a finger on me bare flesh."

Bertha nodded in full agreement. She looked at Millie with a puzzled frown. "What's wrong with him, anyway? He seems to be a bit soft upstairs." She cocked her head to one side, the bewildered expression still on her face. "There's some little thing wrong with him, whatever 'tis."

"More than a little thing, if ye asks me," Millie retorted, cutting another slice of molasses cake for Bertha and piling it high with freshly churned butter. "If he gets a notion into his head, right or wrong, there's no gettin' it out." She related the sort of things he did that made him the joke of the Cove. "If he got the notion to go cuttin' wood, he'd take the axe and go, whether it was seven in the mornin' or seven in the evenin'."

When she passed the cake to Bertha, she giggled saucily. "Did ye notice the way he sniffs all the time?" She screwed up her nose and gave one of Vince's sniffs, and Bertha doubled over laughing. Millie, realizing she was committing a sin by making fun of the poor in spirit, sobered almost instantly. "God forgive us," she said, traces of laughter still in her voice. "We shouldn't be makin' fun of a poor creature with a mark, but he does make ye think ye left old socks lyin' around some-where."

"That's the truth," Bertha answered and began to laugh all over again. She mimicked Vince herself, twisting her head to the side and sniffing out of one nostril.

"I spose 'tis jest a habit," Millie said. "As far as anyone knows, there's no real reason fer it." She dropped her voice to a confidential whisper. "Ye knows what they sez happened to him? They sez he fell off a stool when he was a baby and put a dent in his forehead as big as a twenty-five-cent piece." She tapped her forehead over her temple. "Everyone sez Mrs. Selena blames herself because she left him alone fer a minute. And that's why she always made Ned look after him, even though Ned was younger." She poured herself another cup of tea and kept on talking. "And that's why Ned can't get away from the Cove for very long. He's tried, but he always has to come back. Mrs. Selena gets one of her spells. But the truth is she needs him around to look after Vince as well as herself."

Bertha was unmoved by Millie's story. "No matter how he got that way, he still gives me the creeps, and he better keep away from me."

Millie giggled. "Ye knows what they sez as well? 'Twas old age. Mrs. Selena was almost thirty when she got married. And when Vince was young, he had sort of foxy-coloured hair." She blushed beet red just thinking about what she was going to say. "They sez it was rust. That's the talk around here. They sez that's why Ned is all right. Vince took all the rust with him."

Appalled at her own tongue, she abruptly changed her tone.

"Hard to know what happened. Maybe it was jest God's will."

—⊰◆⊱—

After that conversation with Millie, Bertha was extra careful never to be alone in a room without keeping a watchful eye on the door. And she always made sure Vince was off somewhere in the fields before she went to the henhouse or to the clothesline or anywhere outdoors where he could come upon her unawares and corner her. Now, whenever Ned teased her in Vince's presence, she felt uncomfortable, especially if he gave her that watery-eyed look.

Ned would often jerk her braids when he passed her or call her molasses head. Once, Vince pulled her hair, trying to act like Ned, and it made the skin on her spine shrivel. She had tried to hide how she felt because she didn't want to anger him unnecessarily, but she was certain from the look on his face, he knew he repulsed her. She became even more determined to keep out of his way.

But for all her wariness, she didn't dodge him for long. One afternoon she was in the pantry getting things ready for supper. Mrs. Selena was still having her nap, and Ned had gone to the store for horse feed. Bertha was taking the butter from the churn and stuffing it into individual wooden moulds. It was one of a few remnants of finery Mrs. Selena still retained from the days when she was a sea-going skipper's wife. She wouldn't stand for having the butter look, as she put it, like a cow splatter on a plate.

Vince had sneaked into the pantry as silently as a rat. He grabbed her from behind and held both her breasts captive in his big clumsy hands. She screamed and dropped the mould she was filling. It crashed against an earthenware jug and sent particles of butter over the bench and all over the wallpaper. Vince never even flinched, but held her in a death grip. He knew his mother took pills and potions and sometimes a nip of brandy whenever she went to bed. A thunderbolt wouldn't wake her. He manoeuvred Berth up against a wall, and turning her to face him, he suctioned his lips across hers, taking big gulps like a horse drinking from a bucket. She struggled to get away from his clutching mouth, but the more she struggled, the harder he pressed against her. She could feel the heat of his loins against her stomach. It repulsed her even worse than his lips crawling over her face like wet slugs.

Finally, she managed to pull one of her arms loose when he momentarily slackened his grip. She clenched her fist and punched him with all her might in his Adam's apple. He gasped and staggered back. While he was off guard, she grabbed an iron pot and held it threateningly above her head. She told him she would smash it into his face if he as much as took one step closer. She backed her way towards the door, never once taking her eyes from him, watching for his slightest movement, ready to hit him with all her strength.

When he saw she was getting away, his eyes got the watery look again, and he squatted down on the floor and began to cry. He gave big, sloppy sobs, mumbling and sniffing at the same time.

"Why can't ye pretend I'm Ned?" he whimpered. "Ned don't even know yer alive." When he realized she was running out of the room and not listening, he shouted after her. "He can get nicer lookin' girls than ye any day he wants. They falls all over him when he plays for dances."

Bertha made no attempt to clean up the butter mess. She not only ran out of the pantry, she ran out of the house and over to Millie's.

Millie huffed her outrage. "The likes of him. He should be put away." She made Bertha stay away from the house until Ned got back. She insisted she tell him everything that was going on. "I think ye should even tell Mrs. Selena. I knows there are times when she hasn't much more sense than Vince, but she has her days."

"I can't tell anyone but you," Bertha said hopelessly. "They'd send me home. They couldn't very well send Vince away. So I'd be the one."

"Then go home," Millie stated, anger and fear still in her voice. "Get to the divil out of there. Go back to yer father."

Bertha shook her head slowly and fresh tears welled up in her eyes. "I can't go back. Father can't afford to keep me. That's why I'm here in the first place."

But her unwillingness to give her father another mouth to feed was not the only reason. There was also her pride. How could she tell anyone why she had left her job? Would anyone believe her? Would even her father believe her? She was certain Mrs. Selena wouldn't go against her son in support of a servant girl, even if she had sense enough to fully understand what had happened. And it wasn't likely Ned would publicly brand his brother a skirt chaser or an old ram. Even if he would do such a thing to Vince, he would have to think about himself. No servant girl would ever come to work there if the truth got out, and without a servant girl, Ned would be tied to the house as tightly as Mrs. Selena was.

"I can't go back," she said resolutely, swiping her eyes with the back of her hand. "I have to make the best of it here. I couldn't stand to have everyone at home staring at me and whispering behind my back."

Millie disagreed with her reasoning, but she knew there was no way to convince her otherwise. The best she could do was to let her know she could come to her whenever she felt the need.

They lapsed into silence, each thinking of a way out of Bertha's predicament. Millie was the first to speak. "I thinks I got a better idea than chancing telling Ned. 'Tis true he might send you packin' if he smelled trouble brewin'." She explained her idea.

"The first chance ye gets, tell Vince that my Aloysius knows what's goin' on. Say that Aloysius is goin' to report him to the magistrate if he tries anythin' else. He's frightened to death of Aloysius ever since he let their cow eat up our cabbage. Aloysius put the fear of God in him then. And he's more afraid of the magistrate than the divil is of holy water." She said that the best thing to do was face him down. "He's a coward down deep. When push comes to shove, he's got no more guts than a caplin."

Millie elaborated on Vince's fear of the magistrate. "All Mrs. Selena had to do when he was growin' up was say she was goin' to turn him over to the magistrate, and it was enough to frighten him out of a year's growth."

In spite of her troubles, Bertha had to laugh at Millie's way of putting things. And besides, she now had hope. Perhaps it was possible for her to stay in the Cove and not be at the mercy of Vince. She went back to the house more at ease than she had been in weeks. If Vince felt about Aloysius and the magistrate like Millie said, perhaps that would be enough to make him keep his distance, even if he was full of hop beer. Although when he had a few beers in him, he seemed to be afraid of nothing. Still, it was worth trying, anyway.

Ned was back from the store by the time she returned to the house. He was in the kitchen stoking up the fire. She had stopped by the clothesline on the way across the yard and pulled off an armful of dry undershirts. She made believe she had just gone outside to bring them in.

"'Tis hard to get the clothes dry today," she said offhandedly. "Too much fog."

"Don't set a place for Vince," Ned said by way of reply. "He just left and said he was goin' to try and hunt down some hop beer." He gave her a sharp look. "But for the love of God, don't tell Ma. She'll tirade all night."

Later that evening, after the supper dishes were cleared away, Bertha asked Ned if he would be staying home. "If ye weren't goin' anywhere," she said shyly, "I'd go over to Millie's. Aloysius said he'd play a game of cards with us."

"Go ahead," he told her easily. "I'm goin' out later to help Pat Kervan mend his fishin' nets. But not until his crowd of youngsters are in bed. And ye'll be back by then."

As soon as she got Mrs. Selena settled into bed, Bertha threw off her apron and headed for Millie's, half-sorry she had promised to go. It wasn't often she had a chance to be alone in the kitchen with Ned. Even if they never exchanged a word for the whole evening, she felt good just being in the same room with him.

At Millie's, the talk got around to Mrs. Selena's dead husband. Bertha asked what he had looked like and whether the picture in the Corrigans' parlour was a good resemblance.

"But surely ye've seen Ambrose in person," Aloysius said, his voice a question mark. "All the other servant girls did. He's always hoverin' around upstairs." He explained quickly. "I means his haunt is."

"Aloysius, stop that and put yer mind on yer cards," Millie chastised sharply. "Don't start that foolishness with Bertha."

"Start what?" he asked innocently. "I only said I'm surprised she hasn't seen Ambrose's haunt yet. How's that startin' anything?"

A part of Bertha knew Aloysius was only teasing her, but another part believed him. She herself believed in ghosts, and certainly her room was dreary enough to have a haunt or two wandering about. She shivered visibly, and Aloysius, seeing her reaction, carried on even more.

"Yer room is at the very back of the house, ent it, Bertha?" he asked, knowing very well where her room was situated because Mrs. Selena always gave the servant girls the small room.

Bertha nodded and said in a small voice, "Yes, 'tis."

"The very one," Aloysius said ominously. "That was Ambrose's room."

Bertha looked puzzled, and Aloysius explained. "Ambrose used to use that room when he came home from sea. That was before they had servant girls. Surely they told ye it was his room and that he might come around sometime? Surely they did?"

She shook her head. Her hands had become cold and clammy. "I thought it always had been a servant's room," she said, her voice trembling. "'Tis so far away from the other rooms. And 'tis so dark and pokey."

"Don't be so foolish, Bertha," Millie interjected sternly. "He's only tryin' to get ye goin'."

Bertha looked at her, eyes wide with fear. Millie turned to Aloysius. "Enough, Aloysius! She's startin' to believe ye. Next thing ye knows, she'll be frightened out of her wits."

"And so she should be," Aloysius retorted solemnly, undaunted. "She's got his room, and the least we can do is get her prepared for his visit."

Millie turned her annoyance on Bertha. "If Aloysius don't have sense enough to stop talkin' foolishness, at least ye have sense enough not to listen to him." She levelled a hard look at Aloysius. "And ye, ye old fool. Ye wouldn't know Ambrose's room from Ned's room." She got up to put the kettle on to boil, and as she did, she threw a barb over her shoulder at her husband. "Besides, if Ambrose did come back, ye'd be running from this house with yer tail between yer legs. Ye wouldn't even stay this close to his ghost. Yer as big a coward as any of the girls."

"That's what ye thinks," Aloysius retorted, smarting from the truth. "And I do know which room is which." He spoke persuasively to Bertha. "Ye sees the way it was, girl. After Selena had Ned she told old Ambrose there was to be no more youngsters. Two was enough for her at her age. So after his fishin' jaunts, he was banished to that little back room."

Later that night, when Bertha climbed into bed, she hesitated momentarily before blowing out the lamp. She felt uneasy in the dark. Maybe there was more truth than lies to what Aloysius said. She huddled down into the centre of the bed and pulled the quilts over her head. If Ambrose did visit, she had no intention of seeing him, and if she were nowhere in sight, maybe he'd go back to wherever he had come from.

She slept fitfully, waking every few minutes. She was suffocating under the mound of bedclothes. Then she sensed someone in the room. Not only was someone there, someone was sitting on her bed. She could feel the uneven keel of the mattress. Her body went ramrod straight. Ambrose's ghost! She was certain it was. She hardly dared breathe in case the haunt would know she was there. She didn't know what a haunt was capable of doing, but she had heard plenty of tales back home, and they weren't the type to put a person's mind at ease. One man was turned into a babbling fool because he was given such a fright by seeing his dead mother on the stairs. Another man's hair turned snow white after he met a haunt on the road on his way home from a dance.

Bertha lay as still as the grave, breathing only in small breaths so the bedclothes wouldn't stir. The haunt shifted its position on the bed. For an instant, her hopes rose. Perhaps it was getting tired of sitting and was going to leave. Maybe it had only come to see who was using its room now.

She felt the quilts slowly being lifted from her body and the cold air hitting her raw legs where the nightdress had slid up her thighs. Ever so gently the quilts were raised. First from her legs, then from her body, and finally from her face. She kept her eyes squeezed shut, not having the courage to see what was stripping her. She could feel it staring at her. She wanted to pull her nightdress down over her naked thighs, but her arms refused to move. She wanted to shout a piercing, deafening scream so even Mrs. Selena would get up to see what was wrong, but her throat was parched and no sound would escape.

She tried to inch herself towards the far side of the bed so she could run out the door. Her limbs refused to budge. Terror manacled her mind and body. It even shackled her soul. She tried to pray, but no words would form.

"Bertha! Bertha! Wake up!" The haunt's voice was so close to her face she could smell the rancid odour of stale hop beer.

"Come on, Bertha. Be nice to me!"

Fingers roved over her nightdress, pawing as they went. They searched for her breasts, grabbed her nipples and pinched hard.

She remained mute, paralyzed into silence.

Sniff! Sniff! Sniff! "Little Bertha, wake up." *Sniff! Sniff!*

Vince! Bertha's body and mind sprang alert, and she sat bolt upright, her disgust overshadowing her fear. How dare he barge into her bedroom. It was bad enough that he would stalk her in the pantry, but to enter her bedroom, especially when her door was closed, was totally disgusting. Back home, a closed door was as sacred as the church. And after she had let him know that day in the pantry that she would not stand for him pawing her flesh, how dare he touch her again. In the light from the window, she saw he was naked, and her revulsion heightened. "Get out! Get out before I shouts out for Ned or Mrs. Selena!"

Instantly, Vince clamped his hand over her mouth so hard he knocked her back down on the bed.

"Now we'll see who's goin' to scream," he sneered. "Ned won't be back for hours. And Ma wouldn't wake up if ye set off the foghorn in her ear."

The greatest terror of her short life closed around her. She suddenly realized he didn't just intend to paw her body. He intended to savage her! The knowledge was so horrifying she knew instantly she would struggle to the death to protect herself. A cunningness overtook her. Her mind searched for escapes. Millie said he was a coward. She would tell him about Aloysius. About the magistrate. She struggled to free her mouth, but he kept squeezing her jaws together until she thought her flesh would leave her bones. He sprawled on top of her and with his free hand began ripping her nightdress, snapping the buttons down to her waist with one brutal yank.

"I'm not goin' to hurt ye, Little Bertha," he slobbered, sniffing after almost every word. "Jest want ye to give me a snuggle. Jest a snuggle."

His clammy nakedness repulsed her bare flesh, and she writhed out from underneath him. He yanked her back single-handedly and said contemptuously, "Oh no ye don't, Little Bertha. Yer goin' to be my girl tonight. I'll make ye forget all about Ned. Ye won't need to go moonin' over him no more. Not at all. No more."

Like a bird that knows it is captured and its only hope is in pretending it is dead, she lay very still, waiting for him to slacken his grip for even an instant. Then she would roar so loudly Mrs. Selena would hear her even if she were dead.

Taking her lack of struggle for surrender, Vince eased the pressure of his hand, and she jerked her head out of his grasp.

But she wasn't quick enough, and he clamped her mouth shut again before she could even get an intake of breath.

"Call Ma if ye can," he taunted. "Or if ye dares. She'd send ye home in a flash." Her near escape served only to frenzy him, and he tore the nightdress all the way down, scattering the pearl buttons she had so carefully sewn on the night before she left Salmon Head. He continued to maul her, wet-kissing her neck, her breasts, her thighs. Seconds before he impaled her to the feather bed, he grabbed a pillow and stuffed it into her face to stifle the shriek he must have known she'd make when he ripped her right up the centre.

In the aftermath of his violence, she lay splayed out like a codfish drying on a flake. Her ears pounded with the sound of his voice. "O Little Bertha," he whimpered, brushing her hair back from her forehead and running his hand soothingly over her face. "I didn't mean to hurt ye. I didn't mean to." He babbled remorsefully, as if his repentance were important to her. As if anything would ever again be important to her.

He slunk out of the room, sniffing and whimpering something about her not telling his mother. Her ripped nightdress was humped beside her. Her mother had always told the children, but particularly the two girls, that cleanliness was next to godliness because the body was a temple of God. The temple, she had said, should be kept clean, and all its adornments should be clean.

"Always be sure to keep yer underwear and yer night clothes in good order, Bertha dear," she had said many times. "Ye never knows when ye'll have to call a priest or a doctor in a hurry, and we wouldn't want them to see a dirty temple."

Bertha arched herself up on her elbow and reached over the tangled quilts and tenderly stroked the familiar worn cotton of her nightdress. She lifted it to her cheek and buried her face in it. The scent of Vince flooded her nostrils. She pitched the nightdress away from her as if it were in flames. She fell back down on the bed. Her body gave big, convulsive shivers, like a ship in the aftermath of a swell. She wanted to cry, but no tears would come. She wanted the tears to wash her clean of Vince. She thought about all the sad things that had ever happened to her. About her mother's death, about leaving Bessie and her brothers. Her mind slipped from one sorrow to another, a litany of heartaches. Her stomach heaved with sobs. Her soul throbbed with a pain so terrible she could barely catch her breath. Her eyes stayed as dry as the glass beads of her rosary.

Her teeth chattered from an icy chill that had settled inside her, and she groped her way across the dark room for her heavy winter coat hanging from a nail on the back of her door. She hauled on the coat and wrapped it around her naked body. It then occurred to her that the door was unlatched and she was still prey for Vince. She tried to force it shut, but it jammed, as it always did, against the frame. She fumbled for matches on her lampstand and lit the kerosene lamp, but even in the light she couldn't find anything to wedge against the door to keep it closed. The chair and lampstand were too easy to push aside if Vince wanted to get in, and the bureau was too heavy for her to move across the uneven floor. She huddled on the edge of the bed, whimpering, and waited for morning.

Daylight still hadn't broken by the time she had made her decision to go back home. She contemplated the outcome of returning. The worries that she had voiced earlier to Millie were still fresh in her mind. Would her father believe her? Would Mrs. Selena and Ned believe her? And even if they did, would they admit to the truth in public? And what was she to tell the people back home as to why she returned? She doubted she could convince her father to lie on her account and give a false reason for her leaving the Cove. He always preached that a liar is worse than a thief because you can lock against a thief, but you have no protection from a liar.

But when everything was weighed, the shame of going home was considerably less painful than the horror of staying in the Cove. It was like comparing purgatory with hell. Being in Vince's presence, cooking his meals, washing his underwear, making his bed and always anticipating the next time her mattress might be bowed under his weight was to her mind no different from suffering the tortures of the deserving damned.

Once her decision was made, she dressed quickly so as to get away before daybreak and before Ned came back. By leaving right away, she wouldn't have to explain things face to face. And she wouldn't have to see Vince again. She would leave a note propped against the sugar bowl so Ned would see it when he came home or as soon as he came down for breakfast. She didn't have to worry about Vince finding the note and destroying it because he could barely read and write his own name, much less someone's handwriting. Besides, he always clung to the bed until Ned pulled him out. She was determined to leave a note because she didn't want to be accused of slinking away without a word, as Mary Cosgrove, the last servant girl, was supposed to have done. Her excuse would be simple: she was homesick for her family.

The night's fog had seeped in through the leaky window frame and her room was damp and raw. But she didn't feel its chill. The cold inside her had numbed her so completely she could have been standing in a snowbank and it wouldn't have made any difference to her flesh. She filled the washbasin from the jug of cold water she had made a habit of bringing to her room every night. She washed her hands and her face and every inch of her body with the harsh, homemade soap she used for washing her clothes, hoping the lye would cleanse away the stench of Vince.

She dressed in her travelling clothes — the fringed petticoat and the blue calico skirt and waist she had worn the day she arrived, which she had kept for Sundays and special occasions. Because she had decided to tell no one — not even her father — why she had left the Cove, preferring people to believe she didn't have the gumption to stay away from home rather than finding out what had really happened, she took extra pains with her toilet. Her outside appearance would in no way be a reflection of the uproar going on inside her. She brushed her hair and braided it so no wisps poked out. She made certain her fingernails were clean, and she put new laces in her boots. As a final touch, she tucked a neatly folded cotton handkerchief into the wrist of her long-sleeved waist.

Just before picking up her suitcase and leaving forever the scene of her destruction, she peered into the dark mirror over her bureau. From the reflection of her fully dressed self, she was certain there was no way anyone could tell what had been done to her. But it was visible to her. It was as visible as the beacon on the foghorn point. She was shrouded in it. It was in her eyes, in the slope of her mouth, in the hunch of her shoulders. She knew she would never ever be free of it.

Hatred for Vince rose in her throat as thick and as bitter as the sour curd she used in her biscuits. Her soul burned from the pain of its mortal sin. Whenever the Mission Fathers had come to her parish, they always preached about the mortal sin of hating others. They pointed out that there was a distinction between disliking a person and hating him. This distinction could be tested. They said that if a situation arose where the person in question was in danger of death and if it were within your capability to save him and you knew with certainty that you would not, then you could be sure you hated that person.

As Bertha crept gingerly down the stairs, she knew beyond

a doubt she wouldn't move a finger to save Vince. If he were drowning and she were in a dory nearby, she wouldn't even reach out an oar to haul him aboard. She shivered under the weight of her sin and hated Vince all the more for the eternity of hell's flames he had secured for her.

Even though it was dark and cold in the kitchen, she decided against lighting the lamps or building a fire. Because she was owed three weeks' wages, she felt no compunction about dipping into the grocery money crock for her train fare. She moved stealthily into the pantry and rummaged on the shelves for bread and jam. The breadknife was always kept on the second shelf, and her fingers had just curled around its handle when she heard her name being whispered.

"Bertha! Is that ye, Bertha?"

The blood stood still in her veins, and her hand clenched the knife handle. *Vince had found her!* Instantly she knew what she would do if he came near her. She would plunge the cold steel blade into his heart! She would not be savaged again. Not by him. Not by anyone.

She turned quickly and looked towards the doorway. Even though it was still dark, she could distinguish Ned's form. Relief drained the strength from her legs, and she had to ease herself down on the backless chair she used to hold the churn when she made butter.

"What in heaven's name are ye doin' up so early? 'Tis not even daylight!" Ned exclaimed.

"Oh Ned," she said weakly, barely able to utter the words. "'Tis you."

"Of course 'tis me," he replied, his tone light and bantering. "Who were ye expectin' at this hour? Bishop Whalen?"

She made no answer. Ned, sensing something was wrong, stepped inside the pantry to see what was going on. When he did so, his foot hit the suitcase she had propped up against the door casing. He reached down and picked it up.

"What's this?" he asked, staring from Bertha to the suitcase, anxiety already beginning to form knots in his stomach. "What's wrong? Where're you goin' at this hour?" He saw she was dressed in her Sunday clothes. She *couldn't* be leaving! Not when she was his only hope of ever getting out of the Cove. And leaving like Mary Cosgrove had left, without a word to anyone.

Pointing at her Sunday attire, he repeated, "What's up? Where are ye goin'?" He constantly lived with the fear that someday he wouldn't be able to find a replacement for the servants who left as quickly as they came, and when that happened, not only would he be confined to the Cove, he'd be confined to the house tending his mother. His mind flitted to his mother's sour temper, and he knew what had happened. She had had a fight with Bertha and sent her packing. He felt relieved. He'd patch everything up later, but first he had to get Bertha to stay.

"'Tis Ma, ent it," he said, making it a statement more than a question. "She's been in one of her tirades again. Hasn't she?"

Bertha didn't answer. She hadn't even heard him. The relief she had first felt at seeing it wasn't Vince had turned into a sickening realization that now she would have to face all of them. She could no longer get away with just leaving a note. She would have to face everything head on — Mrs. Selena's scornful tongue. And Vince!

"When did ye come in? And why ent ye in bed?" she asked, her voice heavy with despair.

"I jest got home a short while ago, and I lay on the couch in case I woke up Ma going upstairs." The sight of Bertha looking so forlorn and downcast softened his voice. "What's up?" he repeated. "Why are ye leavin'?" He looked at the suitcase he had set back down by his feet. "If that's what yer doin'?"

"That's what I'm doin'," she replied, her tone still dead and cold. "I'm goin' home." She added lamely, "I was goin' to leave a note."

"Sure ye were," he retorted. "Jest like Mary Cosgrove did." He reached out angrily and took her arm to make her stand up and look him squarely in the face.

She stood up and stared defiantly into his eyes. "I'm goin' home," she repeated, determination in every word. "I'm goin' home before Mrs. Selena gets up."

When Vince had clamped his hand over her face, her teeth had cut her lip. She had carefully cleaned all traces of blood away when she had washed herself in her room, but the cut had started to bleed afresh. She could taste the blood trickling into her mouth. She hastily swiped her hand across her face so Ned wouldn't notice.

But she was too late. He saw the blood trickling down her chin. His stomach sickened. "God in heaven, Bertha! Is that blood?" he asked, knowing very well it was. "Did Ma do that? Did she get in that much of a rage?" He moved closer to get a better look and reached out and gently tipped her chin upwards, scrutinizing the wound.

Bertha jerked her face away. The cold sliminess of a snail had more appeal for her than the touch of his hand. Any man's hand. Just a few hours earlier she would have considered herself in paradise just to be alone in a darkened room with Ned. Now her flesh crawled from his closeness. Vince had killed *everything* within her. It was just another reason for hating him with every fibre of her being.

Ned didn't notice her recoiling. He was so concerned with his mother's brutishness that he only wanted to find out what had caused her to lose such control. He knew his mother was contrary and unreasonable, but he had never known her to raise a hand to anyone.

"Why did she smack ye, Bertha? What brought it on?"

Bertha stared at the floor, her head shaking back and forth to give lie to what he was saying.

"Come on, Bertha," he cajoled. "Ye can tell me. I won't even tell her ye told me if ye wants it that way." When she didn't answer, he persevered. "Ye might jest as well tell me first as last, Bertha, because I'm not goin' to let you out of this room until I gets to the bottom of this."

"Vince," she mumbled, her eyes still on the floor.

Ned wasn't sure he had heard correctly. "*Vince?*" he repeated. "*Vince?*"

She nodded, this time more forcefully.

Ned's face blanched with fury. It was possible he could have found an excuse for his mother but not for Vince. His mind reeled in confusion. "What fer?" he demanded. "Fer God's sake, what fer?" Sometimes people laughed at Vince for the shuffling way he walked or for the way he had of talking as if he had a hot potato in his mouth. Whenever he heard them making fun of him, he would fly into a rage. But Ned wouldn't have thought for an instant that Bertha would have poked fun like that. She knew her place better, if nothing else.

"Ye didn't make fun of him, did ye, Bertha?" he asked tentatively. "Surely ye didn't do that."

Anger replaced Bertha's shame. How dare Ned suggest it was her fault. How dare he make excuses for Vince. She wanted to smite Ned's composure by spitting out words that would send him reeling. *He savaged me! He savaged me!* She kept silent, hoping only to get away without any more fuss.

"Out with it, Bertha!" Ned grabbed her arm again. "If ye don't tell me, I'll go wake up Vince right this minute and get the truth out of *him*. I'll bring him down to the kitchen and worm it out of him right here and now."

Bertha flinched. She never wanted to see Vince again, much less to be in the same room with him when he was relating what he had done. She had no recourse but to tell Ned what had happened and hope he would let her leave.

"He . . . he came to my room and . . . he . . . he . . ." The words wouldn't leave her lips. Her head drooped.

"Oh Sweet Jesus!" Ned whispered, the full implication of what had taken place hitting him. "Sweet Jesus. Sweet Jesus. Sweet Jesus," he repeated.

He now understood Mary Cosgrove's whipped-dog look the day before she left. Her wilted face burned in his mind. Had the others suffered the same fate? The answer was too terrible even to consider. He left the pantry and paced the kitchen, pounding a fist into the palm of his hand as though he were pummelling Vince. "I'll kill the bastard. I'll strangle the blood of a bitch." He stopped pacing and started to go upstairs to pull Vince out of bed. He stopped abruptly. No matter how he felt, he couldn't do any of the things he threatened. He slumped into a chair, defeated. As always, he would have to cover up for Vince.

He got up slowly and went back to the pantry where Bertha stood looking as mesmerized as a jacked deer. He spoke softly, telling her to come sit in the kitchen and he would get a wet cloth for the cut on her lip.

"I haven't time," she protested, her voice trembling. "I can't be here when he gets up. I can't lay eyes on him ever again."

Cold sweat broke out on the back of Ned's neck. He couldn't let her go. The only way to contain the scandal was to have Bertha remain in his mother's service. He thought about what it would be like for him if everyone in the Cove knew what had gone on. He wondered if people would think he was as bad as his brother. And he was certain he would never be able to get another servant girl. He would be stuck in the Cove. He would be shackled to his mother forever. And Vince would be sent to jail for the Lord knew how long if Bertha's father found out about the rape. Ned saw his dream of going back to Grand Falls to work in the paper mill with the rest of his buddies dissolve before his eyes.

He pleaded with Bertha to stay. "Stay fer my sake, Bertha," he begged, his voice soft and persuading. He knew Bertha had taken a fancy to him just by the way she flushed whenever he was around her. He despised himself for using that knowledge to promote his own ends now, but he had no choice. He reached for her hand. It was as cold and clammy as a dead fish. She snatched it away as though he had touched her with a flaming match. She reached for her suitcase.

"I'm goin'," she said, heading for the door. Her features showed no emotion — not even fear.

"Wait!" He ran to the door and blocked her exit. "Let me fix yer lip. 'Tis bleedin' again. Ye can't leave with blood streamin' down yer face." He pulled a handkerchief from his pocket and began to daub at her lip. "Wait," he said again. "It needs to be wet." He went to the stove and poured water from the kettle over the freshly ironed handkerchief Bertha had put in his room the evening before. "Press it against yer lip," he urged.

She mutely accepted the cloth and daubed it against her mouth and then held it close to the cut for several seconds. When she pulled it away, there was no fresh blood. "I'm goin' now," she said, passing the handkerchief back to him. "I've got to get away before they gets up."

He searched for something — anything — that would convince her to stay. He said in a calculating voice, "If ye goes back now, everyone there will know what happened to ye. The news will spread like wildfire. Some people might even say ye led Vince on."

He saw her wince, and he knew he had taken the right tack. "I'll help every way I can if ye stays," he said quickly. "I'll get ye a job in Grand Falls just as soon as I can line up another girl for Ma. I've lots of buddies in Grand Falls, and they're always tellin' me how the grand houses — the ones the high-ups in the company live in — are always needin' servants." He lied without a qualm. He had read somewhere that servant girls in grand homes wore uniforms and collars and cuffs. "Jest think, Bertha," he said hurriedly, not giving her time to protest. "Ye'd come downstairs to serve breakfast in a black shiny uniform and spic-and-span white collars and cuffs. And a little doodad on yer head." He circled his head with his index finger. "A little white frilly doodad. Ye'd look some good. A little cap on top of that red hair." He thought of another enticement. "And ye gets every second weekend off. Jest think, Bertha! In great big Grand Falls where there's everything to do . . . a whole weekend to yerself." He rushed on. "And ye can save up yer weekends until they becomes a week, and then ye could go home to see Bessie and the boys, and ye'd have plenty of money to take the train back and forth because the wages are high — sky high."

While he had been pressuring her to change her mind, Bertha had been sorting through the options open to her if she went home. They ranged from limited to none. He had said the right thing when he offered the possibility of the Grand Falls job. The prospect of working in a rich home was tempting. And it was certainly better than going back to Salmon Head. But there was one stumbling block to accepting Ned's offer. She asked, "How could I stay on here for even a couple of weeks with him in the house? I'd never be safe." Fear made her voice shake. "I'd never know when . . ."

Ned knew he had won, and he said expansively, "Leave Vince to me. I'll take care of him. When I'm through with him he won't even glance sideways at ye. I'll tell him I knows about Mary Cosgrove and the others, and they'll come to be witnesses when I goes to the magistrate." He hardly paused for breath, he felt so elated over being saved from a lifetime of suffocating confinement. "And I'll keep him on tenterhooks about spillin' the beans to Ma. And I won't go out in the evenings and leave you alone. I'll pay someone, Millie maybe, to come stay with you." He crossed his heart and said earnestly, "'Pon my soul, Bertha. Ye won't regret stayin'." He hoped that if she stayed for a couple of weeks and saw that there would be no more trouble from Vince, she would settle in to staying permanently and forget about going to Grand Falls. He felt certain he could put enough fear into Vince that he would never attack her again. Besides, at the worst, if she did leave after a few weeks, there would be time to let the furor die down, and the scandal wouldn't have to break wide open.

"Will ye put a bolt on me bedroom door," she said in a small voice. "I wants to be sure he can't get in again."

"This very afternoon," he told her. "Right after Ma goes fer her nap." His voice was buoyant. "I'll get a piece of steel from the stable and fashion it into a latch that even Old Nick himself couldn't get in through."

Bertha thought of another concern, this one not for herself.

"How can I let another young girl come and take me place without even warnin' her?" she asked plaintively. "I couldn't live with meself if I did that. It would be wrong."

Ned had a ready answer. "I won't hire another girl. I'll hire an old hag. Someone who has a face like a boiled boot and arms like a stevedore. Jest the look of her will frighten Vince out of a year's growth. I may have to pay her a little more, but I'll see to that."

Bertha capitulated. She wasn't overjoyed with staying, but she recognized that it at least offered better possibilities than going home. She picked up her suitcase and went back upstairs to change into her working clothes.

That same afternoon, true to his word, Ned went to Vince, and, as he told Bertha later, put "the fear of the divil" in him. Afterwards, Vince skulked around the house as furtively as a weasel. He never even glanced in Bertha's direction. And also true to his word, Ned made a bolt for Bertha's bedroom door.

He made it out of a piece of steel left over from the time he put the new runners on the Sunday sleigh, and he fastened it on her door as soon as Mrs. Selena went to bed for her nap.

But Bertha didn't put all of her trust in the bolt any more than she put all of her trust in Ned's talk with Vince. Each night, as soon as she entered her room, she pulled her bureau up against the door. To do so, she had to take out the drawers and position the bureau on a mat so she could pull it across the room. She always replaced the drawers and let them dangle in such a way that they would fall to the floor at the slightest jar. Vince would never again get in her room without her knowing. And if he did get in, she would have plenty of time to shout out for help, or if worse came to worse, to break the window and jump out on the porch and onto the ground where she would race across the meadow to Millie's. And even should all else fail, he would never again get off scot-free if he entered her room. She had smuggled a piece of cast-iron pipe up to her bedroom and each night just before going to sleep, she checked to see that it was underneath her pillow, lying in wait beside her rosary beads.

Bertha had never heard of the word *rape*, but she knew there had to be a special word for such a horrible act. She recalled once overhearing a magistrate talking to her father about a girl who had been savaged coming home from a dance one night. The magistrate had said that even a woman of the streets deserved better than to be *outraged*. Bertha had heard talk about the case, and although then she didn't know exactly what had happened to the girl, she had had a hazy notion about what had taken place and now thought that *outrage* was a fitting name for it. She called Vince's foul deed an outrage, and although the word never once left her lips, it was as familiar to her as if she recited it every day.

Her outrage gave her a reference point from which all other events could be calculated. From that day onwards, every occurrence was pinpointed in time as having taken place either before, after or around the time of her outrage. Her father had two such reference points. One was the burning of St. John's. Whenever anyone was wondering about the date of some happening, he would say, "Oh that was around the time of the Great Fire," and he would proceed to give the day, month and year of the fire. His wife's death was the other reference point. Many times Bertha had heard him say, "Such and such an event couldn't have happened in February because poor Carrie hadn't been buried more than a week when it happened," or, "That was just before Carrie died because she was with me setting the potato garden at the time."

Bertha knew that if in years down the road someone were to ask the exact date when recruitment for the First World War took place in the Cove, she would be able to supply day, month and year. Of course, she couldn't say it took place four days short of three months from the day of her *outrage*. But she could say with certainty and conviction that the recruitment officer came to the Cove on August 16, 1914.

The news that England had gone to war with Germany didn't cause much of a stir in the Cove. England was a long way away, and even though it was the Mother Country, there was little filial devotion given to it. After all, what had England ever done for them? However, when the recruitment officer arrived, preceded by the rumour that fifty able-bodied men were required to swell the numbers in the regiment, the Newfoundland government had pledged to England's cause, interest picked up, especially when it was learned that the soldiers would get paid thirty dollars a month. Everyone was talking about who was joining up and who wasn't.

"Thirty dollars a month!" Vince announced at the supper table, sniffing his awe at such a staggering amount. The only time he saw so much money was just after the lambs and calves were sold in the fall. Even then he had to turn it all over to his mother or Ned, and they doled him out a couple of dollars a week for spending.

Neither Ned nor Mrs. Selena picked up on Vince's conversation, but he wouldn't let well enough alone. "That's what they pays. Thirty dollars! That's what Billie Connors told me today. I went to Murphy's right after I mowed the lower half, and Billie was there on his way back from joining up."

When he still didn't get a response, he repeated, "Thirty dollars *every month!* Just think how much that would come to in a year." He looked from Ned to his mother, expecting their eyes to pop open at such an enormous sum. All the way home he had kept trying to calculate how much thirty dollars a month would mean in a year, but the arithmetic had befuddled his brain, and he decided to just remember how much the pay was per month and let Ned figure out the yearly salary. It always made him sulky when neither Ned nor his mother paid attention to his news because they said he always had everything so mixed up it was a waste of time listening. This time he had the correct information, and they still weren't listening.

"They're joinin' up left and right," he said, waiting for the lull that always came when Bertha cleared away the plates and brought in the tea. He could tell by the way his mother buttered and rebuttered her bread that she had heard him clearly. She slathered on the butter as if she was puttying the windows, making sure no air holes remained. Then she cut the bread into squares. Vince took several loud sniffs and repeated, "I said they're signin' up left and right. And no wonder. *Thirty dollars a month!*"

Whenever Mrs. Selena got agitated, her bronchial tubes sounded like a wave drawing away from the landwash, and she would then have to gulp to get her breath. She put a square of bread in her mouth and gulped several times before she even began to chew it. Ever since she had heard about the recruiting officers, she had been terrified Ned would want to go. She had deliberately not broached the subject in case she put the notion in his head.

"Billie Connors is joinin'." Vince threw the words across the table and then glanced furtively at his brother. He couldn't understand why Ned wasn't interested, never mentioning it even once all the time they were mowing the meadow.

Mrs. Selena shoved the last square of bread into her mouth and swallowed it almost whole. She had to flex her neck to ease the crust down her throat. She gave Vince a hateful look. Because of him her tubes would be smothering her all night, and her supper would still be stuck in her craw.

"Well, good riddance to Billie Connors," she barked, flinging her words at Vince, but looking at Ned to make certain he understood his place was at home with her. "If Billie Connors wants to desert his poor old mother in her time of need, let him." She punctuated her sentences with exaggerated wheezing. "Ned is stayin' right here."

Vince, abashed by her words, dropped his head closer to his plate and began forking the food into his mouth. He didn't know what he had said that had made her so angry. He was never able to determine what would please her and what wouldn't. He stayed silent for the rest of the meal.

The following evening when they again sat down for supper there was a tension around the table as thick as the beans Bertha had ladled up. It was one of Mrs. Selena's good days, and although she felt the heavy silence, she had no inkling what it could be about. To get the conversation going, she asked almost pleasantly, "Did ye get all the hay cut on the foghorn meadow? And was it heavy?"

Vince sniffed several times but made no answer.

"Yes, real heavy," Ned said, not meeting her eye but concentrating on sopping up the bean juice with a heel of bread.

Vince sniffed loudly and scraped his beans angrily into a hump in the centre of his plate. Why, he wondered, wasn't Ned telling her what had taken place? He sucked in a deep breath and gave several sniffs. Maybe Ned could wait for a better time to tell her, but he couldn't.

"Joined up, Ma. This afternoon. Joined the regiment." Vince's words shot across the table with the speed of a bullet and ricocheted off the forkful of beans Mrs. Selena had been lifting to her mouth. The fork tipped upside down, and the beans landed in a clump on her plate.

"I did join up," he repeated emphatically, not knowing what else to say and realizing she probably didn't believe him. "I did so. Right after Ned came back from joinin'."

Mrs. Selena dropped the fork as though the handle were white hot. She stared open-mouthed at Vince, and he knew that as soon as she regained her composure she would tongue-lash the both of them, but especially him because he had taken her by surprise. To ward off her attack, he became petulant. "If he could join up why couldn't I? Why is he always able to do everything he wants and I can't?"

"Ma!" Ned said warningly, soothingly. "Ma, take it easy. Ye'll bring on an attack." He gave Vince a withering look. It was just like him to splurt out the news without waiting for a better time. "I was going to tell ye, Ma. After ye had yer supper. After ye had settled away for the evening."

Vince started to say something, but Ned quashed him with a deterring look before he had time to even get out the second sniff. Ned was furious with Vince, but he was even more furious with himself. He should never have told Vince he had joined up. He had left the meadow on the pretext of going to the store, but once he had the papers in his pocket, the secret was too good to keep to himself. As soon as Vince saw the enlistment forms, he dropped the scythe right in the winnow and ran off to the recruiting office. Ned hadn't minded Vince's going because he was certain he would be turned down. He had been more concerned with how lazy and sulky he would become when he found out he wasn't allowed to join up. He had almost fainted when Vince came running back waving the signed papers.

Mrs. Selena continued to stare from one son to the other. She was livid at Ned for joining up and doing so without her permission, but she was aghast that Vince had even tried, much less succeeded. Anyone, she felt, could see he was a poor fool. His upstairs wasn't finished. She would have to set the recruiting people straight in the morning. Mowing or no mowing, she would make Ned hitch up the horse and carriage and take her over to wherever the recruitment station was set up.

She levelled her eyes on Vince. "Tomorrow ye'll *unjoin!* The both of ye." Finding her voice seemed to have jolted her back to herself. "And that's as sure as God made beach rocks." The disgust in her voice was for all the stupid tricks Vince had pulled — this one was the most stupid of all — and for Ned, who would not only go behind her back to do something she disapproved of, but who would haul his poor, not-right brother along with him.

"Ye can't make me," Vince snapped. He gave a triumphant smile. "And ye can't use the excuse that ye have no one to look after ye." He looked at Bertha. "I told them ye would look after Ma."

A lump as big and as cold as an iceberg formed in Bertha's stomach. She bored her eyes into Ned's, imploring him to say she would be going to Grand Falls in a few weeks. Not that she could go to Grand Falls even if the opportunity did come, and besides, she was already beginning to surmise that the work in Grand Falls was just so much talk on Ned's part. For several weeks she had lived with the sickening realization that there was nowhere for her to go but back home to her father's house. It was the only place for a girl in the family way.

Ned took no notice of Bertha's imploring look. He pretended to concentrate on his plate of beans, moving mounds from one side to another. When the silence got too heavy and Mrs. Selena's wheezing was the only sound in the room, Ned addressed his mother. He looked at her apologetically. "Everyone my age has joined up, Ma. If I had told you I wanted to join ye'd have kicked up such a fuss I'd end up not goin'."

When Mrs. Selena made no comment, he continued. "I wants to go, Ma," he said earnestly. "I really do. More than anything in the world." He turned towards Vince. "As God is me judge, I didn't encourage him to join up. I never thought . . ."

Mrs. Selena half-rose from her seat and hunkered at the end of the table like an animal ready to spring. "Don't try to soft soap me, young man," she snapped. She whipped her gaze from one son to the other. "Yer both a pair of lunatics. I brought a pair of lunatics into the world." She riveted her eyes on Ned, letting him know that he wasn't the same type of lunatic as Vince, and because of that she had expected more from him. "Yer worse than he is. Yer completely off yer head." She grabbed her dinner knife and with her thumb measured out a portion of the steel near the very tip. "*Not that much* consideration for yer poor old mother." The tip was barely visible. "Not *that* much."

After the first rush of her anger, Vince began to revel in his mother's tirade. It was so rare for Ned to be under attack. It bolstered Vince's courage. "We're goin' to fight fer our country, Ma," he said patronizingly. "That's what the recruitin' officer said. And ye should know that too, Ma."

Mrs. Selena's eyes blazed. How dare he talk to her as if she were the one who didn't know daylight from dark, or whether her arse was bored or burnt, reamed or augured. She pounded her fist on the table. "Fightin' fer yer mother country, my backside," she scoffed. "Ye jest wants to go gallivantin' around the world. Get out of yer responsibilities." She tossed her head in the direction of the chimney. "If ye wants to go fightin' something, go up on the roof and fight the damn soot in the chimbley before it catches fire and burns to the ground and us with it."

She dropped back down in the chair, wheezing, but with strength enough left to continue. "I'm goin' over to the recruitin' office tomorrow and if ye won't drive me, I'll get Aloysius to take me. I'll have both of ye taken off the list."

Vince waited a few moments for Ned to explain that once you signed up there was no way anyone could get you off the list. When Ned didn't contradict Mrs. Selena, he spoke up himself. "Ye can't do that, Ma. They won't let ye." But even as he said the words, he didn't quite believe them. There was always a way his mother could get things done. He wished Ned would confirm what he had just said. It would make it more true if Ned said it.

"We'll see," Mrs. Selena jutted her chin in the air and sneered. "*Hrrmph*. We'll see. Ye have a stable full of animals, not to mention a sick mother." She pointed to Bertha. "She's only a child. She can't look after me, much less the animals."

"But England is our Mother country." Vince's voice held the patriotic tone he had heard the recruiting officer use. "Newfoundland has to give so many men. And we're goin'."

Mrs. Selena's agitation had risen to such a fevered pitch that it was hard to hear what she was saying above the noise in her bronchial tubes.

"Mother country, me starn. England wouldn't give a cup of piss for either of ye. And I jest bet no one in England would leave a poor sick mother in the care of a wet-behind-the-ears youngster and poor divil animals to the mercy of the wind."

Ned spoke gently. "We're not leavin' ye with strangers, Ma. We're leavin' ye with Bertha." He beckoned his head in the direction of Aloysius' house. "And I stopped by Aloysius's on the way home and arranged about the cow and horse. He's goin' to look after them in return for the use of our pasture land. And Millie said she'd give ye all the butter and milk ye needed."

"And what about the sheep," Mrs. Selena accused. "I spose they'll look after themselves until ye get back, whenever in the name of God that is."

Ned hastened to assure her that his stay wouldn't be long. "We'll only be gone a month or so. That's what the recruitin' officer said. We mightn't even have time to get trained and overseas before the war'll be over." He paused. "Anyway, I'm goin' to sell the sheep. We've been talkin' about doin' that for the last two years. They're more bother than they're worth with ye no longer carding and spinnin' and neither one of us caring about mutton."

He turned his attention to Bertha. "Ye'll stay, won't ye, Bertha? 'Tis like I said. Jest fer a short time. We won't be gone long at all." He tried to keep that disappointment out of his voice. He hoped the recruitment officer was wrong. He wanted to see England and maybe Europe as well.

Bertha fumbled with the edge of the tablecloth, not answering. She didn't even lift her eyes. They were all talking about a war over in England, and she had her own war raging right inside her. The battle continued night and day. At night, she plotted strategies that fell apart at dawn. She saw no way out. Nowhere to turn. She wished she had the courage to jump over the cliffs — the high rocky ones out by the foghorn point. She wanted only to mangle herself on the beach and then have the tide wash her away from the Cove. She wanted to be sucked down by the undertow so she would never be heard of again.

She felt Ned's eyes boring into her, waiting for her answer, expecting her to say yes. She raised her head slowly and stared at Mrs. Selena's hands knuckled up against her old face. Big bloated veins stood out underneath the wrinkled skin like fat, purple earthworms criss-crossing a patch of sun-baked ground. The sight of the gnarled hands made the nausea that usually restricted itself to early morning rise up in her throat. She ran to the back porch and leaned over the railing of the veranda. Retching convulsed her body, and her supper tumbled out onto the bachelor buttons that grew beside the steps, bending their purple heads. When her stomach had emptied, she sat down and placed her head between her legs, like she had often seen her mother do to stop the dry heaves.

Anger slowly began to replace the nausea as she thought about the conversation that had taken place inside. How selfish they all were! The lot of them only considered themselves. Even Ned. It had never dawned on him that she might not want to be saddled all on her own with a contrary old woman who had a bad memory. Mrs. Selena was always mislaying her pipe or tobacco, and sometimes she argued she had never been given breakfast an hour after she had eaten enough toast and tea to fill a horse.

For the hundredth time or more, she wished she had someone she could confide in. She had come close to telling Millie. One day she had asked her if it were possible to get in the family way from being outraged. Millie had looked at her, puzzled but concerned.

"I thinks ye can," she had replied, "but Aloysius sez ye have to enjoy it before ye can get in the family way." She had given her a piercing stare. "Is there somethin' ye'd like me to know, Bertha? Whatever it is, it would stay with me as long as ye'd want it to."

That opening had been her chance to tell, but she had hurriedly backed away from confiding. She quickly assured Millie she was just being curious and that there was nothing to tell. She lived with the hope that the baby would flush itself, and if that were to happen, the less who knew the better. Several of her mother's babies had flushed during the first four months. It was the hope that she had inherited her mother's weakness in birthing that had kept her from notifying her father — that and the fear he'd be so angry with her he wouldn't let her come home.

"Bertha! Bertha! Come quick!" Ned's urgent voice reached her from the kitchen. "Quick, Bertha. Ma's havin' a spell."

Bertha ran in and saw Mrs. Selena slumped down in her chair, her mouth opening and closing like a beached dogfish. Her eyes were wide open.

Vince was stoking the fire, trying to get the kettle boiling to raise steam, and Ned had gone upstairs to get some pillows. When he returned and tried to bolster Mrs. Selena's head and it just kept flopping sideways, he looked at Bertha with fear in his eyes. "Don't think 'tis her asthma. Not this time. She needs the doctor." He snapped at Vince, "Harness the horse!" The urgency in his voice made Vince move quickly. Ned shouted after him, "I'll be out to help as soon as I gets her upstairs."

It was after midnight before the doctor left. He said Mrs. Selena had suffered a slight stroke, and it was a blessing she wasn't paralyzed. But her mind was confused, and if she didn't show signs of getting better in a couple of days, it was unlikely she would ever recover fully.

Bertha stayed with her until she fell asleep, and by then she was so tired that all hope of sleep had been beaten from her. She went to her bedroom and sat by the window and stared listlessly out into the night. The foghorn bellowed, and she could feel the dampness seeping in. When she had first come to the Cove, she used to think of the foghorn as an animal lying in wait for the fog to come creeping in, and it was the foghorn's job to snarl the fog back out to sea. She had visualized its rear end twitching, ready to spring. But one day she had visited the point with Millie, and the lighthouse keeper blew the horn for her even though there wasn't any fog in sight. Afterwards the horn was only a dreary noise that signalled the makings of a dreary day. She absently rubbed her stomach, patting the bulge that was discernible only to herself.

She thought about Angela Foley from back home. Everyone said Angela had gotten herself in the family way, and they said it as though she had done it all by herself. Angela had come home from teaching down the bay, and she never left the house until long after the baby was born. When company came, she stayed hidden in her room, peeking out through the curtains, watching for the visitors to leave.

Bertha could now feel Angela's shame as her own. She visualized herself going to church, walking up the aisle with her stomach stuck out ahead of her as big as a puncheon. She thought about Millie's remark that some people believed you had to have enjoyed the outrage if it got you in the family way. Her face burned with humiliation.

She recalled how it had been for Angela after the baby's birth. Whenever she took the child out in public everyone scrutinized its face, searching for resemblances. At the store there was always dirty talk after she left. Someone was sure to turn to one of the old weather-beaten men lounging on the molasses kegs and say, "Sure looks like ye around the gills, Bill. What were ye up to a year ago this time?" Other raw remarks would follow, each person trying to outdo the other.

Bertha knew she could expect the same treatment if she were to return home. But she had no alternative. She couldn't stay in the Cove even if she wanted to. As soon as Mrs. Selena got her senses back and found out why she couldn't look after her while the boys were away to the war, she would certainly send her packing.

Wearily, Bertha climbed into bed. She took her rosary from underneath her pillow and absently let her fingers pass over the smooth glass beads as she searched for a way out. There was only one hope. Maybe if she prayed hard enough, *He* would help. He was her last chance. She started the rosary.

"In the name of the Father and of the Son and of the Holy Ghost." She began the mysteries. "The First Sorrowful Mystery, the Agony in the Garden . . . Hail Mary . . ."

Before she had gotten to the Fourth Sorrowful Mystery, the Carrying of the Cross, she dropped off into a fitful sleep. She dreamed she had crawled into the wood box behind the stove to get warm but had no sooner gotten comfortable when Vince began piling wood in on top of her. She could smell the freshly cut green spruce, still wet with sap. She shouted at the top of her lungs, but no one could hear her over Mrs. Selena's rasping breath. She struggled to pull herself out, but she couldn't grasp the sides of the box because her hands were bound together. After a few futile tries, she lay back under the pile of wood as helpless as a belly-up bluebottle fly and resigned herself to death. But no sooner had she become resigned when some force within her made her struggle one more time, and she pushed with all her strength until she rose head-first up through the knots and sticky bark. She rose until she could breathe the stale goose grease of Mrs. Selena's kitchen.

She sat up in bed, wide awake, perspiration dripping from her armpits. She removed the rosary that had tangled itself around her wrists and began reconstructing the dream, wondering if it were a sign she was going crazy. Being crazy was almost as much of a shame as being unmarried and in the family way. She felt that if she didn't tell someone soon, she would end up in the lunatic asylum, a double disgrace to her family.

She finally decided to confide in Ned. It was possible he would be able to come up with a solution she hadn't thought about. It would be embarrassing telling him, but it was her only way out. Having made her decision, she fell back to sleep.

The next morning, as soon as she got up, she went to Mrs. Selena's room. The old woman was sitting up in bed, looking around the room as though she had never laid eyes on the place before.

"Who are ye?" she asked, bewildered when Bertha asked her if she would like to have something to eat.

"I'm Bertha, Mrs. Selena," she told her gently. "Ye knows me."

"What are ye doin' in this house?"

"I works here, Mrs. Selena. I'm goin' to get ye cleaned up, and then I'll make ye some breakfast."

Mrs. Selena threw off the quilts and began to get out of bed. "I've got to get the children off to school."

Bertha ran downstairs to get Ned. She found him in the kitchen stoking the fire.

"Yer mother's not right," she said breathlessly. "Ye've got to get up there and make her stay in bed. She thinks she has to feed the children."

Ned dropped the poker and ran up the stairs. He was able to finally cajole his mother back into bed. When he returned to the kitchen, he told Bertha in a dejected voice that his mother's mind had gone back to the time when he and Vince were young boys. "She thinks I'm Father. Called me Ambrose and asked if Madeline had fed the children." He explained, "Madeline was a servant girl we had when we were young. She stayed with us for years." He sat down on the couch and wiped his forehead with the back of his hand. "Maybe she'll snap out of it like the doctor says," he said hopefully. "Maybe in a couple of days."

Bertha realized then that she would have to wait another few days before presenting her own problem to Ned. When three days went by and Mrs. Selena was only slightly improved, she knew she couldn't put off telling him any longer. Both Vince and Ned were still making plans to leave, just as if Mrs. Selena was in her right mind, and they were counting on her to look after the old woman while they were gone.

The following morning the opportunity to tell Ned arose when she went out to feed the hens. She emptied the contents of the enamel pan into the hen yard and then stood for a few moments watching the hens jostle one another to get at the boiled potatoes and bread. She heard voices and looked up towards the sheep house to see Ned in conversation with the man who had come to buy the sheep. The realization that everything was moving so fast almost made her feel faint, and she had to clutch at the empty pan for support. She held it tight against her like a breastplate.

She bolstered her courage and decided she would tell Ned as soon as the business with the sheep was finished, just before he went back to the house.

She waited until he left the sheep house and started down the path before she came out of the hen yard. She timed it so he would be far enough away and out in the open so Vince couldn't come up on them unawares. Her whole body was rigid with the expectation of his anger, and she walked woodenly, the pan still clutched to her breast. Just as she came beside him, she burst out crying. The tears came on as suddenly as the heartburn she had been having for the past two months. She tried to hold back the sound, just as she had tried to swallow back the bitter stomach gas. But nothing she did would stifle it. She even sat down and placed both hands over her mouth, but the sound escaped through her fingers.

Ned was so happy with the price he had gotten for the sheep that he almost sprinted down the path. Everything was finally under control. In just a few more days he would be gone. The doctor had assured him his mother was in no worse health than she had been before the stroke, except that her mind was lodged back in the days when she was a young wife. He whistled as he hurried along the path fingering the roll of worn bills in his pocket.

He saw Bertha sitting on the grass all hunched over in a huddle of misery. When he got closer, he could hear her crying and see her shoulders heaving underneath her cotton dress.

"What's up now?" he whispered under his breath, annoyance furrowing its way into his good feelings. His instincts told him to veer off the path so he wouldn't have to deal with whatever was wrong. It was what Vince would have done. Vince believed if you didn't acknowledge trouble, then there was no trouble. But he wasn't Vince.

"What's up, Bertha?" His irritation was barely concealed under the civil words. "What's the trouble?"

Bertha began crying all the harder.

"Is it Ma? Is she callin' ye Madeline and tellin' ye to bring the children indoors again?"

Bertha shook her head, never once raising her eyes from the ground.

"What is it then?" His irritation surfaced. "What's wrong?" As soon as the words were out, his insides tightened. *Vince! Surely it wasn't Vince again!*

"Is it Vince?" He hardly dared breathe until he had her answer.

She shook her head again.

Relief only sharpened his exasperation with her. "Well, what *is* the matter?"

"I can't . . . stay on . . . when ye leaves." She stammered between sobs.

"Of course ye can," he said easily, his voice belying his sureness. He could understand why she would want to go. His mother's foolish talk was enough to drive anyone away. "I'll double yer salary." He pulled the sheep money out of his pocket and showed her the fistful of bills. "I'll give ye the extra money right now." He peeled off the bills. "Here's two months' pay in case we're away longer than the officer said."

Bertha made no attempt to take the money. "I'm in the family way," she blurted, choking on the words so he could barely make out what she was saying. "I'm in the family way on account of Vince."

Ned slowly put the roll of bills back in his pocket and clutched it tightly. The enormity of what he had just heard could only be absorbed a little at a time. He felt it first in his feet. Perspiration formed between his toes and dampened his socks, sending chills up his calves. The news spread through the rest of his body, and by the time it reached his brain, all strength had been leached from his body, and he had to ease himself down on the ground beside Bertha. Only then was he able to fully comprehend what she had told him and how it would affect him. It would mean no regiment and a lifetime of strangulation in the Cove.

"Sweet Jesus!" he whispered as he rocked back and forth on the grass. "Sweet Jesus!"

He had almost drowned when he was ten years old. He had gone fishing with his father on one of the rare occasions when the skipper was in port long enough to spend time with him. They had gone out jigging flatfish to put on the gardens for fertilizer. He had been so excited about the trip that he hadn't slept the night before, afraid if he closed his eyes something would happen to make the skipper change his mind about going.

They had taken out the smallest of their dories because they weren't going to go very far, and it seemed like no time had passed before it was half-full of slippery flatfish. His mitts had gotten wet, and he had stood up to walk towards the stern to get a dry pair from the oilskin bag. He had only taken one step when he slipped on the pile of fish and lost his balance, toppling over the side of the dory. *Down! Down! Down!*

Even now, fifteen years later, he could taste salt in his spit. He had gulped down the boiling green sea until he was certain his stomach would burst. He only had to close his eyes now to see the horrified look on his father's face when he had bobbed up for the third time. After what seemed like hours, but was really only minutes, the lurching dory came close enough so the skipper could reach out an oar. He had shouted at him to grab hold.

Now as he sat on the grass that was still damp from the night's fog, he grasped the sheep money every bit as tightly as he had grasped that oar. His fingers, stiff and cold, dug into the soft paper.

"Hold on! Hold on! Hold on!" his father had shouted, but with the wind and the slap of the waves, he appeared to be only mouthing the words. Still he was able to feel his father's desperation as he shouted the noiseless words. It was powerful enough to make him hold on even though his mitts were as stiff as boards.

He tried now to save himself. Perhaps Bertha had misjudged her problem. He had heard about women who had made that kind of mistake. "Sweet Jesus, Bertha. Are ye sure?" he asked, willing her to shake her head. "Yer not jumpin' the gun, are ye?"

She made no move. He searched the slump of her shoulders and her tear-streaked face half-hidden under her hands for some sign that she was not certain.

"I'm not jumpin' the gun," she said softly, her voice as hollow as an empty church.

"Yer sure, then," he repeated uselessly. "There's no mistake."

It angered Bertha to have him suggest she wasn't certain of a thing like that. Had she not seen her mother often enough vomiting up her insides in the mornings and having to run outdoors to gulp fresh air after she rendered out the fat pork for frying eggs? And she knew other signs as well. And she had them all. "I'm almost three months gone," she stated in the same dead, empty voice. "There's no mistake. But I wish to God there was."

Ned began rocking back and forth on the grass, comforting himself the way he used to do when he was a child and Vince would torment him. It had been no good going to his mother because she would just say that Vince didn't know any better and everyone had a cross to bear and Vince was theirs. Sometimes, when he complained too many times in the run of a day, she would begin to wheeze, and he would run outdoors feeling guilty at having brought on her asthma.

Once, he had almost killed Vince. They were both young men at the time. Vince had raced the horse home from church on a winter Sunday and then left it standing in a lather of sweat outside the stable door. He had come upon the poor beast shivering in the cold without even a blanket across its back. He had gone immediately to get Vince and had found him in the kitchen stuffing biscuits into his mouth, crumbs dribbling down his vest onto the tablecloth. He grabbed him by the throat and banged his head up against the wall.

"Don't ye ever do that to that poor beast again, or I'll kill ye fer sure." He had kept banging Vince's head until his mother ran into the room and threw her shawl over their heads like she'd do for a hen fight, separating them. She had tongue-lashed both of them, but mostly him, saying that he had to make allowances for Vince because he didn't have good sense and that he, Ned, had to have sense enough for the two of them.

But he was sick and tired of making allowances for Vince, sick and tired of taking responsibility for him, sick and tired of his mother's demands. And now with Bertha's problem there was no way he was going to take anything else from either of them. It was bad enough when he learned that he and Vince were going to be in the same regiment, let alone have Vince get away from the Cove while he stayed home and took over the burdens that Vince had caused.

"Don't worry about drivin' me to the train," Bertha said, interrupting his thoughts. "I walked here. I can walk back."

Ned sat up with a jolt. "Ye can't leave! Not now! Not when I only have a few days left. I'd never get another girl in that short a time."

When she didn't answer and he couldn't read her face, he began groping for a way out. He lit upon the possibility of making Vince marry her. It might even entice Vince to stay home, and that way it would solve two problems at once. He discarded the idea without even broaching it to Bertha. She would never accept marriage to Vince. He had seen the hatred simmering in her eyes every time she had to go near him to serve him meals, or whenever she had to pass by him in the kitchen and inadvertently touched against him. Just suggesting the possibility of marriage to Vince might make her run home all the faster.

He absently fingered the worn bills while he searched his mind for options. Then it hit him. The answer was money! Lots of money. Of course! Why hadn't he thought about it right away. He quickly pulled the wad of bills out of his pocket and held them out to her. "I'll give ye all of this," he said eagerly, "if ye'll stay until I gets back." He flipped the bills like a deck of cards. "The whole hundred and ten." He laid the money on the grass, sheltering it between his legs so the wind wouldn't blow it away. He began counting. "Ten . . . fifteen . . . twenty-five . . . thirty . . ."

Bertha stared in stunned fascination. In her entire life she had never seen that much money, and all she had to do to get it was to agree to stay a month longer in the Cove. Or two months at the most. Going home with that kind of money, she reasoned, would mean she would be able to pay her way, and that would certainly make her father feel a lot better about her being there. And she would be able to have her own bank account. Just like

Mrs. Selena, although Mrs. Selena never went to the bank. Ned did all of that.

Ned mistook Bertha's silence for rejection of his offer, and he upped the ante. "I'll give ye a like amount when I gets back. I'll even set up an account for ye here so me allotment check can go into it."

For a few moments Bertha was tempted to accept Ned's offer, but then she came to her senses and realized that no amount of money could help her. "There's no way I can stay here," she said, her voice still flat and dead. "When I starts to get big, Mrs. Selena will send me home. She'd never believe it was Vince's fault."

"Who said anything about tellin' Ma? No need to tell her. Ma doesn't know whether she's in dry dock or on the high seas, so she's certainly not goin' to know yer in the family way." He nodded confidently. "Besides, I'll be back before ye . . . before ye . . . gets . . . ." He finished, embarrassed, "Before ye knows it. In a month or so."

Bertha plucked at clumps of chickweed, her gaze still not able to meet his. "But what do I say to others? Like Millie?"

"Nothin' at all. That's what. Because there's no need to." He was becoming impatient with her obstinacy. "When I gets back, I'll take ye to the train. I'll pay yer way, and I'll give ye some money to take to yer father to stop him from makin' a fuss. Ma has plenty salted away." He quickly explained it wasn't stealing from his mother because, if she had her senses, she would be the first to want to keep things covered up so Vince wouldn't get hurt.

"But what if ye don't get back in time?" Bertha persisted. "What am I supposed to do then?"

Instead of answering, he reached inside his bib overalls and pulled a copy of his enlistment papers from his shirt pocket. "See!" he leaned towards her, pushing the form in front of her eyes. He pointed to a section halfway down the page. "Until the duration and not longer than a year, it says." He hurriedly interpreted. "But the enlistment officer said that the duration would probably only be a month or so. He said there was only an outside chance that we'd be away longer than a month. Two would be the outside limit. Said we'd probably jest get trained and the war would be doused and we'd have to come back." He folded the form and put it back in his pocket, satisfied he had convinced her.

"So 'tis all settled then," he said confidently and pressed the bills into her hand so the feel of them would keep her from changing her mind.

Bertha's hand closed loosely around the money. In three or four months, she knew she would be as big as a barrel. If Ned stayed away that long, people in the Cove would know she was in the family way. And she didn't know how she could go up to Murphy's store to buy food if her stomach was sticking out in front of her. But how could she go home without the money Ned was offering? Depression closed in around her.

"I wish I had done away with meself like I wanted to do in the first place. I wish I had." Her voice was as empty as if she were already dead. "I should have leapt over the cliff."

Ned stared at her, horror-struck. "Sweet sufferin' Jesus, girl, don't go thinkin' of pullin' a stunt like that. It'd be the end of all of us." He looked at her vacant face staring down at the mounds of chickweed. His voice gentled. "Everything will work out for the best, Bertha. Trust me. I'll make all the arrangements for ye here so ye can look after things while I'm gone, and I'll be back well before the snow blows."

Bertha mulled over the pros and cons of Ned's proposition and then sighed resignedly. "I spose I'll stay," she said. "I don't know what else to do."

Ned jumped to his feet and then reached down to help Bertha up. She ignored his hand and got up unaided. For the first time that morning, she looked directly at him. "Ye've got to promise me something." Her voice was even and controlled. "And if ye goes back on yer promise, I'll leave the minute I finds out ye did, no matter what condition I'm in. No matter what condition yer mother is in."

"Anything! Anything!" Ned said eagerly.

"Yer never to tell Vince. Never! No matter how much ye'd like to fling it in his face." She used the one threat she knew could reach him. "I'll kill meself fer sure if I found out he knew. I'd do it right in this house if I had to."

Ned promised, even though he felt Vince was getting off too easy by not being told. "'Pon me soul, I won't tell. As God is me judge. I'll never tell anyone unless ye wants me to."

Bertha made no reply. She stooped down and picked up the empty feed pan. There was plenty of work to be done, and Mrs. Selena was probably already shouting out her foolishness about getting the children's breakfast. She could feel the weight of the bills in her apron pocket as she made her way back to the house.

⇒•◆•⇐

About two weeks after the boys left for the training camp at Quidi Vidi Lake, a letter arrived from Ned. He wrote that it was raining day and night and there was mud a foot deep outside their tents. He and Vince were not only in the same unit — they were in the same tent.

Because Mrs. Selena was unable to read, Bertha had to read the letter to her, and when she came to the part about Ned and Vince being in the same tent, the old woman said wistfully that she hoped young Ned would look after little Vince because the poor child needed someone. There were occasional days when it appeared as though Mrs. Selena understood that the boys had joined the regiment, but mostly she thought that they were away visiting relatives, as they used to do during the school holidays.

Ned's letter never mentioned returning to the Cove, and a knot of apprehension began forming in Bertha's stomach. Three weeks later when he wrote again, he talked once more about unimportant things. He said they had received their uniforms, but because there hadn't been enough khaki material in St. John's to make their puttees, these had to be made out of a dark blue material. Vince, he said, was concerned about the odd sight they would make when they got to England and found they were the only soldiers in the war with puttees not matching their uniforms.

When Bertha finished reading this letter aloud, she passed it to Mrs. Selena, who stuffed it in her apron pocket alongside the first one. Bertha went outdoors and sat on the porch steps. She rubbed the bulge in her stomach that was pressing against the too-tight waistband of her underwear. She was sick with worry. There was still no mention of the war being over, and worse still, Ned talked about the possibility of their going to England. And she was sick with fury as well. Here she was, neither sleeping nor eating, thinking about the possibility of her stomach beginning to show before she could leave the Cove, and Vince's only worry was how odd he'd look over in England wearing the blue puttees, and Ned had nothing more important to write than to tell how Vince felt about his uniform. At that moment, she hated both of them.

Several times each day, Mrs. Selena asked Bertha to reread Ned's letters.

"Read me what Neddie said, Madeline," she'd ask in a whining voice and with a faraway look in her eyes that made Bertha wonder whether the old woman knew who Neddie was or if having the letters read to her was just a habit she had gotten into as a means of getting attention.

Bertha no longer bothered to tell her that she wasn't Madeline. After she had her dressed and fed, she would go to Murphy's store and bring back whatever news was on the go about the regiment. Mr. Murphy often went to St. John's to get supplies for the store, and he usually brought back news. Besides, he had the St. John's paper, *The Evening Telegram*, sent out every Thursday when the train came to the Cove.

Mrs. Selena missed her children, and she kept waiting for them to return. As soon as Bertha would go into her bedroom in the morning, she would ask, "Will Neddie and Vincey be home today, Madeline?"

Sometimes Bertha's patience would be so frazzled from lack of sleep that she would answer irritably, "I don't know when they'll be home, Mrs. Selena. I've no more idea than the man in the moon."

Just after the middle of October, Bertha read in the newspaper that the first five hundred men from the regiment had sailed for England on the *Florizel*. A list of names followed. Ned and Vince's names were close to the top.

By now her clothes had gotten so tight she had to go around with the waistband of her skirt unbuttoned. All hope of Ned getting back to take her home had gone with the *Florizel*. She knew that any help she was going to get would have to come from her own resources. She decided to tell Mrs. Selena. She reasoned that even if the old woman wasn't able to understand what she was saying, just telling her — telling someone — would help her keep her own sanity. Every night she resolved that the next day she would tell Mrs. Selena, Millie and the priest. She held the faint hope that Father Flannigan could help her. She knew there were homes for people in her condition, and perhaps he could get her into one. By dawn her resolve always waned, and she would convince herself to wait one more day. Perhaps the war would be over. Besides, she would ask herself, how can anyone help me? Millie would probably scold her for not telling her when there was time to do something and for being foolish enough to listen to Ned's bribery. Mrs. Selena was too senseless to do much of anything, and she'd never have enough nerve to tell Father Flannigan.

Ned wrote from Salisbury and from Edinburgh. Each letter was just a scribbled note saying there was no use in writing to him because he was on the move so much he rarely received mail. He wrote again from Egypt, but by the time that letter arrived in the Cove, the newspaper had already reported that the regiment had moved out of Egypt to a destination unknown at the time the paper had gone to press. In his last letter, Ned had made reference to Bertha's condition. A line at the bottom said, "I'm sorry Bertha but I don't know when I'll be out of this mess. I keeps hoping each day to get word that it is all over."

Bertha stayed more and more to herself. She wore her biggest clothes whenever she went to the store and never, never took off her coat until she was safe in Mrs. Selena's kitchen. She seldom went to Millie's, making the excuse that she didn't like to leave Mrs. Selena alone unnecessarily.

Millie, though, didn't accept that excuse, and she was very troubled by the way Bertha was acting. The only time she now came to visit was when Millie would be out in the yard, and she'd stop her on her way back from the store. Even then, she would only stay a few minutes and would sit hovered on the edge of her chair ready to take flight. She would keep her coat wrapped around her no matter how much heat was in the kitchen.

One day as Millie watched Bertha walk back to her house, it suddenly occurred to her what was wrong. She could tell just by the way Bertha walked, as if she were heavily laden.

She waited just long enough for Bertha to get her coat off

before she made her trip to the Corrigans'. She knew Mrs. Selena would still be sleeping, although, as she told herself, it wouldn't matter if the old woman were sitting in the room with them, her mind was that far gone. Millie wasted no time in getting to the point of her visit.

"I didn't come here to natter," she said when Bertha offered to make a cup of tea. "I came to find out what's goin' on with ye, although I thinks I knows what 'tis."

"What do you mean, goin' on with me," Bertha stalled. "There's nothin' goin' on with me."

"Yer well along in the family way, that's what's wrong," Millie said with her usual forthrightness. "I can tell jest by the way ye walks."

Bertha set the teapot back on the stove and began to sputter indignantly that Millie must be out of her mind to think such a thing, but she no sooner got the words out of her mouth when she burst out crying.

"Yer right," she sobbed. "And I've nowhere to turn. I wish I was dead and gone. I wish I'd never been born."

"Oh God help us," Millie whispered sympathetically before turning her anger on Vince. "It was that bloody Vince, wasn't it? He attacked ye. I could tell from the things ye said and from the things the other servant girls hinted at."

Bertha looked at Millie wild eyed. "Please don't tell anyone," she begged hysterically. "I'd probably be forced to marry him. And I'd kill meself fer sure before I'd do that."

"Don't be ridiculous, Bertha. No one's goin' to force ye to marry anyone," Millie assured, anger at Vince still in her voice. "No one would force ye to marry that soft-brained divil, but he should be forced out of the regiment and made to face up to things."

Bertha's protest was almost a scream. "No! I don't want to see him. Not ever again. Ned promised I'd never have to see him again."

"What!" Millie said incredulously. "Ned knows! And he left ye stranded!"

Bertha related the conditions under which she had consented to stay. When Millie spoke again her tone had softened a little.

"Ye were a foolish girl, Bertha. Ye should have told me or Aloysius. We'd have helped. We wouldn't have let those two get away."

The telling of the circumstances helped Bertha get control of herself, and when she had calmed down, she forced a promise out of Millie not to tell Aloysius who the father of the child was.

"Ye swore, Millie. Ye said, ''Pon me soul I won't tell,' so ye won't, will ye. 'Twould be a mortal sin if ye did, wouldn't it?" she prodded.

"I won't tell," Millie answered, irritated for having been persuaded to do something so foolish. "But who will ye say is the father?"

"I won't say. No one can make me. And that way I won't be forced to marry anyone. Father would think Vince was a good catch. This big house and all that land. And Vince don't look foolish. And he likely wants to get married." She added, "To anyone who will have him." She shivered, recalling the touch of his clammy hands. "If ye tells anyone, Millie, ye'll be responsible for me death because I'd much sooner be dead than to have to take up with Vince."

Frustrated by being blocked on all sides from offering help, Millie said in exasperation, "But what do ye intend to do? Have the youngster on yer way to the store and leave it in the ditch?"

"Now yer bein' ridiculous," Bertha snapped. "I'm goin' to write to me father. Or Bessie most likely because father probably isn't back from the lumber woods yet. I'll tell her about my condition and that I have to come home. But I won't say a word about Vince."

When Millie said that her father would probably persuade her to tell who the child's father was, Bertha shook her head firmly. "No I won't. There was this girl at home. Angela her name was. She had a youngster. And she never told who the father was."

Millie posed another barrier to Bertha's leaving the Cove, one Bertha had thought about and had tried to dismiss. "But if ye goes home, what will happen to Mrs. Selena? Ye can't leave her all alone, and ye'd never get anyone to take on that much responsibility. Even if ye offered double the salary Ned paid."

Bertha began to cry again, hopelessly this time. There was no way out. There was no use fooling herself into thinking there was. She couldn't leave Mrs. Selena to fend for herself, and Millie was right in saying that no one else would want the job.

Millie searched frantically for some solution, even a partial one. "Stay on here," she offered. "Mrs. Selena won't be any the wiser, the poor soul. Write yer father and tell him about your condition, but if Ned doesn't get back in time to get ye home, we could get Mrs. Hartigan — that's the midwife — to come in when yer time comes. And when Ned comes back, go home then." She looked sternly at Bertha. "And be sure ye gets the money he promised ye. Don't let him get away with that." She added in a softer tone. "Not that I think he'd try to gyp ye. He's not that kind. But still, money does strange things to people."

That night, for the first time in months, Bertha slept well. She even began to make plans for when she got back home. Bessie could go to work if she wanted, but if she didn't, she could stay home because there would be enough work and enough money for both of them. And she liked Millie's suggestion that she not just settle for the lump sum cash Ned had promised but hold out for a monthly settlement. The Corrigans, Millie said, owed her that much, and certainly Ned would be willing to put out rather than have a scandal break open.

———⊰•⊱———

Bertha's child, a girl, was born in mid-February, and if everyone in the Cove was buzzing with the gossip, Bertha was unaware of it. She had long before stopped going to the store and depended upon Millie and Aloysius to get her groceries. She had even given up going to Mass on Sundays.

She called the child Carmel Elizabeth — Carmel after her mother and Elizabeth after her sister Bessie. Mrs. Selena called the child Neddie and talked to her in baby talk just as she must have done when Ned was young. Millie and Aloysius were godparents, and when they came to take Carmel to the church for baptism and christening, Millie gave Bertha the form to fill out for the parish records. Bertha took the paper and without a moment of hesitation filled in the spaces.

Name of Child: *Carmel Elizabeth*
Date of Birth: *Feb. 16, 1915*
Mother's Name: *Bertha Mary Ryan*
Father's Name: *Edward Francis Corrigan*

From the moment Carmel had given her first cry, Bertha knew she loved her too much to subject her to the shame that Angela's child had had to endure. She resolved that no old men lounging on molasses barrels would look at her daughter and search for resemblances. And she certainly had no intention of giving her a halfwitted father like Vince. The Corrigans, she reasoned, owed the child a father, and Ned was the obvious choice.

All along, Aloysius had surmised Ned was the father. He knew Bertha had taken a fancy to him, and he knew Ned had a reputation with the women. His face registered no surprise when he read the form. Millie's, on the other hand, registered shock, disbelief and finally comprehension.

"Ye can't do this, Bertha," she protested vehemently when Aloysius went to get more wood for Bertha's bedroom stove. "'Tis wrong."

"So 'tis wrong," Bertha said coldly. "'Tis no more wrong than have the child grow up without a name."

Millie handed the form back to Bertha. "'Tis slander, Bertha. I'd do a lot fer ye, but I can't be a party to slander."

Bertha realized she had to have Millie's cooperation if she was going to do right by Carmel. She had to think of some way to get her to go along with her plan. She looked over the child's head at Millie and said innocently, "Who sez 'tis slander. Who sez I wasn't lyin' to ye before. I sez Ned is the father. And that's all ye have to go on. No sin on yer soul whether I'm lyin' or tellin' the truth. And one more on me own won't matter."

⟫◆⟪

Only two letters had come from Ned after he left for Egypt, and both of these were hurriedly scribbled while he waited in a trench for the fighting to start afresh. In each one he asked how Bertha was managing, but he never made any outright mention of the baby. Bertha never replied. Although Mrs. Selena still hoarded Ned's letters in her apron pocket, maternal instinct still clinging to corners of her clouded mind, she never asked that Bertha reply to them, and Bertha felt no desire to do so of her own accord. Mrs. Selena continued to confuse Carmel with her own babies, and whenever the child cried, she would rock back and forth in her chair, her arms cradled with a make-believe Neddie or Vincey.

The newspaper accounts of the war were still very important to Bertha, although she had a difficult time trying to make any sense out of them. She often was none the wiser for having spent half an hour reading about the various invasions, the names and places of which were so strange-sounding that she couldn't even pronounce them, much less determine in what part of the world they were.

On the last day of June, Father Flannigan came to the house. When Bertha caught sight of him driving up the laneway in the two-seater black carriage, she frantically crossed herself. "Oh please, God!" she prayed. "Don't let it be fer me. Don't let it be somethin' wrong with Bessie or the boys."

She mustered enough strength to have the presence of mind to bring the priest in through the front door and seat him in one of the high-backed chairs in the parlour. As soon as he was seated, he reached inside his coat pocket and took out a black-bordered envelope and said he wanted to speak to Mrs. Selena. "I have terrible news for the poor soul," he said solemnly. "I hope she's up to hearing it." He indicated the telegram. "Just got the word this morning."

Bertha knew then that either Vince or Ned had been killed. She began to tremble. What if it were Ned? She'd never get out of the Cove. And how could she stay in the same house with Vince?

"'Tis not Ned, is it Father?" she managed to ask. "Dear God above, please tell me 'tis not Ned."

Father Flannigan, understanding that the child had been fathered by Ned, coughed in embarrassment. He felt guilty that he had never talked to the servant girl about her child being conceived outside of marriage, and he solaced himself by saying he intended to wait until Ned returned from the war. But he knew the real reason was that he was no good with dealing in other people's sins of the flesh. He spoke gently to Bertha.

"No, my dear. Not Ned. The child's father is safe as far as I know. It's her oldest boy. Vince."

He looked out towards the kitchen. "Can you bring Mrs. Corrigan in here, or would it be better if I went to the kitchen?"

Bertha was so relieved it wasn't Ned that her voice shivered from after-fright. "She's up havin' her nap now, Father. But she don't come down much no more. 'Twould be best if ye went up to her."

She turned to lead the way upstairs. "She don't understand a lot, Father," she explained as they mounted the steps. "She might not know what yer talkin' about."

Father Flannigan sat on the side of Mrs. Selena's bed and awkwardly tried to give her comfort. But the more he talked, the more laboured her breathing became. He looked at Bertha, his eyes filled with alarm.

"Oh my heavens, she's choking to death. Get the doctor!"

Bertha quickly went to bolster Mrs. Selena's head up on the pillows. "The doctor can't help, Father." She said calmly. "Just steam. I'll get the kettle boilin', and I'll get ye to help me bring her down to the kitchen."

After her breathing had eased and Father Flannigan had left, Mrs. Selena's mind took the bad news she had been given and reworked it in her own fashion. She suddenly stood up and looked wild eyed around the kitchen.

"Madeline! Get Vincey. He's up on the sheep house roof. If he falls, he's goin' to kill hisself. Hurry Madeline!" As if she couldn't wait for Madeline to save the child, she, herself, started for the outside door. Bertha became frantic.

"No! No! Mrs. Selena. Ye can't go out. Yer sick. Vince is dead, Ma'am. He was killed in the war." She grabbed her by the arm. "Come back and sit down. Vince is in heaven. Ye heard Father Flannigan. He said young men who spilled their blood fightin' godless nations are God's special children." The words almost stuck in her throat. If Vince were in heaven, it was just as well her hatred of him had forfeited a place for herself there.

Mrs. Selena flung off Bertha's restraining hand. "Git out of me way," she screamed. "He'll fall and kill hisself. I can't let him fall."

In desperation, Bertha grabbed Carmel who was sleeping in her cradle at the far end of the kitchen and thrust her into Mrs. Selena's arms, making sure she kept hold of the child herself. "Here's Vincey, Mrs. Selena. See! He's not on the sheep house roof. He's safe right here. Sit in yer chair and rock him."

The old woman became quiet instantly, and Bertha gently led her back to her chair. Mrs. Selena rubbed the down on Carmel's head and began to sing a lullaby in a soft, almost youthful voice.

⋘◆⋙

Vince had been the first war casualty from the Cove, but others followed. Shortly afterwards, the newspaper was filled with an account of an offensive that had cost the regiment many lives.

"Wiped out almost the whole regiment." Mr. Murphy couldn't seem to stop telling what he had heard in St. John's that day, and he repeated it to everyone who came in the store. "Mowed them down jest as if they were stalks of hay. Everyone is up in arms about the scandalous slaughter. The poor New-foundlanders sent to the front to be killed like rats." He shook his head, horrified anew by the number of men killed, no matter how many times he told the news. "Over in France. A place called *Somme*."

A few days later Father Flannigan returned to see Mrs. Selena, but this time he only told Bertha and left it up to her to break the news to the old woman.

Mrs. Selena was sleeping when he arrived, and he said it would be best if she heard the news when her mind was fresh from her nap. Ned had been wounded on July 1, 1916 in the Battle of the Somme, and he had been relocated to a hospital in London, England.

Although Bertha assured Father Flannigan she would tell Mrs. Selena when she woke up, she changed her mind as soon as he left the house. There was no use in upsetting the old woman needlessly. If Ned got better, she need never know he had been wounded, and if he died, it was time enough for the bad news.

That night Bertha took her rosary beads from underneath her pillow and prayed for Ned's recovery. She knew it was a selfish prayer because without Ned's safe return she would be stuck in the Cove forever. And all the while she prayed for Ned, Vince's face filled her mind. "God forgive me," she breathed, "although now I know I wouldn't lift a hand to bring about his death, and I might even save him if I had the chance, I'm still some glad he's gone. For me own sake and for little Carmel's sake, I'm some glad Ye took him."

In due course Mrs. Selena received a letter offering official condolences on Vince's death. Bertha read it to her.

On behalf of myself and the government, and indeed on behalf of the whole of the people of Newfoundland, I desire to tender you sincere sympathy on the great loss which you have sustained, a loss that is not only yours, but the whole country's.

When she finished reading the message, she handed it to Mrs. Selena to stuff in her apron pocket. Mrs. Selena took it, but instead of folding it many times and then carefully finding a place for it beside the other letters, she opened the damper of the stove and dropped it in amongst the fiercely burning green spruce.

"Piss!" she said as she watched it burn to ash. "Piss!" She then sat back in her chair, her old, creased face drooping.

Bertha looked from Carmel sleeping peacefully in the corner of the kitchen away from drafts to Mrs. Selena huddled in her black shawl. "Poor Mrs. Selena," she said softly. "Poor Mrs. Selena." She put her arm around the old woman's shoulders. "I'll make ye buttermilk biscuits fer supper. That'll make ye feel better."

⟫⟪

Ever since the day of the christening, Bertha sensed a hair-like break in her friendship with Millie. She knew Millie didn't believe her when she said Ned was the father of Carmel, and although they never once mentioned the duplicity that had taken place that afternoon, it always lurked just underneath the surface.

Bertha saw Vince's death as a way of making things right with Millie. Now that she no longer had the threat of being forced to marry Vince hanging over her, or worse, the threat that Vince would somehow claim Carmel, she could afford to make a clean breast of things. She decided to tell Millie that as soon as she got word that Ned was out of the hospital, she would write to him and confess what she had done. She also intended to tell her that she was willing to do whatever Ned felt was necessary to clear his name. She didn't know exactly what clearing his name entailed, but she was fairly certain it would at least mean getting the priest to change the church's records. She had also come to the realization that since Vince was dead, and had died in the war, he could be presented to Carmel as a brave man who had given his life for his country. She could tell her he was her father, and she would make up some story about the circumstances of her conception. She would never tell her she had come into the world as a result of an outrage by a dimwitted fool.

But Bertha was never given the chance to write Ned about clearing his name. He never returned to the front but was sent home directly from the hospital, with papers to show he was unfit for battle. The doctors agreed they were able to cure the bullet hole in his rectum, but they could do nothing about the rips and tears in his mind.

The Ned who returned to the Cove bore little resemblance to the Ned who had left there three years and two months earlier. His frame was gaunt and his hair thin. Even his eyes were different. Although they were the same intense blue, the light had gone out of them. They appeared to be in perpetual mourning, as if they suffered a sorrow too terrible to be shared even with the rest of his body. When he laughed, which he did at irregular intervals and for no apparent reason, his eyes stayed sober. When he cried, which he did often, his eyes stayed dry. And when he stared out through the windows, which he did almost constantly, his eyes remained empty.

Bertha brought a chair down from his bedroom and set it up on the other side of the stove from Mrs. Selena. They looked past each other over the top of the tea kettle, Mrs. Selena searching the wallpaper for her sons and Ned searching the meadows for only God knew what.

Bertha told Millie she now had three children to look after and that Carmel had more sense than the other two put together. She said she was tempted to take the money due her from Ned and go back home. But she couldn't reconcile leaving them to fend for themselves. Besides, there wasn't much of a home to go back to. Bessie had written that her father was remarrying a widow with three children. Even Bessie found that intolerable and said she was going to the United States to work in service for a family who wanted a girl just to look after the children. Bessie said she might as well get paid for looking after someone else's children rather than doing it for nothing.

Millie advised Bertha to stay in the Cove on the grounds that the devil you know is better than the devil you don't know. At least in the Cove she was head of the house, even if she was so only because the real heads were poor fools.

One week after that conversation with Millie, Mrs. Selena died. She ate her supper and then sat back to light her pipe. According to what Bertha told Millie, the old woman had barely time to take a draw from her corncob when she keeled over in her chair, clutching at her shawl with a death grip.

The people from the Cove came in droves. They came partly to offer help and to pay their last respects to Mrs. Selena, but mostly they came to view Ned. There had been much talk about men returning from the regiment with "the shell shock" but they never had seen anyone with it and wondered what effect it had on a person.

When the visitors walked out of the front parlour where Bertha had Mrs. Selena's coffin propped up on four chairs, they always stopped in the kitchen to speak to Ned. They told his unhearing ears that his mother looked lovely. Just grand. Just like herself. As soon as they got outdoors, they looked at each other and exchanged shocked whispers.

"Poor Ned," they'd say. "God help him. He looks more dead than alive. Not a bit like hisself."

After Mrs. Selena's funeral, Bertha's workload lessened enough for her to re-cover the old woman's chair. She went up to Murphy's to pick out some chintz and stopped at Millie's to drop off Carmel. She said she was driven to cover the chair because every time she looked at it she saw Mrs. Selena hunched over in her shawl. "'Tis enough to drive ye to the madhouse," she confessed. "Ned always lookin' like he's jest seen a ghost and me tryin' to keep me eyes off that chair."

As the winter progressed, Ned appeared to get a little better and when people asked Bertha about him, she always said, "Oh, he's comin' along fine. Once in a while he'll go to the stable and for a walk around the meadow. And now he only shouts out when he sleeps. But by the stuff he shouts, he seems to be carryin' around a terrible torment."

As spring came on, Bertha tried to pry Ned away from his almost constant sitting and staring. "The hen yard is fallin' down," she'd complain, sounding much like Mrs. Selena. "Why don't ye try to fix the pickets." Sometimes she would try to coax him out of his chair. "'Tis a grand day, Ned. Not too warm. Not too cold. Not a bit of fog. Why don't ye go out and get some fresh air." And when he complained about his wound, she did what the doctors advised — offered him no sympathy.

"'Tis all in yer head, Ned," she'd snap, worn out from his constant presence. "The doctors sez so. They sez if ye'd get yer behind off that chair and go mix with people, ye'd be a lot better off."

Often after she snapped at him, she would recall how kind he had been to her when she first came to the Cove, and, repentant, she would get a hot brick out of the oven and wrap it in old towels and tell him to sit on it. "'Twill ease the pain," she'd say, knowing that even if there was no pain to ease, the heat would make him fall asleep, and that was as good for her as it was for him.

Father Flannigan often asked about Ned when he stood in

the vestibule of the church after Mass. On a couple of occasions he came to visit, but Ned always seemed to sense when visitors were coming, and he'd spend the day in the stable waiting from them to leave.

"Oh Father, ye made the trip for nothin'," Bertha always apologized, not having the nerve to say Ned was hiding. "He's just gone off somewhere. Just wandered off a little while ago."

Father Flannigan always looked more relieved than disappointed. He asked Bertha about Ned's health, and she would repeat the same thing she had said in the vestibule on Sunday. "He has terrible nightmares. His mind is still over in France somewhere. It was jest the casing of him that came back, Father."

"Well, shell shock is a dreadful thing," Father Flannigan would allow. "Takes a long time to get over it. The mind has been tortured, you know. But in time and with God's goodness, he'll recover."

"Ye'd think there was a battle goin' on in his room, Father," Bertha would add. "Calls out to some captain and to a fellow by the name of Jimmy Hennessey. And always to Vince."

The third trip Father Flannigan made to the Corrigans' on Ned's account had nothing to do with the state of his health. People were beginning to gossip. Father Flannigan had little patience with the local gossips, but when scandalous talk affected the church, he had no choice but to do something.

As usual, when he arrived Ned was nowhere in sight, and Father Flannigan heaved a sigh of relief. He quickly got to the point of his visit, hoping to get away before Ned returned.

"There's talk," he said, "about you and Ned living together and not with the blessing of the church." He hurriedly said he knew there was nothing to the talk, Ned being as sick as he was, but because she was a young and pretty girl and on account of what had gone on before the war about Ned being the father of her child, there was enough grounds for gossip. He made his position clear. "The look of the thing. That's important, you know. The church must be kept away from even a hint of scandal."

Bertha's mouth gaped, and her crimson face showed both her embarrassment and her anger. "Glory be to heaven, Father," she flustered. "I'm jest here lookin' after Ned. He's jest like a child. He needs as much lookin' after as Carmel."

"I understand. I understand," he assured her, as embarrassed as Bertha. He twisted the brim of his felt hat. "Maybe you should get yourself another berth. Maybe what Ned needs is an older woman. An older woman wouldn't give rise to any talk."

As soon as the priest left, Bertha grabbed Carmel and went looking for Ned. Father Flannigan's visit had left her with two options: marry Ned or leave the only home she had. She didn't see how she could bring herself to do either.

She found Ned sitting in the hayloft, biding his time until he could come back to his chair beside the stove. She repeated what Father Flannigan had said, and the only indication she had that he understood what she was saying was that he put both hands over his face and began to cry.

"Don't leave me alone. Don't leave me alone," he begged over and over again.

Bertha went to him and patted his head in much the same way she would pat Carmel's. "Poor Ned," she said gently. "Poor Ned. We won't leave ye alone. Don't worry about that. And I won't have Carmel lose her home either."

Ned had no more interest in getting married than he had in getting the fields ready for haying or in fixing the leak in the roof or, for that matter, in shaving. Bertha, though, kept after him to keep himself clean, and every morning she put out a pan of hot water along with his razor and towel, and she never gave him a moment's peace until he washed and shaved.

It wasn't that Ned liked to be rumpled and unshaven. He just didn't have the energy to waste that way. He used up all his spare energy keeping the war at bay during the day — something he failed to do at night. The instant his eyes closed he had to cut Vince down from the barbed wire fence and drag Jimmy Hennessey to the safety of a shell hole, always stepping gingerly over the rutted ground to avoid walking on Jimmy's insides that had spilled out from the wound in his stomach. And he had to listen to the sounds of the captain's life draining away.

He went along with the marriage because it took too much effort to do otherwise. Besides, he needed Bertha to look after him. And he needed the child. She filled the kitchen with noise, and that noise drowned out the sounds of the captain's last gurgling breath and Jimmy's cries of pain. Her presence also blocked the sight of Vince slung up on the barbed wire fence like winter underwear hung out to air.

Aloysius and Millie stood up for them. They were married in Mrs. Selena's kitchen, with Mrs. Selena's ring. When Ned pushed the wide gold band on Bertha's finger, she felt as though he had put a yoke around her neck.

They slept separately, just as they had done before the marriage. When Mrs. Selena died, Bertha had taken over her room so she would be nearer to Carmel, who was sleeping in Vince's old room. Ned was in his own room. Neither of them discussed changing the sleeping arrangements. They just went back to the way things had been all along.

Ned's emotional state ebbed and flowed over the next three years. For a time he stopped shouting out in his sleep. Once or twice he even took an interest in the house and puttied the window frames and cleaned the chimney. He was always gentle with Carmel, and sometimes Bertha caught him looking at the child, love replacing the usual sadness in his eyes.

On those occasions, Bertha felt something for him akin to love, and she would work extra hard to ensure he was comfortable. She would bake something special for him or warm the cushion for his chair. Sometimes she encouraged him to take Carmel for a walk.

During one of these ebbs and flows, Ned moved into Bertha's bedroom. Just as they never discussed sleeping separately, they never discussed sleeping together, and the night he asked her to move over and make room for him in the big old feather bed of his mother's, she acquiesced easily. In the nights that followed, they reached out to each other like a couple of shipwrecked strangers who know that, through no fault of their own, they are entirely dependent on each other.

—————

Bertha's second child, Martin, was born on a lovely day in May. The fact that the foghorn didn't blow during the first week of his life was an omen to Bertha that he would have clear sailing throughout his life.

Bertha had nursed the hope that Martin's birth would make Ned whole again. She confided in Millie that if there was anything that could turn Ned back into his old self it would be the child. She imagined Ned restocking the stable and working the fields, just as he had done during her early days in the Cove.

But Martin's birth didn't cause a ripple in Ned's life. If anything, he regressed. Although he never resumed the nighttime raving and shouting that he had done when he first returned home, he became even more withdrawn. Bertha could tell from his distant, hollow stare when he looked out through the window that he wasn't seeing the hay bent down from the rain and from want of mowing; he was, instead, seeing the fields of Beaumont Hammel and the raging battle of the Somme. He appeared not even to have noticed that Bertha moved to the servant's room — the little room at the back of the house — and left him to sleep alone in his mother's feather bed.

————⊳◆⊲————

With each passing year, Ned's mind became more and more turned in upon itself. His old friends still came to visit, out of loyalty and charity, although they only stayed ten or fifteen minutes. These visits, Bertha noticed, always seemed to lift him out of his darkest moods, although she wasn't sure what cheered him up: the companionship or the bottle of hop beer they usually brought along. But as she said to Millie, she wasn't going to quibble about which was which. She was just happy that after the friends left, Ned would vacate the chair for the first time that day. Sometimes he would even go outside and bring in wood for the fire.

One day, having come to the conclusion that it was the bottle of hop beer that lifted Ned's mind out of the darkness, Bertha went to Murphy's and bought the ingredients for making home brew. She thought that by having the beer on hand, Ned could not only have a bottle when he wanted one, but he could also have something that would bring his friends back for more visits.

Ned delighted in making the beer. It was the only thing that could sustain his interest for more than five minutes, and Bertha was thrilled at having hit upon something that gave him some pleasure and her some relief from his eternal staring.

But Ned refused to share his brew. He never offered even as much as a glassful when his friends came to the house. He brewed a batch, drank it, then brewed another. When Bertha saw what was happening, she refused to buy the ingredients, thinking that would put an instant stop to his drinking. She was mistaken. He went for two weeks depending upon the sporadic gifts from his friends. Then he started visiting the friends, asking for a glass of beer as soon as he was inside the door.

Once he went to the Tobins', where Carmel was playing. Carmel was mortified. She ran home with tears streaming down her face, telling how Ned had begged for a glass of beer even when Mr. Tobin insisted he hadn't any.

After that incident, Bertha gave him money each week and told him if he wanted beer he would have to go buy the makings himself. For five days the money lay on the windowsill, but on the sixth day, he got up in the morning and without waiting to shave or even to eat breakfast, he took the money and went to Murphy's. After that first venture, he made regular trips. Sometimes he went twice a week. The extent of his drinking began to worry Bertha. She tried not giving him the money, but he would get snarly and surly and keep the house in an uproar. She considered asking Mrs. Murphy not to sell him the hops, but she knew if she did that, Ned would just go around the Cove begging for beer and shaming the children. At least when he stayed home to drink, he exposed neither himself nor the family to public scrutiny, and Carmel's feelings, delicate as fine china, were left unscathed.

Carmel's Story

Carmel tried to scrunch her slight frame into itself in the hope of making it small enough to disappear into one of the many gouges in her wooden desk. She also tried to pretend she had neither heard nor seen her father dart into the classroom as quickly as a lizard darting into the night. He stood just inside the door, his back pressed against the heavy wooden panels, and surveyed the room, trying to sort out where he was. The staring eyes, the shocked faces and the tittering whispers confused and frightened him. He darted back out, none the wiser as to where he had been, knowing only that it wasn't Murphy's store.

Everyone saw him come in. Everyone saw him leave. Everyone, that is, excepting Sister Rita. She had her back to the door, hunkered down by Peter Emberley's desk helping him with his additions. When she heard the commotion, she straightened up to tongue-lash the class into silence, and as she did so she caught a glimpse of the back of Ned's head disappearing out the door.

She flicked a glance from one desk to another, looking for someone who had taken an unexcused trip to the toilet. Seeing all seats were occupied, she inquired hastily, "What was that all about?"

"Shell-shocked Ned, Sister," Clifford Collins volunteered, casting sly glances in Carmel's direction. "I think, Sister, he thought he was goin' to Murphy's because he had a molasses

can in his hand. Goin' fer the fixin's fer his home brew, Sister."
More tittering followed.

Sister Rita gave her veil a violent toss over her shoulder,
signalling that she had taken just about all she was going to
take. "Stop this nonsense immediately! Get back to work this
minute! The lot of you haven't enough sense to work unless
someone is standing over you with a ruler."

She was furious with herself. She had played right into their
hands and added to poor Carmel's humiliation. She glanced
pityingly towards the child and thought, What a cross she has
to bear, having Ned for a father. And so undeserving of that
cross. Sometimes, Sister Rita pretended Carmel was her child.
She had all the fine qualities a daughter of hers would have
had. Driving. Meticulous. Sombre. Dedicated. Sensitive.

"Carmel, dear," she cooed sweetly, forcing softness into her
voice. "If you've finished writing out your spelling, come over
here and I'll test you on them."

Carmel had her head bent so close to her desk her nose
almost scraped against her scribbler, and she clutched her pencil
so hard her knuckles were white. She picked up her scribbler
with row after row of words written in perfectly formed letters
and went to stand beside Peter Emberley's desk. Sister Rita
took the scribbler and quickly scanned the page. She held it up
to the classroom.

"Class! See!" She waited until all eyes were focussed on the
scribbler. "Beautifully formed letters. Not hen's tracks! No dirty
thumb smudges!"

The conscripted oh's and ah's doused some of Carmel's
white hot shame, but she still slunk back to her desk in the
pure knowledge that death would be preferable to enduring
such an incident again.

But other incidents did follow, and none of them brought
merciful death. In his haze of hop beer and shell shock, Ned
often mistook the school for Murphy's store. The buildings

were in adjacent meadows, and distinguishing one from the other usually taxed Ned's power of discrimination beyond its limit. Carmel's humiliation was frequently so intense it pulsated like a festering wound.

Because of Ned she kept her friends away from her house, although that in itself wasn't very difficult. Most of them were afraid of Ned anyway and would run into lanes rather than pass him on the road. Only Eileen Tobin wasn't afraid of him. She lived close by, and she had gotten used to him before she was old enough to realize he was different.

But Eileen mocked him. Sometimes she did this in Carmel's presence. On these occasions, Carmel cringed with shame for not having the courage to make Eileen stop her disrespectful treatment of Ned. Sometimes she pretended she didn't hear the remarks because Eileen was the only companion she had, and if she lost her, she would be left with no one except Martin. On a couple of occasions, her mother had caught Eileen making fun of Ned. She had been singing the war song Ned sang, and she always sang it in the same loud, tuneless way he did. For Carmel's sake Bertha, too, pretended not to hear, but later she always chastised Carmel for associating with Eileen.

"Yer father fought for his country. Don't let the likes of Eileen Tobin poke fun at him." She stressed how Ned Corrigan's children had no reason to be ashamed because their father had had the courage to go to war when others didn't. The others included Eileen's father, Tom Tobin. She would whip the dishcloth over her shoulder in much the same way Sister Rita whipped her veil back when she was angry. "Yer Father's a fool because the war made him one, not because he was born one."

Despite her mother's admonishments, Carmel never tattled on Eileen. She never told even when Eileen taunted Martin by singing a vulgar song about his name, a song that on one occasion made him so furious he picked up a rock and let it fly in Eileen's direction. Only it hadn't struck Eileen. It had lodged instead in Carmel's forehead, just a hair's breadth away from her temple. Eileen was still chanting the song when Carmel ran screaming into the kitchen, calling for her mother.

Martin, Martin, went to bed fartin',
Got up stinkin', went away winkin'.

"Sacred Heart! Sacred Heart!" Bertha shouted when Carmel pulled her hand away from her head and exposed the three-cornered rock embedded in her flesh. Bertha tried to yank it out with her hands, but the rock was shale, and a small piece — too small to be grasped by her fingers — stayed in the wound.

She shouted to Martin. "The pliers! Quick, bring the pliers!"

Martin, still frenzied from having hit Carmel by mistake, scurried around trying to help, not knowing what to do.

"Never mind! Never mind! They're in the stable. I left them there yesterday when I was framin' the picture."

Bertha grabbed Carmel's arm and raced to the stable. Along the way she took turns scolding God and chastising Carmel.

"God up in heaven, ent saddling me with Ned enough! Ent Ned enough!" She moved from God to Carmel. "And you, ye young divil of a thing. Haven't ye got any sense in yer head? A twelve-year-old tormenting a five-year-old. And dirty talk too! Not like ye at all. What's comin' over ye, girl?" Her eyes saw again the rock embedded in Carmel's temple, and her voice softened. "I hope, me child, it don't kill the roots and leave a white streak. Like I've seen happen."

Carmel didn't defend herself by telling that it was Eileen who had sung the song. She hoped that by the time she got back to the house, Martin would have gone off playing, and the incident would be forgotten.

But Martin had been too scared to go out to play. He remained huddled underneath the kitchen table, whimpering. He expected to be punished when his mother got back from the stable. And he was afraid Carmel would have to go to the doctor. He changed his whimpering to loud crying in the hope his father would hear him and tell him everything was going to be all right.

Ned heard nothing. He sat in the barrel chair by the stove with a glass of hop beer in his hand and stared through the window at the stretch of no man's land that separated Company A and Company B from the Germans. He shook his head to get a better grip on his surroundings, and when he did, the movement unsteadied his hand and his beer sloshed over the hot stove, making a hissing sound.

"Down! Down!" he shouted, certain the hissing was from a shell about to hit the ground. He dropped to the floor and quickly searched the kitchen to make sure all of his fellow soldiers were face down in the mud. When he hit the floor, his beer glass crashed against the leg of the stove. "Oh, Sweet Jesus," he whispered as the shells from the battle raging in the Somme pelted down like an early fall hailstorm in the Cove.

He shook his head again to bring the present into clearer focus. It *couldn't* be the Battle of the Somme. Had he not heard his buddy, Jimmy Hennessey, scream for the pliers? His lips moved in a little smile. No matter how many times he corrected Jimmy, he always called the wire cutters *pliers*. If that had been Jimmy shouting for the pliers, it must mean that it was the scouting party that was underway and not the July Drive. He shook his head again. Of course it was the scouting party. He knew exactly where he was. He even knew the date. It was June 28, 1916. He and Vince and Jimmy Hennessey were among the volunteers who had offered to cross no man's land to cut the barbed wire fence protecting the German Line. The cutting of the wire was in preparation for the big drive that was coming up to wipe out the Germans once and for all.

He whispered to himself as he skulked across the piece of shell-tortured ground, his wire cutters at the ready. "Sweet Jesus, 'tis a dark as the grave. Sweet Jesus keep the bastards asleep for a few more minutes. Kiss me starn, Kaiser Bill." He always told the Kaiser to kiss his starn just before he had to turn up his collar and hunch a shoulder to face into the shower of shells. It gave him courage in much the same way whistling did when he walked home from a dance and had to pass by the pasture that was supposed to have a ghost or two wandering about.

"Oh my Christ, 'tis already cut. The bastards! They know we're here."

"Shh! Maybe the shelling this morning did it."

"Now what?"

"We'll go through. We'll shoot every last blood of a bitch right in his own trench."

"Sweet Jesus! A flare! 'Tis as bright as day! *Look out! Down! Down!*" Bang! Bang! Bang!

"Oh God, they got us cornered. More flares!"

"Someone's slung up against the fence!"

"Sweet Jesus, 'tis Vince!"

"Cover Private Corrigan!"

"I have to get Vince. I promised Ma."

"I'll help, Ned. Me pliers! I dropped me pliers. Somebody bring the pliers!"

Bang! Bang! Bang!

"Shut up, Pop! Shut up!" Martin stopped his whimpering long enough to bring his father back to his senses. He used the same nettled tone his mother used for the same purpose, although knowing nothing would make Ned stop shouting if he was of a mind to do so.

"Yer home in the Cove, Pop. Be quiet!"

Ned didn't hear Martin. Instead he heard the voice of the nurse in the London hospital.

"Be quiet, Private Corrigan. You're safe in the hospital. We've got to dress your wound, and we can't do it if you keep thrashing about. Lie still!"

But how could he lie still when he was crouched in a shell hole in no man's land and listening to the dying sounds of Jimmy Hennessey and Captain Larsen, who were lying near him, face down in the chewed-up mud. The shelling from the Battle of the Somme had ended, and in the heavy silence that descended, he could hear Jimmy whimpering for his mother, sounding like a lamb in the pasture, separated from the old ewe. Captain Larsen's breath was gurgling out through the shell hole in his throat. He had to get to them and haul them to safety. He would get Jimmy first. He couldn't leave him out there, ripe for a sniper's bullet. Jimmy's insides were hanging out.

"I'll get ye, Jimmy. Kiss me starn, Kaiser Bill."

He eased himself out of his hiding place and crawled towards Jimmy. He had to stick his own backside up in the air in order to get leverage to inch Jimmy's body over the humps of mud.

"Kiss me starn, Kaiser Bill. Kiss me starn, Kaiser Bill."

Bang!

One of the Kaiser's snipers obliged and kissed his starn with a shell that sent shrapnel up his back passage.

"Shut up shouting, Pop! Go for a walk on the beach. Go sit in the stable."

Martin's voice finally penetrated Ned's war-scarred brain. He pulled his gaze back from no man's land and raised himself up on an elbow and looked around the empty kitchen. Where was everyone? He was all alone. He hated being alone. He sat upright and shouted loudly enough to be heard in any room in the house.

"Bertha! Where are ye, Bertha! Get me pills. Me starn is painin'."

—◆—

In the time it took to have the stone removed from her forehead and the wound cleaned and bandaged, Carmel made a decision to tell Eileen Tobin that she was no longer welcome in her house. She convinced herself she didn't need people her own age. In a few years she would be finished school, and she would then go to the United States. Her Aunt Bessie had promised to sponsor her. Her life would begin when she left the Cove.

Millie Morrissey filled the gap left by Eileen. Whenever Carmel couldn't tolerate another moment of being alone, or of listening to Ned wage war at the Front, she would run across the meadow to Millie's.

"On the rampage again today, is he?" Millie would say as she portioned out slices of gingerbread to go with the hot cup of tea she always had on hand.

"Something shocking," Carmel would stammer, fighting back tears. "He's been up since five and hasn't stopped his shouting and singing." She would toss her long red hair in disgust. "And drinking. Swilling down the hop beer as if there's going to be a drought."

Millie's mouth would curl in disapproval. "'Tis the beer. That's what sets him off worse than he is." She would sigh resignedly. "But nothin' can be done about that. He'll find a way to get it one way or another."

"That's for sure. He's started to keep an extra keg up in the stable. He caught on that Mother waters it down when he keeps it in the house. Now he hides it on her."

Millie always ended these conversations about Ned's

problems on a compassionate note. She said she knew the person who was inside Ned's skin before the war ruined him. And, like Bertha, she worried about him spending so much time in the stable. "I knows what heartache it gives yer mother, him being up there. She's sure he's goin' to stumble over the loft and break his neck." As if carrying on a debate with herself, she would say, "Not that everyone wouldn't be better off, himself included, if he did go quick. But still the poor divil deserves to go in his bed like we all want to."

When Millie described the Ned who went to the regiment, she left it up to Carmel to make the comparison with the Ned who came back.

"As responsible as they come," she would say, nodding her head to affirm the truth of her own assertions. "Looked after his mother even though he'd gladly have given his elbows to leave home as soon as he turned sixteen. Yes, girl. A responsible young man. Took responsibility for Vince, and God knows that fellow was a fish or two shy of a quintal." She would elaborate on the root cause of Ned's problem.

"Awful stuff that shell shock. Never heard tell of it till the war. Now it seems every other fellow who was over there has it." She would give first-hand testimony to the reality of these others. "Heard of a fellow in Crossman's Harbour by the name of Renfrew. Went over a fine specimen of a man. Came back a raving maniac. And a Whalen fellow. Related to the Whalens from here, but living down the bay. Went over as fit as a fiddle and hasn't spoken a word since coming back. Sits in the kitchen like a dead man."

Carmel always felt better about herself after talking with Millie. Having her say Ned wasn't always the person he had become was comforting. She surmised she had been conceived out of wedlock, although nothing had ever been said about this. She just had a feeling she had come before Ned and Bertha's marriage. That was bad enough in itself without being conceived by a fool as well. Once she had tried to tie down dates and asked her mother how long she was married. Bertha's dismissive "Too long for me own good" didn't encourage Carmel to probe any further.

———⟫•⟪———

Although Carmel carefully avoided bringing any of her school friends to her house, and they just as carefully avoided coming of their own accord, the day came when their presence at her place could not be prevented. She was sixteen and in her last year of school. A June bazaar was going to be held at the church. It was to take place after Sunday Mass, and Carmel's class had been told they were to provide cakes for the sale. The class had been divided into groups of three, and lots were to be drawn to see whose kitchen would be used for the baking. Carmel fervently prayed that the lot not fall to her kitchen. She promised litanies and rosaries by the hundreds. She even promised never to yell at Martin for leaving his clothes strewn around the house. All of her supplications were in vain.

The girls were supposed to be at her house at two o'clock, and it was already close to one. Carmel's anxiety was so high she could barely catch her breath. Her father was still in the stable. He had been there ever since breakfast. For the last couple of days he had rarely shouted or sung his song and had spent most of his time in the stable. Still, no matter how early or late he stayed up there, he always came back to the house for his meals. He didn't appear to know night from day, but he had a real cunning sense of mealtime.

Carmel had hoped he would have come down for his lunch at his usual time, and if so, he would be back up in the stable by the time the girls arrived for the baking. But twelve o'clock came and went and he failed to make his appearance. She visualized him walking into the kitchen when they were in the middle of baking. She could see him staggering across the floor and beginning to sing at the top of his voice, his hands waving to keep time to his tuneless song:

> *And when those Newfoundlanders start to yell, start to yell,*
> *Oh Kaiser Bill, you'll wish you were in hell, were in hell.*
> *For they'll hang you high in your Potsdam palace wall,*
> *You're a damn poor Kaiser after all.*

Carmel cringed at the very real possibility of her impending mortification. Every line of the song and every gesture of Ned's hands burned into her brain. He always mispronounced *Kaiser*, calling *Kassar*. And he usually ended his singing with a postscript, "Kiss me starn, Kassar Bill." After he ran through his performance, he would sit in his chair with his ear cocked, listening for the sound of a shell slicing through the air.

She often wished her father had died nobly at the Front instead of dying in bits and pieces in the Cove. Once she said to her mother that it was unfair of God to take her Uncle Vince so quickly — when he wasn't all there anyway — and to leave just the casing of her father, a man who had once been of sound mind and body. And she felt that the unfairest trick of all that had been played on the whole Corrigan family was her father's ignominious wound in his seat. The site of that wound often prodded Eileen Tobin to say Ned had gotten shot running away from the fighting. Bertha's answer to Carmel's lamentations of what should and shouldn't have been was always a curt, "We all don't get what we deserve, nor for that matter deserve what we gets."

Carmel got out the cooking utensils and then paced the floor, her agitation growing with every passing second. If only her father would come down from the stable in time to get fed and be back up there out of the way before the girls arrived.

"*Mother, please! Please!*" she agonized, her misery as visible as the pots and pans that were lying in wait for the girls. "Can't you get him to come down. Send Martin after him. You know what's going to happen. He's going to smell the baking and come in and make a fool of us all in front of Jane and Marie."

Bertha was tired out from trying to ease everyone's burdens and to keep peace in the household. Carmel spent most of her time proving she in no way resembled Ned. She fussed about her clothes, making sure they were spotless. She corrected every second sentence Martin uttered trying to get him to use proper English. It was as if she felt the rest of the family had to make up for Ned's lack of sense. She fretted Martin so much that Bertha wondered if she was going to damage his happy-go-lucky nature.

But as much as Carmel exasperated her at times, Bertha also felt sorry for the child, knowing that feeling sorry wasn't going to help anyone. She couldn't change the conditions of Carmel's life any more than she could get Ned to come down from the stable if he didn't have a mind to do so. Ned moved according to his own clock. She herself had accepted that much, and she always had a pot of something heating on the back of the stove for whenever he decided to eat.

"Mother!" Carmel wailed impatiently. "Can't you send Martin to the stable? He'll come for Martin. You know he will."

Martin sat in the middle of the kitchen floor arranging his fishing tackle. He was hurrying to get out of earshot of Carmel. She was always wanting him to do this or that, mostly nonsense stuff, like hanging up his coat when he was going to use it again in a few minutes.

Bertha looked at Martin who was seemingly unaware of the confusion that constantly went on in the household. She knew he was the only person who could manipulate Ned and get him to do something he had no intention of doing.

"Martin, boy," she said cajolingly, pushing some of his tackle out of the traffic route with the toe of her shoe, "before ye do anything else, run up to the stable like Carmel wants and get yer father to come down fer a bite to eat."

Martin kept on rearranging his tackle. Bertha's patience ran out.

"Move, Martin! I've got enough to put up with without having a disobedient youngster on me hands. Get up to the stable this minute!"

Martin got up slowly, shooting a spiteful glance at Carmel. "Fusser! Fusser!" he hurled the words across the kitchen just before he scurried out the door. He raced up the narrow path hoping, as he ran, that his father would come without too much coaxing. He didn't want to waste any more time before going fishing with his buddies, and he had arranged to meet them at the brook by half-past one.

He rushed into the stable, letting the heavy outside door slam shut behind him. He ran past the empty stalls and scampered up the ladder to the loft. He knew exactly where his father would be. He would be sitting on the haymow loft with his legs dangling into the empty mow.

"Pop!" he shouted, even before he reached the top rung of the ladder. "Maw says come down. She has beans."

There was no answer, but Martin hadn't expected one. Ned never answered him. He always called out just to rouse him out of his daydreaming because he hated seeing the distant stare in his father's eyes being replaced by a startled, frightened look. Whenever he was startled by voices or unexpected noises, Ned would begin to tremble as though his life were in danger.

"Pop! Pop!" Martin stepped out on the loft and waited an instant for his eyes to adjust to the small stream of light from the half window in the haymow. He walked across the loft and searched the spot where he knew his father would be sitting. Ned wasn't there.

Martin went to his father's second choice resting spot — behind the barrels of harness that long ago had been gathered together and stored out of the way. He called as he looked. "Pop! Pop! Where are ye? Maw got beans ready."

Ned still didn't answer. Martin started to go down the ladder again. Whenever Ned couldn't be found in the stable, he was certain to be down on the beach wandering up and down the landwash, staring into the sand as though he were looking for something he had dropped. Once Martin had found him there. He wasn't wandering then, just sitting in the sand. His legs were soaking wet because the tide had changed while he sat. His mother said if he hadn't found him when he did, he would have drowned for sure because if the cold water hadn't been enough to arouse him out of his stupor, nothing would.

As he backed down the ladder, Martin mumbled his disgruntlement. He wasn't going to be the one to go searching the beach. Carmel was the one who would have to do that. It didn't matter to him what time his father came to eat. He was never embarrassed by him. And his friends knew better than to poke fun at him. But even as he grumbled, he knew he would have to go to the landwash. His mother would see to it that he was the one. If he balked, his mother would wheedle. "Ye run along like a good boy. It'll save me the trip, and yer younger than me."

When he got to the bottom of the ladder, he turned to open the heavy door. He saw him then. He was dangling from a nail on the back of the door, a piece of hemp rope circling his neck.

For an instant Martin was too paralyzed even to take flight. He just stared at Ned's inert body hung up on the spike that used to hold the horse's collar. When he could move, he started to run back up the ladder. But then he realized he couldn't get out that way. The only way out was through the door that held his suspended father.

He moved gingerly towards the door. Ned's hand had flopped, palm up, like a dead trout, over the latch. Martin took the hand, but it was so cold and clammy he let go of it immediately. He reached out again and this time snatched the sleeve of Ned's shirt and pulled the hand free of the latch and hauled the door ajar.

He raced to the house so fast he was sure his lungs would burst. He tore into the kitchen and leaned against the door frame unable to speak. His mouth worked frantically, but no sounds came out.

Bertha saw his chalk white face and the terror in his wide-open eyes. "Sacred Heart! Sacred Heart! What's wrong, boy! What's happened?" Even as she shouted at him and shook his shoulders trying to get him to speak, she knew what had happened. "Sacred Heart of Jesus, he's stumbled over the loft. Come quick, Carmel! Come quick!"

Martin began to shake violently, and his words came out in a shiver. "He's . . . he's . . . he's" — he cupped his hands frantically around his throat — "he's . . . he's hangin' . . ." As soon as he squeezed this out, he spewed vomit across the floor.

"Sacred Heart! Sacred Heart!" Bertha's agonized scream filled the room. She crossed herself in rapid succession to keep at bay the horror of what she was hearing. "What to do! What to do!" She raced back and forth across the kitchen, frenzied. She had to save him. He couldn't die by his own hand. She shouted at Carmel to get Aloysius and the priest and the doctor. She snatched the butcher knife out of the cupboard drawer and ordered Martin to follow her to the stable.

Martin recoiled and backed himself further into the wall. "No! No! No!" he shrieked. "No!"

Bertha grabbed him by the arm and half-dragged him to

the stable. Martin vomited continuously as he stumbled along the path.

Once inside, Bertha continued to snap orders. "Get that old harness box! Upend it so ye can reach."

Martin obeyed, dazed. Bertha handed him the butcher knife. "Ye cut, and I'll press against him to break his fall." She grabbed the milking stool — the stool Ned had used to take his weight while he was rigging the rope — and pushed it back underneath his feet. Martin hacked at the rope, and in a few minutes, Ned's body slid down the door.

By the time they had dragged the body outside, Millie and Aloysius were coming up the path, and Carmel came into sight, breathlessly shouting that the priest was on his way, but the doctor was out of the Cove on a case.

Aloysius took the rope from Ned's neck and straightened the body so there wouldn't be any trouble later getting it in the coffin. He knew death when he saw it. Carmel rushed to the house and came back with a pillow and a blanket. She raised Ned's head and slipped the pillow underneath it and gently tucked the blanket over him.

In less than ten minutes, Father Myrick was kneeling beside Ned. He had been ordained only a little over a year when he was sent out to the Cove to help Father Flannigan, but within a few weeks of his coming, the old priest died, and Father Myrick had been left on his own. Already he was wishing the parish was someone else's responsibility.

He had raced his horse so fast to the Corrigans' house that by the time he reached the spot where Ned was laid on the ground, the animal was in a lather of sweat. He leapt from the carriage and dropped to his knees beside Ned. He felt for a pulse. Feeling no throb at the wrists, behind the ears or at the temples or ankles, he put his mouth to Ned's ear and demanded, "Blink your eye if you can hear me." He searched Ned's wide-open, bulging eyes for the slightest sign of movement.

Ned remained motionless.

"Squeeze my finger!" He grabbed hold of Ned's stiffening hand. The hand remained inert.

Father Myrick quickly took his stole from his inside coat pocket, and after hastily kissing the embroidered cross, slung it around his neck.

"Say after me, Ned," he commanded, moving his face closer to Ned's. "Oh my God, I am heartily sorry for having offended Thee . . ." He looked at Ned's silent lips. "Think the words, Ned! *Think* them!"

He began the Act of Contrition again in the hope it would prod Ned's thoughts, but when he looked at the lifeless body, he knew it was pointless to carry on. He squatted back on his heels, ready to accept defeat. Then he remembered what he had been taught at the seminary. *If there was the slightest chance, you must never give up.*

He shouted out. "Bring a looking glass! Quick!"

Carmel ran to the house and returned with the shaving mirror from the porch.

"Let there be a spark," Father Myrick prayed as he held the mirror to Ned's mouth. "Let there be a spark." It came away bone dry.

He began the ritual of conditional anointing and conditional absolution. "*If you are living,*" he began, the Latin rolling easily off his lips, "*Si vivis, per istam, sanctam unctionem indulgeat tibi dominus quidquid deliquisti. Amen.*" He dipped his thumb into a vial of chrism and made the sign of the cross on Ned's forehead. "May the Lord Jesus save you, free you from sin and raise you up." The oil glistened on Ned's pallid flesh.

He took Ned's hand to anoint it, but the fingers had stiffened inward, and he had to pry them open to get at the palm. When the anointing was completed, he began the Papal Blessing, slicing the sign of the cross over Ned's face, and racing his words to get them said before Ned's soul departed.

He stopped abruptly in the midst of the blessing. *Who was he trying to fool?* Ned was as dead as a doornail. By denying an obvious suicide, he was making a mockery out of the most precious of sacraments. He leaned wearily back on his haunches and removed his stole, hauling it off as though it weighed a ton. He folded it slowly, once again kissing the embroidered cross before placing it back in his inside coat pocket. He beckoned to Bertha to come to the house. The children followed.

Knowing the hell and damnation that followed suicide, he wondered what he should say and what he should do. He had never before run up against anything even remotely relating to self-destruction. He grasped at straws. Perhaps there was still a chance Ned could be given a Christian burial. If it could be shown Ned was insane at the time of the act and that the insanity hadn't been self-induced, then Ned could be given a burial from the church. He decided to act on that.

Bertha sat on the couch whimpering, some of the impact of Ned's deed beginning to bear down on her. "Oh my God, he done away with hisself, Father. He done away with hisself."

Father Myrick looked at the terrified faces of the children, and he asked Bertha if they could go to the parlour. He directed Carmel to wait in the kitchen and make a cup of tea for all of them. He told Martin to go sit beside the stove because he looked very cold.

Martin didn't move. The only chair by the stove was Ned's, Mrs. Selena's having long ago been relegated to the back porch for the times when Ned wanted to sit in a cool part of the house.

As soon as they were alone, Father Myrick let his consternation show. "God help us all, Mrs. Corrigan. What's to be done?" He rubbed his hands across his face, wishing he hadn't been so eager to have a parish of his own. He wanted to put the right words in Bertha's mouth without actually saying them first. He prodded, hopefully.

"Would you say Ned was insane?"

Bertha couldn't see how Ned's sanity had anything to do with his death. He was dead by his own hand and that was shame enough for the children to bear without adding lunacy as well.

"He was shell-shocked, Father, but I wouldn't consider him off his head or anything like that. He brooded a lot, and the hop beer always set him off on a ravin' spree."

"Yes, I smelled the beer all right, and he must have spilled it over himself." Father Myrick rubbed the front of his suit jacket as though feeling the sopping wet of Ned's shirt. "His whole front was soaking wet."

He plunged into the reason for wanting to see Bertha alone. "Ned can be buried *inside* the church if it can be shown he was insane — that he was off his head even before he got drunk." Getting drunk, he explained, was a wilful act, and Ned would have to be held responsible for that.

"What do you mean *inside* the church, Father?"

"I mean buried in the cemetery, beside his mother."

"Of course he'll be buried on Dickson's Hill. The rest of the family is already up there," she retorted. "I don't understand why yer askin', Father."

Bertha hadn't had the advantage of a convent education to teach her the finer points of her religion. And she had never known anyone who had taken his own life. She only knew that suicide was a terrible sin.

Realizing the extent of Bertha's ignorance. Father Myrick gently explained the church's stand on suicide. "Of course he can be buried on Dickson's Hill, Mrs. Corrigan, but not in the consecrated part of the cemetery. It will have to be in a place not blest. Not if he killed himself while in sound mind." He outlined the reason for such a stand.

"It's the Outward Sign," he explained, the words coming almost verbatim from his seminary text. "Holy Mother Church can't condone the sin of Judas. Only God can give life and only God can take it. We can't throw His most precious gift back in His face."

Bertha said nothing, just kept staring at her lap. Father Myrick continued. "Suicide is the most heinous of crimes," he said gently. "It can't be condoned because it puts the person outside God's love. That's why we can't even *appear* to condone it. Even if there's the slightest chance — I mean the *slightest* chance — that the person died by his own hand while in sound mind."

When she finally understood, Bertha considered retracting her statement about Ned being shell-shocked and not insane. She had no idea there would be such public condemnation of a suicide. Public shame! Still, she really didn't consider Ned insane, and if she were to say otherwise she would be lying to the church. How could she do that even for her children? She was convinced Ned *wasn't* insane. She had heard about people having to be wrapped in canvas and taken to the lunatic asylum. One man had grabbed a knife and threatened to slice up the whole family. Ned had never acted like that. He was as harmless as an old dog.

She stared into her lap, pondering the pros and cons of the lie. It was her sin or the children's shame. After a long, heavy silence she spoke.

"Who am I to say, Father? I'm no doctor. Perhaps he *was* off his head, and we didn't know it." She faltered. She couldn't continue with the lie. There were enough sins already in the Corrigan household. She wasn't going to add to them. She looked straight into Father Myrick's face. "The truth is, Father, there was some little thing wrong with Ned brought on by the shell shock, but he certainly wasn't off his head."

She explained how she had asked Dr. Mahar to send a letter to the government in St. John's saying Ned had lost his senses on account of the war and that he would never get any better. The letter, she said, would have meant an upping of Ned's pension. The doctor, however, wouldn't do it for her. He insisted there was nothing wrong with Ned that would keep him from working if he was so inclined. He told her that lots of men had returned from the war and hadn't sat around feeling sorry for themselves. He cited his own son as one such person. He had seen front line action, and now he was a doctor with a practice down the bay.

Bertha looked shamefaced at the priest. "If ye'll pardon the expression, Father, his exact words were 'there's nothing more serious wrong with Ned than a congealed fart.'" She hurried to explain that Ned kept complaining about his rectum paining, but the London doctors had said the wound was healed and the St. John's doctors agreed also. She added sombrely, "They all said the pain was in Ned's mind and not in his backside."

Father Myrick's tone remained as sombre as Bertha's. "I'll go see Dr. Mahar myself. I'll talk to him about getting some sort of statement saying Ned had problems with his mind."

Bertha gave a resigned nod of her head. "Ned'll be crawling with blowflies by the time ye gets hold of Mahar, Father. The housekeeper told Carmel she was supposed to say he was away on a case. The truth is he's gone to St. John's on another of his week-long benders. Won't be back until his hands are too shaky to tip the glass to his mouth."

Martin sensed that something terrible — something even more terrible than his father's death — had been discussed in the parlour. He could tell by the hushed voices and by the drained look on his mother's face when she returned to the kitchen. And he could tell by the woebegone way Father Myrick took his leave, saying he would come back in the evening, although there was nothing he could do in the wake room.

Carmel knew exactly what had been discussed. She had learned it in her Christian doctrine courses. Her father's body could not be taken into the church before the burial. There could be no rosary in the wake room and no prayers at the graveside. She knew, too, that in death, her father was going to cause her even more humiliation and even more agony than he ever had in life. Although she had never really loved him in the way she would have liked to love a father, the thought of him burning in hell for all eternity was a torment that would follow her as long as she lived.

And her heart ached for Martin. She knew he loved his father. She had often seen him going and sitting on his lap and putting his hand over his mouth to get him to stop singing.

"Stop singin', Pop," he would whisper quietly into his ear. "I'll go fer a walk with ye if ye'll stop singin'."

As well, she knew that Martin would one day also understand the agony and shame of his father's death.

Martin crawled underneath the table and began to cry. Carmel scolded.

"Shut up your blubbering, Martin! There's enough to do around here now without having to listen to you blubbering."

"Shut up, yerself," he retorted. "Leave me alone. I'll blubber all I like, and ye can't make me stop."

"Children! Children! Can't ye even be civil to one another at yer poor father's wake," Bertha asked in a careworn voice. "Try to keep yer tongues civil for the next couple of days. We have to pull together now."

When Ned's body was set up in the parlour, people from the Cove once again came in droves to the Corrigans' house. His body was kept three days, just like anyone else's would have been to make sure he was really dead. But similarities ended there. Candles were burned in the wake room, but they were burned only to keep the odour down. They were just plain wax candles and not the ones that were blest by the church on Candlemas Day. The rosary wasn't said and when people visited, they didn't kneel by the coffin and say a prayer for Ned's departed soul. His body went directly from the parlour to the cemetery and no prayers were said at the gravesite.

On the way back from the burial, Bertha confided to Millie that her feelings had dried up. "I don't feel a thing, girl. Not a blessed thing. I don't feel sad. I don't even feel relief."

"'Twill all come in due time," Millie comforted. "'Tis too soon fer feelings, especially under the conditions."

Carmel and Martin trudged behind their mother.

"An awful thing, suicide. Awful fer those left." Bertha spoke in a sad voice. She looked over her shoulder to see the distance between the children and themselves. She lowered her voice. "Do ye think it will warp the children?"

"Hard to say," Millie answered honestly. She searched for something more comforting. "Carmel is old enough to understand. She's too far along to be warped. And besides she's a sod of sense." She looked back at Martin who was kicking a rock along the cemetery path. "And Martin is so full of mischief, so come day, go day, the divil take Sunday, that he won't dwell fer long on what happened."

The heaviness in Bertha's heart lifted slightly. More than anything else, she didn't want Ned's sin to reach beyond the grave. She wanted it to be contained in the little plot of unconsecrated ground on the rim of Dickson's Hill. She hoped Ned had found peace. She hoped God considered him insane even if she couldn't have. Before the funeral, Father Myrick had come to the house and given her a measure of comfort. He told her that they had done for Ned what their conscience had told them to do. They would have to leave the rest up to Him because He had a wider view than either one of them.

———◆———

Martin inherited his father's good looks. He had the same easy smile and the same ash blond hair that in July always turned the colour of ripe hay. And he had the same piercing blue eyes.

Sometimes when Bertha came upon her son unexpectedly, he reminded her so much of his father — the Ned she had known when she first came to the Cove — that her breath would catch sharply. Always in those surprise encounters, she would feel again the magic of those early weeks when she was in love with Ned. Even though those relived moments were fleeting, she could smell the smells, hear the sounds and see the sights of those past times, just as if the years had not intervened. As if there had been no rape. No war. No marriage. No suicide. She used to try to hold on to the moments to relish them later, to rub her face and hair in them and fondle them with her mind. But they always vanished as quickly as they came, leaving barely a memory of a memory.

Just as Millie predicted on the day of Ned's funeral, life began to touch Bertha again. Little by little, her emotions uncorked and she began to take pleasure in her house and her land and her children — especially her children. She loved the children so much she was determined they would both leave the Cove when they grew up and make a fresh start somewhere else.

———◆———

When she was growing up, Carmel talked about little else besides going to the United States to live with her Aunt Bessie. She would get a good job there and have nice clothes and plenty of friends. From the time he was old enough to read geography books, Martin said he was going to Canada. The two children often spent hours arguing the merits of one country over the other.

When Carmel finished school, though, and had the opportunity to go to the States, she wasn't at all anxious to leave the Cove, and instead, took a job as teller in the bank. She justified her change of mind by saying she would save up enough money to pay her own way to the States, and she would only have to depend upon her Aunt Bessie for a sponsor.

Bertha surmised Carmel didn't want to leave Martin and her behind and so, from time to time, she would nudge her to leave and not to stay on their account. "Don't go waitin' around here on account of us. Martin will go as soon as he turns eighteen because he promised me he'd wait till then. And I've no intention of uprootin' meself from here. I'm here till I leaves feet first for Dickson's Hill."

The year Carmel turned twenty-two she began working on her immigration papers. She had no doubt her twenty-third birthday would be spent in Boston. Just thinking about being away from the family made her lonely enough to curb her tendency to nag Martin and to snap at her mother for always giving in to him. Not that being nice to Martin helped his temperament any. He seemed to take delight in wrangling with her, and he was perverse enough to do exactly what she didn't want him to do. His tongue, as she put it, was "dirty" from his foul language and, even worse, he was always using excuses to stay away from Mass, particularly the annual Mass that was held in the cemetery.

Each year on the Sunday closest to the fifteenth of August, the Mass for the Souls in Purgatory was held on Dickson's Hill.

For days, sometimes weeks prior to this event, the people in the Cove refurbished their family graves. They weeded and painted and planted and transplanted until each grave was a monument suitably befitting a soul preparing to enter heaven.

This particular year, because it was likely the last one they would be together as a family, Carmel wanted the three of them to be at the Mass. Martin, though, had other ideas. He had usually managed acceptable excuses for not going, but he was beginning to realize these were running thin. He hoped the service would have to be cancelled on account of rain.

The first thing he did when he woke up on the Sunday morning of the cemetery Mass was to note with dismay that the sun was shining. He hauled the quilts over his head. The Mass would be held and he had no excuse for staying home. And there would be a row with Carmel. She would badger him to go and then upbraid her mother for accepting his lame excuses. He knew the house would be in an uproar the whole day. He dreaded coming downstairs to get his breakfast.

"Stomach cramps again?" Carmel asked when she overheard him tell his mother he wasn't feeling well.

"Now, now, Carmel!" his mother admonished gently, hoping to avert a repeat of last year's fight. "Let things be."

Carmel gave her head a toss so that her long red hair whipped out behind her. Her eyes blazed. "Let things be! Let things be! That's all you ever say." She gave Martin a withering look and then turned back to face her mother.

"I'm sick and tired of lying for him. I'm ashamed he's my brother." She snapped a quick look at Martin and then reconstructed last year's conversation with Father Myrick. "No, Father, Martin isn't here." Her voice was pretend sweet. "He couldn't come today. Stomach trouble. Something he ate, we think."

Recalling the indignity of that conversation, she challenged her mother.

"Why can't you make him go, cramps or no cramps? I'm sick and tired of his lies. Just because he's too afraid to go to a graveyard."

"Be reasonable, girl. I can't very well make him go if he has stomach cramps, can I? What if he gets short taken. There's no place up there fer him to go."

Martin, nettled by Carmel's slur about him being afraid of a graveyard, put in quickly. "That's right, Carmel. What do ye expect me to do. Be like old Peter Fitzgerald? Shit in me hand and throw it over the cliff?" He waited for his vulgarity to raise Carmel's hackles.

"Dirty-tongued youngster," Carmel hissed, rising to his bait. "It's about time someone did something about your vulgar mouth." She gave her mother a disgusted look. "I don't know how you have the stomach to listen to him." She gave a toss of her hair and walked towards the door leading upstairs.

"But you *do* have the stomach to go up to the bone yard and pretend yer father isn't dumped out there over the fence like a bloated horse!" Martin's words shot across the kitchen like a shell from Ned's war rifle. They penetrated Carmel, stopping her in her tracks. Her fingers froze on the door knob. The words pierced Bertha. She drew in a short, stitch-like breath and dropped into a chair. She clamped her hand over her mouth as if she could contain Martin's words and stop them from flying loose over the kitchen.

For years Martin had wanted to pelt his father's name at them. He wanted to scourge them with questions. He wanted to ask them why it was that every evening when they said the rosary they prayed for uncles and aunts he had never known or seen and yet never said as much as "Lord have mercy" for his father. They prayed for neighbours. They prayed for the sick and the dying, for the poor in spirit, for the weak and the wayward, the hungry and the needy, the lame and the lazy. But his father's name never passed their lips. His anger had festered, but he had never gotten nerve enough to ask why it was they could pray for lunatics and losers and not for a poor bastard who had choked the breath out of himself with old Bess' tether.

Even Martin couldn't believe his own ears. Had he actually said what he said? He stared down at his hard fried eggs, mute with shock.

Carmel was the first to speak. Her voice was flat and dead, all the spit and fire drained out of her. "Do you think I relish going up there? Do you think I relished going up there all these years?" Her eyes glistened with the pain of many Augusts. She didn't even toss her hair.

Instantly, Martin wished he had kept his mouth shut. He really hadn't wanted to hurt either of them. He had just wanted to jolt them to their senses. He wished he could say he was sorry, but soft talk wasn't his way — nor theirs for that matter. Not knowing any other way to act, he snapped, "Sure seems that way. Ye two heads up to the cemetery every year carryin' bottles of nasturtiums for Grandmother's grave and shit-all fer Pop."

His words hovered over the table like a cold fog. Carmel let the vulgarity slide by without even flinching. His mother said in a faraway voice, "Ye don't know what yer talkin' about, boy. Ye don't understand at all."

For once, Martin had no urge to contradict her. He even listened without making smart remarks when Carmel uncomfortably recounted the agonies she had endured through the years.

"I would go up there, and Eileen Tobin and the others would be with me, and when we'd pass Father's plot to get to Grandmother's, they would look at me to see if I was going to glance out over the fence. But I never gave them the satisfaction. I never let on I knew what they were looking at me for."

"But no one forced ye to go," Martin said, although not in the sarcastic tone he would have ordinarily used. "Why did ye go? Why did ye want to torture yerself that way?"

"Because she's a good Catholic, that's why," Bertha interrupted. "She's not the type to let a little hardship keep *her* from Mass."

Martin winced at her jab but he continued his questioning, his voice sad even though his words were bitter. "Why did ye let them do it, Maw? Why did ye let them treat him like that?" He turned to Carmel and said in a sparring voice, "You were old enough to order me around, so why couldn't ye have put a stop to what they were doin' to Pop?"

Carmel began to explain. "It was suicide, Martin . . ."

"Suicide, me arse," he interjected, his old blustering way returning. He gesticulated towards the stable as though Ned were still swinging from the doornail. "He was out of his mind, that's what the man was."

"On hop beer. Drank a full keg of beer that morning. Sensible enough he was before that." Bertha's voice was harsh, more from her anger at Ned's deed than from Martin's question. She had never talked about Ned's death because she had thought it was best for all of them. And she had never wanted Martin to know about the hop beer. But it was time the truth came out. She couldn't let him direct his anger at Carmel or at the church.

"I knew he had the hop beer. I knew all along." His tone was accusing. "I didn't need ye to tell me. I even asked Millie about it. She told me he never touched a drop before the war — at least not enough to get polluted the way he did afterwards. So how can ye all hold him responsible for what the war did to him?"

"True enough. True enough." Bertha sighed heavily, wishing the conversation had never reached this stage.

Martin's voice turned bitter. "If 'tis so true, then how come the poor blood of a bitch who went over to fight for England when the rest of them here were too shitless to go gets thanked by being buried like a load of fish guts?"

He didn't give them time to protest or to offer excuses. "He gets the hell shot out of him and comes back with a sliver of a mind and half of an arse and what thanks? He gets loaded on a dray and dumped over the fence like a pile of cow shit."

"That's not the way it was at all, boy," Bertha's voice was faltering. "He was hauled up the hill with a horse and wagon — Paddy Whiffen's — jest like everyone else." She began to cry. "Ye makes it sound like I treated him like an animal."

Once more, silence fell. Carmel still stood by the hall door, her shoulders slumped. Martin wished she would chastise him for using vulgar language or berate him for upsetting his mother. He was so ashamed of his outburst, and now she was permitting him no way to bluster out of what he had gotten himself into. If Carmel would rage, everything would be back to normal. Or if his mother would laugh, everything would be smoothed over. He tried to think of something outrageous to say or do, but nothing came to mind.

Carmel broke the silence. "I guess we all suffered." Her voice was subdued. She looked at Martin. "I didn't know that was why you stayed away."

After Carmel and his mother had gone upstairs to get dressed for church, Martin went out and sat on the back doorstep, hoping to avoid seeing either of them when they left. He felt dejected. He felt ashamed. After all the years of wanting to hurl his father's name at them, he had finally done so, and it had given him no satisfaction whatsoever. It was a conversation, he was certain, that would never surface again. It had caused enough pain as it was.

Shortly after the upset over the Mass on Dickson's Hill, Carmel told her mother she had her immigration papers complete except for her chest X-rays and that before the week was over she intended to go to the TB sanatorium on the outskirts of St. John's to get these taken. Bertha asked her to convince Martin to go with her and have his lungs X-rayed.

"He's still got that cough he got with the wet pleurisy in the winter. I think he's getting worse instead of better." She was sewing buttons on Martin's shirt. She snipped the thread off with her teeth and laid the shirt aside. "I'm frightened by that cough. Especially with so much consumption around."

Carmel had been hemming a dress to wear to work the next day. She screwed up her face to show her distaste for her mother's choice of words.

"Mother, no one calls it consumption anymore. Why can't you say tuberculosis or even TB?" Carmel hated coarse and outdated words as much as she hated incorrect grammar, and she always made certain to choose her words correctly.

Bertha gathered up her sewing materials and began to pack them into her sewing kit. "Call it what ye wants. 'Tis still consumption to me." She turned towards Carmel. "But I'd really like ye to talk Martin into goin' to St. John's. Convince him."

"*Me* convince *him*? You know how he acts with me. If I say day, he'll say night, just to be contrary."

Bertha replied crossly, "I knows how he is. No one can tell me how he is. But 'tis mostly bluff. And ye knows he's fond of ye for all his way of actin'. And he'd do most anything ye'd ask." She gave a rueful shrug. "After a spell, of course. He don't jump to do yer biddin'. But if ye cared enough, ye could convince him to go with ye."

Carmel did care deeply about Martin and, she had noticed his cough had worsened. She had even noticed that he had lost weight over the last couple of months, but she didn't want to add that to her mother's worries.

"Perhaps if he'd stop being on the go night and day, he might get rid of the cough," she said, her tone condemning. "Ever since he left school he's been on the dead run."

"Ye forgets when he's playin' for dances he's makin' money. And if he's goin' to Canada next year, like he says, he has to get his passage." She added with a touch of pride, "And ye knows he's the best mouth-organ player in these parts."

Bertha brought the conversation back to the real problem.

"Tell him ye don't want to go by yerself. Tell him ye needs his company. He'll go if ye says ye needs him."

⬥

The next morning when Martin came downstairs for breakfast, Bertha followed his cough step after step. By the time he reached the kitchen landing, she had decided not to depend upon Carmel's intercession.

"Martin, boy, I've been thinkin' perhaps ye should go with Carmel to St. John's when she goes to get her X-rays. She was sayin' last night she was a bit nervous goin' alone." She poured herself a cup of tea and sat opposite him. "Ye knows how 'tis. A strange place. And the san is so big . . ."

Martin took a swallow of tea and then gave her a look that said he had never heard anything so ridiculous in his life.

"How in hell is she goin' to find her way 'round Boston if she can't find her way 'round the san?"

It exasperated Bertha that with Martin there was never a straight yes or no answer. He always had to have some twist to it, always something to make her snarl a retort. "How should I know? I spose her Aunt Bessie will be there to help."

When Martin said nothing, her tone became more interceding. "Ye won't be together much longer. Wouldn't hurt to help each other fer the time that's left."

"Oh, all right," he said grudgingly. "I'll go because if I don't ye'll be on me back for the rest of the year."

Bertha played her trump card. "While yer in there, why don't ye have an X-ray yerself."

He looked at her as if she had taken leave of her senses. "What next will ye think up for the lovin' honour of God. I'm not goin' away till next year. Ye don't have to practice gettin' an X-ray taken."

"I jest thought that as long as yer in there and as long as Carmel is gettin' one . . ."

"Damn good thing Carmel isn't having her leg cut off, or ye'd say I should have mine cut off, too, as long as I was in there, just to keep Carmel company."

Bertha had sparred enough. She came directly to the point. "Ye've got a terrible cough, Martin. A wet cough. It worries me."

He pushed his plate of eggs aside, uneaten, and quickly moved away from the table. "I'd better get the hell out of here, or the next thing ye'll have me with gallopin' consumption."

But Martin did go into the sanatorium with Carmel, making it quite clear before he left that he wasn't having X-rays himself. However, he hadn't reckoned on Carmel's deviousness. When she went to the X-ray department, she explained about Martin's cough to the doctor, who confronted Martin and caught him so off guard he couldn't think up an excuse for refusing to have an X-ray taken.

—◆—

The results of the X-rays came in the mail two weeks later. Carmel's lungs were clear, but Martin had active TB. The letter that accompanied the results said that there was a very long waiting list for a bed in the sanatorium and that Martin should take bed rest at home immediately.

Not since he had found his father hanging on the stable door had Bertha seen him look so terrible, so completely devastated. "Do ye know what this means," he kept repeating as though no one but him could see the terrible significance of the holes in his lungs. "'Tis goodbye Canada, and ye knows how much I wanted to get the hell out of the Cove."

"Not likely, boy. 'Tis not goodbye Canada at all. Not likely." Bertha wasn't going to let a little consumption keep one of her children from realizing a dream. "We'll have ye up and around by the time the six months are up."

Exasperated, Martin shook his head. "Ye don't understand, Maw. Once ye've had TB, they don't let ye in. Ye might as well have leprosy. The immigration people won't touch ye with a ten-foot pole. Ask Kevin Cleary. Just ask him why he never left the Cove."

Carmel and Bertha switched around furniture and made the dining room Martin's bedroom. Bertha said it was easier on her legs than having to climb stairs.

Once Martin was settled in his new quarters, Carmel announced she was postponing her immigration to Boston.

"Are ye off yer head?" Martin blustered. "Yer not goin' to stay home on my account. I'd never hear the end of it. How ye martyred yerself fer me."

"Shut up, Martin! You're an ingrate of the worst kind." Carmel turned away quickly so he wouldn't see the tears she was having difficulty holding back. But she didn't turn quickly enough. To cover his embarrassment over the extent of her feelings, he became even more abrasive.

"Ingrate! Ingrate!" he repeated with forced sarcasm. "Is that somethin' ye puts on toast?" He pointed out towards the chair by the kitchen stove. "I can jest see ye in twenty years' time. All wizened up like a boiled boot and telling everyone ye gave yer life fer yer brother, the ingrate."

"He's right, Carmel. I can look after him meself. No need for ye to give up yer plans." Bertha wanted to reassure herself. "Ye can stand on yer head for six months. And that's all it'll be. No need to ruin yer plans fer six months."

"It might be a hell of a lot longer than six months, Maw. They always tell ye that so ye won't jump over a bridge." Martin turned towards Carmel, and his eyes, if not his voice, held concern.

"If ye stays here, ye'll end up with TB. And we don't need that. We'll have to hang out a sign — *Seaside San*. And ye might as well give up the notion of gettin' into the States if ye gets a spot."

"That's not true, Martin," Carmel protested, suspecting it was true because Martin had much more knowledge about most things than she did. He always had his nose in a book or was talking to people, asking questions.

Following the doctor's orders, Carmel had fashioned a number of cheesecloth masks, and she now reached into her pocket and took one out and tied it over her mouth. Martin stared from her to his mother. "Shit almighty, Maw. Yer not goin' to let her stay around here lookin' like a cursed mummy, are ye?"

Carmel intended to follow to the letter the dos and don'ts of caring for a tubercular patient. The following day she went to Murphy's store and bought dishes that could stand up to a good scalding and wouldn't be mistaken for those used by the rest of the family. When she returned, she sat on Martin's bed and displayed her purchases. He watched as she unwrapped each dish, and when the complete place setting was unveiled and laid out on his quilt, he grimaced. He thought the watery green colour looked much like his morning spit.

He picked up the dinner plate and pretended to scrutinize it, pinging the thick glass with a snick of his thumb and finger. "If ye tried, Carmel," he said, not a trace of humour in his voice, "if ye had really tried, could ye have picked something a little uglier? I don't see how I can face so much beauty after all that spit in the morning." He squinted at the plate. "'Tis the exact colour, ye know. A perfect match. Did ye ask Old Murphy fer spit green dishes?"

In response, Carmel tossed her hair and began to pick up the dishes. Disappointed that he couldn't get a better rise out of her, he craned his neck towards the kitchen. "Maw! Come in here and let me show ye my tu-ber-cul-osis dishes. Spit green." When Bertha didn't make any move to leave the kitchen, he called again. "Maw!"

Bertha had heard him the first time, but she had kept on with her knitting. She was tired of their constant badgering, and she knew if Carmel was going to stay home to help out, she herself was going to have to stay out of their squabbles. "Purl one. Knit two," she recited out loud to block out the voices from the dining room. "Purl two together."

"Get back in bed this instant!" Carmel's sharp voice reached

Bertha. "You know very well you're not supposed to get out of bed."

Bertha dropped her knitting instantly and ran to the dining room in time to see Martin haul his leg back underneath the quilt.

"Martin Corrigan! I'm givin' ye an order right now."

Martin gave a loud groan. "No more orders! Between you and Carmel and the bloody doctors, I'm up to here with orders." He sliced the air underneath his nose.

"I don't care if yer up to *there*," Bertha said, pointing to a spot above her head. "If ye ever puts a leg outside those quilts other than to go to the toilet, I'll break it off at the knee. And then ye'll really have something to groan about."

Carmel and Martin roared laughing at Bertha's ridiculous threat, the squabbling temporarily stopped.

Later that night, when Carmel was getting ready for bed, Bertha came to her room. "He doesn't want ye stayin' around here and getting' what he's got. I thinks he's right, sayin' ye should go to Boston."

Carmel had taken the top quilt off her bed and was folding it neatly. "What would be the good of me going to Boston now? All I'd be doing would be worrying about him." She climbed into bed and said more gently, "Mother, I have no intention of catching TB. I take all the precautions. I wash my hands every time I come out of his room. I sterilize the door-knobs whenever he touches them. And I wear the mask." She looked with concern at Bertha. "It's you he should be worried about. You don't take any precautions."

Bertha waved away Carmel's concern. "I'm as tough as a gad. A germ is more afraid of me than I am of it." She sat on the edge of the bed and absently traced the quilt pattern with her finger. "I thinks I've been around consumption before. I'm sure that's what poor Mother had. That's what made her so delicate." She looked across the room, remembering the goose grease that hadn't helped and the babies that hadn't lived. After a few seconds, she came back to the present. "Don't worry about me. If I was goin' to get consumption, I'd have had it by now."

As Bertha promised, Martin was on his feet within six months. By that time the Second World War had broken out, and many of Martin's friends had already joined up. Martin lamented that he couldn't go with them. Bertha was secretly glad. The thought of him returning home and stationing himself in the chair by the stove was intolerable. She began to see his tuberculosis as a blessing from God.

"Yer still too young to join up, lungs or no lungs," she scolded.

Martin scoffed. "I certainly wouldn't let age stop me. I'd lie if I had to. Lots of fellows lied." He named names. "I'd lie about the TB if I thought I'd get away with it. But there's the damn physical."

Bertha knew that Martin had to get work of some type or else he would sink deeper and deeper into self-pity. But there was nothing around the Cove that didn't involve manual work, and the doctor said hard labour was out for at least five years. Almost all the firms in St. John's, as well as the government offices, had a policy of not hiring ex-TB patients. She wracked her brain for ideas.

"Martin, boy," she asked one evening as they sat listening to the radio, "how would ye like to drive a taxi from here to St. John's a couple times a week. Like Leonard Walsh. They sez on account of the servicemen comin' and goin' there's much more business now."

Before he could snuff out her idea without giving it a thought, she added quickly, "There's big money in it. I asked around. Everyone sez so."

Martin looked at her, a mischievous smile lighting up his face. "And how do ye plan to buy a taxi. Rob a bank?"

"If ye wants a car, we'll get ye a car."

"*We'll* get ye a car," he repeated. "So Carmel is goin' to rob the bank."

Carmel was in the wash porch ironing a blouse to wear to work the next day. "Hear that, Carmel? Maw thinks ye should fiddle the books to get me into the taxi business."

Carmel, who had already discussed with her mother the possibility of buying a taxi, ignored the taunting.

"I'll sell off the meadows," Bertha said, as easily as if she were talking about getting rid of the hens. "They're doin' us no good lyin' there empty. Aloysius might as well have them for pasture land. He's lookin' for extra meadows. He feels that with the men off to war, he can sell more milk and butter because a lot of people have sold their cattle. The women can't look after everything."

Martin barely had time to get his taxi business underway when word spread that an American base was going to be built on the outskirts of the Cove. There would be work for everyone who wanted it. Carmel, who had considered reopening her immigration papers, decided she would give up any notion of going to the United States and, instead, would go to work on the base. She knew her banking experience would be a big help to her in getting work.

Bertha had her misgivings. "'Tis yer life fer sure," she told Carmel. "But better fer ye in the long run to go to the States. Wars don't last forever, and when this one is over, the base will be over, too."

She discussed Carmel's notion of going on the base with Millie, who saw Carmel's side. "The base isn't such a bad idea, Bertha. I hears the girls — and the men too, I spose — will be put up in barracks, so in a way she'll be away from home and still not away." To cement her stand she added, "And she'll make big money. Twice her bank salary."

"'Tis not the money," Bertha replied, miffed because Millie had taken Carmel's side. "Money isn't everything. In Boston she could get married and settle down."

"Who sez she still can't do that? I hears there's thousands of servicemen expected."

"Oh maybe yer right," Bertha conceded, adding with a little laugh, "and I thinks maybe thousands of men is what Carmel needs to make her choice. She sure is picky. Certainly no one in the Cove even comes close to suiting her." She added sombrely, "Not that I wants her to take up with anyone here."

Once more, Millie came to Carmel's defence. "She's particular, that's fer sure. But ye got to remember some of the fellows who wants to court her now are the same ones who used to laugh at Ned right to her face."

Bertha nodded, recalling the numerous times she had seen Carmel coming up the lane, her head held so high you'd think she was the Queen. The higher she held her head and the haughtier she walked, the more she had likely been hurt.

"And maybe her way of actin' now is fer the best. At least she didn't have a rushed-into marriage." Millie addressed Bertha directly. "Wouldye want her to be like Eileen Tobin, married at seventeen and a houseful of youngsters before she was twenty?"

During the first weeks Carmel spent on the base, she came home every Saturday afternoon, and Martin drove her back again on Sunday evening. Gradually, she weaned herself away from the weekend trip and began spending every other weekend in the barracks. When she had been working less than three months, she announced to Bertha and Martin that she was going to be bringing someone home for dinner the following Sunday.

"A man," she said shyly, aware that Martin and her mother would both be taken aback by her announcement. "His name is Ed Strominski. He's American, and he's a construction worker." She added proudly, "He's a supervisor of a crew of twenty."

Bertha took the news with pretended nonchalance and darted Martin an admonishing look to tell him he was not to make any smart remarks that might put Carmel off. However, when Carmel began to outline the things she was going to do in preparation for Ed's visit, Martin couldn't resist asking his mother within earshot of Carmel whether this visitor should be treated like important clergy.

"Don't spose we should build an arch of boughs, do ye, Maw? Like we did when Bishop Riley came in his jubilee year?"

Bertha threw him a rebuking look, which he took great pains not to see.

"Do you think we'll have to kiss his ring and say, Yes, yer Grace. No, yer Grace?"

Carmel acknowledged Martin's taunting remarks with a blazing stare. He was the reason she had put off inviting Ed earlier. She never knew what Martin was going to say.

"So help me Martin, if you embarrass me when Ed is here, I'll never darken this door again while you're inside."

"Me! Embarrass ye! What do ye take me fer? Yer talkin' as though I'm going to piss in the soup in front of this Yank."

Carmel flung a look of fire towards her mother. "See! Did you hear that? He's going to use dirty talk in front of Ed and shame us to death." Just saying Ed's name softened Carmel's voice and to camouflage her feelings she became even angrier. "And another thing. Don't go on about the war. Don't go asking why the United States isn't in it. And don't . . ." She stopped abruptly, not having nerve enough to continue.

"And don't what?" Martin snapped. "Spit it out. What else shouldn't I don't?"

"Don't say you've had TB." She blurted out the words, ashamed of herself even as she said them. "I told him you had wet pleurisy and that's why you're driving a taxi instead of being in the war." Her mouth was so dry she could feel each word as it passed over her tongue. She had lain awake at night wondering how to ask Martin to keep quiet about his tuberculosis, and now she couldn't believe she had actually put her thoughts into words.

"What? Ye told him what?"

It was a warm August day, and Bertha had set up a table out beside the rose tree so they could eat supper away from the heat of the kitchen. Martin had been sitting in a kitchen chair near a bed of Bertha's prized pansies. He jumped up so quickly his chair tipped over and landed in the centre of the flowers, breaking off the purple heads.

"See what ye've done!" Bertha scolded, hoping to diffuse Martin's fury. "Ye broke me pansies."

Martin gave a quick glance over his shoulder to survey his destruction and snarled, "Should break Carmel's head. Although that probably wouldn't do much damage. She has sawdust for brains. Tellin' the Yank I had wet pleurisy."

Carmel's lip trembled, and she tried to fight back tears. "I was afraid he wouldn't want to come. I was afraid he might think it was catching."

The sight of Carmel's tears drained off some of Martin's

anger, and he had to force himself to keep the snarl in his voice.

"Yer off yer head, Carmel. *Wet pleurisy?*" he turned to his mother. "God in heaven, if she wanted to give me an excuse fer not being in the war, why didn't she say I was a Doukhobor or a conscientious objector. That would be something worth lying about." He turned to Carmel and asked, "Is he so stupid he doesn't know we don't have conscription?"

"He knows. I just didn't want him to think you were a coward." She added in a subdued voice, "Besides, I'm not really asking you to lie. You did have pleurisy once."

"That's right, boy," Bertha cut in.

Martin threw up his hands in exasperation. "Shit, Maw. I had cradle cap once, but it wasn't enough to keep me out of the war."

"But 'tis jest stretchin' the truth a little," Bertha cajoled. "And 'tis fer a good reason. Ye knows how people feels about consumption."

Martin had retrieved the chair and was holding it by the legs. He let it drop back down again. He turned his back to them and jabbed his lungs with his fingers. "See!" he said, pointing to his right lung, "I have a hole here as big as a fifty-cent piece. And right here," he said jabbing his left lung. "Ye can drive a horse and carriage through the gap, 'tis that big." He turned around to face both of them. "And sayin' I have a touch of pleurisy is just *stretchin'* the truth! Some stretch."

The exertion of his outburst made him cough, and Bertha agonizingly watched his heaving shoulders. She wondered if he would ever get back to being the strapping man he had been.

"But yer cured, Martin," she assured him, as much to comfort herself as him. "The holes have healed over. All ye have to do is put on a little weight and get yer breath back again. The doctor wouldn't let ye drive a taxi if ye weren't all right."

Martin righted the chair and sat down on it. "I'll never be all right again, Maw. If I was all right I'd be on the base now, not kept away like a leper." He stared at her. "Don't ye know ye are never all right after ye've had TB? Yer a leper." He caught sight of the pitying looks exchanged between his mother and Carmel, and he tried to change the mood back to one he found more manageable. He returned to baiting Carmel.

"Maybe I'll tell this Yank fellow I have gallopin' consumption." He leapt up and galloped across the yard, neighing like a horse.

"Don't be actin' the fool, boy," Bertha scolded. "Be grateful to God yer cured. And stop tormentin' Carmel. Yer not goin' to shame her, and ye knows it." She turned to Carmel. "And ye stop payin' any mind to anything he says. He just delights in getting' ye goin', and the two of ye are wearin' me out with yer nonsense. I'll be ten toes up before ye knows it."

———⟫•◆•⟪———

Carmel had met Ed through her dormitory roommate, Ellen O'Brien. Ellen had recently started dating a fellow who worked with Ed, and it was his idea that she find someone for Ed so the four of them could double date.

Carmel had to be talked into going. She offered the excuse she was tired and had a lot of work to do to get her clothes ready for work in the morning. In truth, she was terrified her inexperience with men would be obvious to all of them, but especially to Ed.

She was introduced to Ed in the lobby of her barracks and in an instant fell in love with him. He was both handsome and charming. "I've a date with the most beautiful girl on the base," he said, extending his hand and letting his eyes rove over her appreciatively. She had shampooed her hair and rinsed it half a dozen times so that it shone even in the artificial light. The soft yellow sweater and skirt she had spent hours deciding upon brought out the deep blue of her eyes. She knew she looked as good as it was possible for her to look, and she was glad she had taken such pains to get ready.

Ed's voice was almost as sultry as the night. And his body had to be the most beautiful one she had ever seen. He had come without a coat, and Carmel had the most outrageous urge to rub her face over the greying hairs that curled out through the open V of his shirt. She had the wayward desire to stroke his bare arms, to press up against his thighs and to run her hands through his thick, slightly greying black hair that was even curlier than the hair on his chest. As they walked along the street to the movie theatre, she wished she would stumble so he would have to catch her, and then she could feel the pressure of his hands on her waist. The brazenness of her thoughts astounded her.

She had no idea what the movie was about. She remained conscious only of Ed sitting beside her and of the way his hand covered hers and how his fingers kneaded the soft flesh around her thumb. That she would let a man — especially a man she had only met an hour earlier — hold her hand in such an intimate way made her face burn, and she was grateful for the darkened theatre.

After the movie the four of them walked toward the girls' dormitory. Ed said good night to her in the lobby, and because males were not allowed to go any further into the building, there were others present when he kissed her. His lips barely brushed her cheek, but his eyes met hers in such a long, private look that she hugged it to her for the rest of the night.

"Good night, Carm," he said huskily. "I'll be in touch."

No one had ever abbreviated her name before, and the heat in his voice was almost as satisfying to her as a passionate kiss. She stayed awake most of the night reliving the moments, more beautiful than any she had ever before experienced.

Later that month, the girls on Carmel's dormitory floor were in her room, chatting and talking girl talk. Mostly they were trying to console Ellen O'Brien because her boyfriend had left her for someone new. Ellen said he left because she wouldn't sneak him into her room and grant him sleepover privileges.

"All Americans are alike," Ellen gloomily announced. "All they want is one thing from the girls around here."

Carmel hotly disagreed. Ed Strominski was different.

"Don't be so naive, Carmel," Ellen flared. "Sometimes I think you're a real babe in the woods even though you're five years older than I am." Ellen's glance swept the room. "I'm right, aren't I? Carmel just hasn't given him enough time yet. She's only been out with him three or four times."

"Six times," Carmel corrected. "And it wouldn't matter if it were sixty times. He likes me for myself." To strengthen her conviction, she confided that she had asked him to her house for Sunday dinner the following week. "He was really pleased to be asked. He wants to meet my mother and brother." She looked at Ellen. "That doesn't seem like a person who has his mind in the bedroom."

Carmel took Saturday morning off from work so she could go home Friday evening and get a start on the housecleaning. She baked and cleaned and ironed until Martin, who had been trying to sleep, complained that it would be easier to sleep in the galley of the *Titanic* just before it went under.

"What's this fellow Ed do fer a livin' anyway?" he asked his mother, when he had abandoned all hope of getting any sleep. "What does he do in the way of work?" He knew very well what Ed did, and he also knew that Carmel was within listening distance.

Bertha, who was trying to bleach a tea stain out of the best tablecloth, answered absently, "Carmel said he was a construction worker. Don't you remember? Ent that right, Carmel?"

Before Carmel had time to answer, Martin broke in. "Naw, he can't be. No one would turn a house upside down for a construction worker. I bet he's with the Department of Health, and Carmel's afraid he'll condemn our place."

Carmel let the remark go by. She had enough on her mind without having a fight with Martin. She was worried that the house wasn't grand enough, that the tablecloth would still have the tea stain even after the several bleachings, and that her mother, who had the habit of pumping strangers for more information, would give Ed the third degree. Or worse still, she wouldn't say his name correctly. No matter how many times she had told her the correct pronunciation for *Strominski*, Bertha always forgot and said something so ridiculous that Martin would keel over laughing.

On Sunday afternoon, on the appointed hour, Ed arrived in a taxi, and when Carmel brought him into the house and introduced him, her mother embarrassed her so much she wished she could disappear.

Bertha extended her hand eagerly and said, "How do ye do Mr. . . . Strum . . . Mr. Ed," she finished lamely. "Come in and make yerself at home."

Carmel pretended not to notice Bertha's name fumbling and introduced Martin. "And this is Martin," she said, giving Martin a pleading look to keep his promise.

"Glad to meet you, Marty. Carm tells me you've been sick." Martin cringed at the diminutive of his name, but he answered without hesitation. "A while ago. A touch of wet pleurisy. But I'm on the mend now."

Dinner had cooked faster than they had anticipated, and it was almost ready to place on the table by the time Ed arrived. They went immediately to the dining room and sat down. Carmel began bringing in the food. Each time she went to the stove to take something from a pot, she heard her mother plumbing the depths of Ed's private life. She stiffened with anger. Her mother had promised not to ask questions!

"And yer family, sir. Are they well?" Bertha's tone was diffident.

"Yes, Ma'am. They're all well." Ed's tone was deferential, but there was a slight edge of uneasiness that only Carmel detected.

"And they live out there . . ." Bertha waited for Ed to supply where "out there" was, and when he didn't, she continued. "Where was it Carmel said yer home is?"

"Oregon, Ma'am."

Carmel tried to break the tension by asking Ed if he wanted more to eat. She even asked Martin several times if she could refill his plate, and when she did, Martin, who was so unaccustomed to such civility from Carmel, looked as though he were going to burst out laughing. But he forced a serious face, just once or twice allowing a devilish smile to tug at his mouth. He thanked her with equally unaccustomed politeness. She was just scooping more potatoes from the pot on the stove when she heard her mother probing into Ed's family again.

"And yer poor mother? Is she living?"

Once more Carmel stiffened. Ed hated to have anyone dig and pry into his life. She recalled one time when she had been coming home with him after an evening at the American Club. She asked him about his relatives. He cut her off short and swift. "I'm here and they're there, so why don't we leave it at that." He quickly apologized for his rudeness by pulling her close and kissing her, right on the street, unmindful that they could be seen by others. He brushed her hair back from her face and gently let his fingertips kiss her cheeks. "Just be satisfied that we're together. For all we know by tomorrow morning Uncle Sam will be into this war, and I'll be pulled out of here to go steam shovel another base into shape in some other godforsaken place."

After that incident she had made herself be satisfied with the here and now of him. Not everyone, she told herself, was bound up in family the way she was. Besides, she had heard that Americans weren't like people in the Cove. American relatives were more independent of one another.

She carried the potatoes back to the table. She could feel the tension. It was as thick as her mother's gravy. Martin had hardly said ten sentences during the whole meal. Her mother kept on talking and prying, and when she wasn't doing that she was pushing food at Ed every time the conversation lulled. Already Carmel could feel a tightening at the base of her neck, the beginning of a headache.

As soon as dinner was over, Bertha told Carmel to take Ed to meet Millie. "Don't bother yerself with the dishes, Carmel," she said evenly, hoping desperately Carmel would take Ed out for awhile so she could eat the rhubarb pie she had pretended not to like in case Ed wanted a second piece. "Millie is jest dyin' to meet Ed."

Bertha and Martin peeked from behind the kitchen curtains at Carmel and Ed crossing the meadow to Millie's. "Well, boy," Bertha asked, unable to contain herself any longer. "What did ye think of him?" Without waiting for an answer, she said, "Meself, I thought he was deep."

"And ye sure tried to plumb the bottom." Martin began to

mimic her probing of Ed's background, exaggerating to the point of ridiculousness.

"And yer poor mother? Did they cremate her or just let her lie on top of the ground until the maggots carted her off?"

Bertha didn't crack a smile. "Someone had to talk. Left all up to me, ye did. Carmel was like a pillar of salt. And yer tongue is usually like the clapper of a cow's bell, yet ye hardly said ten words."

"I'd never hear the end of it if I embarrassed Carmel, would I now? Easiest way out was to keep quiet." He didn't want to admit to her that he couldn't find anything to say, especially after the clipped way Ed responded to her questions.

"See that!" Bertha directed Martin's gaze to Ed's arm tucked around Carmel's waist as they walked across the meadow. "Look at that! Scandalous! Draped all over her in public."

"Oh fer the lovin' honour of God, Maw!" Martin sounded as though he was tired of the whole episode. "He only has his arm around her."

"Well, I don't like him a bit. Not a bit. He wouldn't have mentioned his mother if I hadn't brought her up."

"What's that got to do with him?" Martin retorted irritably, knowing she would harp on Ed all evening. "Ye don't think for a minute if I went to Oregon I'd haul yer name around durin' the meal?"

Bertha's eyes blazed. "I most certainly do think that. I'd certainly hope ye'd mention yer family without someone havin' to drag the information out of ye."

Carmel and Ed had disappeared from her view, and she turned to go do the dishes. "Besides, he's too old for her." She began stacking the dishes, mumbling to herself. "But not much good havin' a worry around here. Everyone is too foolish to take anything serious."

Martin hadn't liked anything about Ed. He disliked his superior airs and his haughtiness and especially the way he said "You folks" when he referred to the people in Newfoundland. It was as though he thought everyone on the island had been stamped with the same personality, all sheep from the same breed. But he didn't want his mother to worry more than she had already, so he kept his feelings to himself. He grabbed a dishcloth from the table and draped it across his face so that only his eyes peeped out. He spoke furtively. "My name is Ed Strominski. I'm a German spy, and I'm going' to turn yer daughter into a Nazi agent."

Bertha's worry over Carmel's choice of young man made her immune to Martin's antics. She grabbed the dishcloth from his face and told him to go carry on somewhere else. "Go out and play yer poker. Like ye do every Sunday," she admonished. "Not a care in the world. Just be back in time to take Carmel to the base."

She washed and dried the dishes, grumbling to herself. "Not even Catholic. A Nothingarian as far as I can figger out. Belongs to no church. And Carmel is so wishy-washy around him. He'll lead her around by the nose if she takes up with him."

As she put the cleaned dishes in the cupboard, she thought about Martin's remark regarding Ed being a German spy. She decided that what he said may not be that far-fetched. The base had only been started a few months when another girl from the cove — Dolly McBride — got herself tangled up with a Yank who turned out to be a German spy. At least that was the rumour. Certainly he had been hauled off the base fast enough to make everyone suspicious.

She wished it was time for Carmel to go back to the base. She could hardly wait to see Millie to hear what she had to say. She chided herself for making mountains out of molehills, because bringing the fellow home didn't mean Carmel was going to marry him. She comforted herself with that thought.

<hr />

"I didn't take to him at all," Millie declared. "I really wanted to. Fer her sake. Even Aloysius didn't take to him. Said he was too old fer her." She looked to Bertha for confirmation of Ed's age. "He's forty if he's a day. Ent he?"

"I'd say so. Old enough to be her father. Too old fer someone like Carmel."

Millie heard the worry in Bertha's voice, and she tried to dismiss the concerns they both had. She gave a silly laugh. "How full of nonsense we are. Carmel brings a fellow home, and already we have her married to him. Worryin' about his age instead of bein' happy she's finally takin' an interest in a man."

"I spose yer right," Bertha agreed tentatively, letting out a long sigh. "Like Martin sez, I'm always lookin' fer the worst."

<hr />

From the first evening Carmel had spent in Ed's presence, she had fantasized about being married. To bring the fantasy into reality, she made herself exclusively available to him, accepting invitations whenever he offered them and keeping her time available in case he would telephone.

Still, despite her infatuation, there were areas of Ed's personality she found troublesome. He was louder than she would like him to be. He was especially loud when he was with Dusty Rankine. Dusty was part of Ed's construction crew, and they often partied together. Dusty had a girlfriend —

Vivian — who had an apartment off the base. When Ed was around those two, he drank too much and became as vulgar as Dusty.

One Saturday night the four of them went to the American Civilian Club. After several rounds of drinks, Dusty began taunting Carmel about drinking only ginger ale. He made her feel childish and awkward. When she tried to divert the conversation, he turned to Ed and gave him a sly, lewd wink,

"Is she that pure in *every* way, Ed?"

Carmel was sure Ed would tell him to clean up his conversation, but instead he winked back. "She's one little Puritan." The conversation gradually degenerated. After one particularly tasteless joke, Carmel asked Ed if he would dance with her.

"I'm tired of dancing," he said, dismissing her and turning his attention back to Dusty and Vivian. Carmel could feel the tears stinging her eyes, but she managed to hold them back long enough to ask him if they could go home.

"Go home if you want, Carm. You know the way as well as I do."

His remark cut her to the quick, and she instantly reached for her purse.

Ed grabbed her arm and pulled her down beside him. "Aw, come on, Carm. Can't you take a joke? Don't you have any sense of humour?"

She wanted to tell him that her sense of humour didn't extend to filthy talk, but instead she said in an uneven voice, "I just want to go home, Ed."

For an answer, Ed drained the last of his drink and summoned the waiter for a refill. "Go if you want, I'm staying." His voice had risen loud enough to attract attention from surrounding tables. Carmel summoned all her courage and dignity and walked across the room towards the outside door. She held her head high and never looked to the left or the right until she was outdoors and could feel the cool air on her burning face.

Before she had gone down the steps to the street, Ed came after her, shouting for her to wait. Even in the dark she could tell he was furious. He grabbed her arm.

"What the hell gives with you, anyway?" he demanded. "You made a fool of me in front of my friends. In front of the whole damn club."

Carmel tried to keep her hurt to herself, but tears spilled down her face. She had expected him to be remorseful but instead he was reprimanding her. She shook off his arm and began walking away. He grabbed her again. "Come back in with me," he demanded. "I bet Dusty a round of drinks I'd get you to come back."

Tears scalded her cheeks, and she made no effort to check them. How could Ed be so insensitive as to take bets on whether he could make her come back? How could he have cared so little about her feelings? A thousand Ed's wouldn't make her face going back into the club.

When he saw she was adamant, he abused her verbally, saying she bored him and that the next woman he took up with would not be an iceberg. He intimated that it wouldn't take him long to find one more suitable.

Carmel couldn't remember anything about walking back to the dormitory. All that filled her mind was that she had lost Ed. She was certain of that. In hindsight, she wished she hadn't left the table, hadn't taunted him into taking a stand. The enormity of her loss wiped out her fear of walking alone after dark and of what people would think if they saw a young woman crying as she made her way home.

Ellen O'Brien said it was good riddance to bad rubbish and that now Carmel would be able to believe that what all Americans wanted from the local girls was bedroom privileges. Ellen predicted that within a week Carmel would be glad she was no longer involved with Ed.

But Carmel knew better. She knew it with such certainty that she felt no need to argue the point. There had never been and there never would be any other man for her. She cried the entire night, stuffing the pillow over her head so Ellen wouldn't hear her. The next day, Sunday, she didn't even have the strength to get out of bed, much less go to church. On Monday, she forced herself to go to work, but for all she accomplished she might as well have stayed in bed. Every time the phone rang she was sure it was Ed calling to offer an apology. When it turned out to be someone else, her disappointment was so acute she would have to hold the receiver for several seconds before she could speak.

In the nights that followed, she lay awake reliving the loving times. Her senses were so unjaded she could reexperience his kisses. He always pulled her so tightly to him she was able to feel the full outline of his body and taste his muskiness. She wallowed in the sensation of his hands rubbing up and down her thighs and in the way he leaned into her when he kissed her good night, his knee gently separating her knees so their two bodies welded into one.

Other remembered moments, ones less pleasant, often crowded out the sensual ones. She recalled the times he had coaxed and cajoled her to spend the night with him at Dusty's. Dusty, he said, would accommodate them by staying with friends. She had always refused him gently and tenderly, caressing his face with both hands, the touch of him so very precious. Her fingers would roam his face, soaking in the soft skin around his eyes, the barely present stubble of beard, the deep creases at the sides of his mouth. Often she would kiss those creases, standing on tiptoe to do so.

"I love you, love you, love you!" She had committed herself many times. "I love you with my whole heart and soul." She noticed he always shied away from any talk which would offer them a future. The nearest he came to commitment was suggesting they live together, not just an overnight stay. "If we love each other so much," he said, his tone almost harsh, "why won't you agree to our setting up housekeeping. Like Dusty and Vivian."

Once she almost capitulated. She had wavered precariously between her spiritual beliefs and her earthly passions. Ed had been wearing one of his V-necked sweaters and she was nuzzling her face in the softly curling hair on his chest, wanting to lick it into deep waves, like a mother cat.

"I love you more than I could ever imagine possible," she had said, her voice soft.

"Prove it!" he said, squeezing her even closer to him, prodding gently. "Prove you love me."

"Please Ed, I can't," she told him and waited for the voice inside her that on earlier occasions had enabled her to say no with conviction. But now she couldn't hear the voice because Ed was running his fingers through her hair, pushing it back from her face with such tenderness that her blood pounded so hard it blocked out all other sounds. She had to summon strength from depths within her in order to refuse him.

When she did refuse, he instantly pushed her away, untangling his hands from her hair, strand by strand until she was completely separate from him. She tried to close the space between them by begging him to understand, but he just left her standing alone outside her dormitory door. He had come back the next evening without an apology and without an explanation for his actions. She had pretended to herself that apologies and explanations weren't necessary, grateful for his return under any circumstances.

But this leaving was different. She could feel its finality. She went to the Cove several weekends in a row. When her mother asked where Ed was, she evaded a direct answer and mumbled something about extra work to get the base completed on schedule.

On her fourth visit to the Cove, Martin, as usual, drove her back to the base late Sunday afternoon. Because she arrived at her dormitory just at supper hour and everyone had gone to the mess hall, the place was empty. As she took out her key, the telephone at the end of the hall began to ring. At first she paid no attention to it, knowing it wouldn't be for her. She went into her room and began unpacking, sorting away the clothes she had washed at her mother's. The phone kept ringing. Finally, in exasperation, she went to answer it.

"Dormitory 126." Annoyance circled her voice. The last thing she wanted to do was take messages about dates for other girls.

"Hiya, Carm. Long time no see." Ed's voice penetrated every nook and cranny of her body.

"Carm!" Ed almost shouted. "I said hiya, doll."

"Hello," she said tentatively, her voice a mere whisper. "Hello, Ed."

"I've got swell news. Swell news. My contract's been extended for two more years."

"Oh." She answered hesitantly, unable to comprehend why he was jubilant about staying for a longer term in Newfoundland. He had never liked the place. Because he was still waiting for her to say something else, she added, "That's nice," although she didn't think it was nice at all, preferring him to have been transferred so she wouldn't have to encounter him with another girl.

"*Nice*! Is that all you can say. *Nice*!"

His words were thick, and she surmised he had been drinking. She took the reprimand without comment and he continued.

"It was here or Greenland, and they tell me if you go from Newfoundland to Greenland to hell, the change is so gradual you don't notice the difference."

He expected her to laugh, but she just let the silence pass back and forth over the line. A hundred questions were crowding her mind, the most important one being whether he had found a woman who wasn't an iceberg.

"Carm," he began. He stalled for a few seconds and began again. "Carm. Let's get married. I've missed you."

She reached out to touch the wall for support but found it wasn't sufficient to hold her up. She clutched the phone and lowered herself to the floor and squatted like a small child in the corner.

"What?"

"Married! I said let's get married." She could feel his annoyance at having to repeat what she should have heard the first time. She knew if she could see him right then he would be scowling. She wished she were near him so she could kiss away the deep lines the scowl made. She wished she were near him so she could kiss his lips into a smile.

She realized the past four weeks had all been for nothing. She had worked at forgetting him, but she had forgotten nothing. Not the taste of him. Not the smell of him. Not the sound of him. She could even remember the heat of him.

She tried to stand up to uncramp her legs and found she wobbled like a newborn lamb. She sat back on the floor and cradled the phone as if it were her lover. She hugged it close to her neck almost feeling the moistness of Ed's breath against the ticklish spot behind her ear.

"Well? Yes or no?"

"Yes," she whispered. "Oh yes, Ed." She wished she could embrace him, run her palms over his face, touch his hair, any contact at all to make her answer more concrete and to give substance to his question. In her fantasies, his proposal had been more tender. More needy. More desperate. A tickle of disappointment entered her heart, and she quickly pushed it aside. Ed was a mature man, and as he himself often said, he was trying to slap a base together for a war. She wished he had apologized for the way he had talked to her the last time they were together, but in the light of his proposal, dwelling on such small things seemed petty and unimportant.

"Yer marrying a total stranger, fer the love of God!" Bertha almost hollered her disapproval when Carmel made a special trip home during the week. "What in the name of heavens do you know about him? A foreigner!"

Later in the evening when Carmel was getting ready to return to the base, Bertha pleaded with her to wait a few more months before committing herself to marriage. "Even Martin thinks yer off yer head." As a final inducement, she added, "Go talk to Millie if ye won't listen to us. Or Sister Rita. Ye always got along well with her."

When Carmel said she knew what she was doing and didn't need the advice of anyone else, Bertha knew the battle had been lost before it even began. "Don't ye see what yer doin', girl?" she asked sadly, although it was obvious to her Carmel didn't see what she was doing at all. She pointed out to her the pitfalls of the marriage. "He's not even Catholic. And yer such a churchgoer. And he's older. Too much older."

⟫⟡⟪

Carmel always dreamed of a large wedding, and she approached Ed with the list of people she was going to ask. He quickly squelched her dreams. The wedding would be small. Her mother and Martin and Dusty and Vivian, and if she insisted, she could have Eileen O'Brien as bridesmaid.

He gently explained his reasons for rejecting her plans. "We're really not supposed to marry the locals. We're supposed to wait until we get back stateside and marry our own gals."

He said he had only six months to go for a promotion, and he didn't want to jeopardize his chances. He said his supervisor was dead against his men taking up with the locals. "Old Hank says it's a good policy because getting involved here takes the men's minds off the job they were sent to do." He shrugged prophetically. "If he finds out after the fact, so he finds out. But I'm not going to rush the news to him."

He explained further why making a public spectacle of their wedding wasn't a good idea. The base, he said, had been put on a priority completion, and he was working around the clock to get the living quarters ready for the army detachment that was arriving within a couple of weeks. Under the circumstances, he wasn't even certain he could get the weekend off for their honeymoon.

"For all I know," he said, his voice soft and persuasive, "Uncle Sam may be tangled up in the war soon." He shrugged as if to say stranger things had come to pass. "What if at the last minute I can't make the wedding because of some emergency here? Look how embarrassed you'd be with all the people invited. Bad enough the disappointment for us."

She had tried to pretend it didn't matter, but her eyes filled with tears. He brushed them away with the heel of his hand. "Carm," he said very tenderly, "you can't go by the book in wartime. Nothing holds up when there's a war going on. Absolutely nothing."

Carmel went to see Father Myrick. He insisted on three weeks' notice so there would be time for three publications of the bans. Before he would consent to marry them, he wanted to meet with Ed to make sure he understood what marrying a Catholic entailed.

Carmel faltered several times before getting the courage to give Ed Father Myrick's message. She was certain he would balk at the restrictions that would be placed upon him. He also would probably bring up the idea of a Justice of the Peace as he had earlier, saying it was a way of short-circuiting all the red tape.

To her amazement, though, Ed agreed to all the stipulations. He had to sign a form attesting he had been baptized and that he was free to marry. As well, he had to agree to bring up the children in the Catholic faith. He was also told that the rhythm method of contraception — and this only for spacing children, not for preventing them altogether — was the only form of contraception acceptable to the church.

Carmel had always known that when she got married it would be with a Nuptial Mass. But just as she had to pass up her dream of a big wedding, the dream of a Nuptial Mass also had to go. It wasn't suitable for a mixed marriage. Neither was the main altar in the church. Rather than be married at one of the side altars, Carmel chose the sacristy and consoled herself by believing that when Ed converted, as he was bound to do, they would get married over again, and this time with the complete blessing of the church.

She went to St. John's to get her trousseau. Since the wedding was to take place in late autumn, she selected a soft wool suit in winter white. The salesgirl's murmur of appreciation told her she had chosen well.

"That fits you like a glove," the clerk said, appraising Carmel's slim waist and narrow hips. "It does things for yer figger." She slid her hands down her own ample thighs and gave a rueful laugh. "Not that yer figger needs anything done to it."

When Carmel explained that the suit was to be her bridal outfit, the clerk said she had just the right accessories to go with it and showed her a soft, ivory-coloured silk blouse and a hat to match that was little more than a wisp of a veil over a velvet bow.

In the dressing room, Carmel couldn't help but be awed at the sight of herself in the three-way mirror. "I look exactly the way a bride should look," she told herself. "And ivory is a much better colour than stark white and more practical too." Pretending her purse was a bridal bouquet, she took several steps across the dressing room, humming the Wedding March.

Next she went to purchase lingerie. She had always worn pyjamas, and when she asked to see nightgowns, she could feel a blush starting in the pit of her stomach and working its way towards her face.

The middle-aged salesclerk smiled broadly. "A bride?" she asked. Carmel nodded shyly.

"Can always tell," the clerk said and then turned to another worker. "We always know 'tis for a bride, don't we, Angie? The unmarried ones wouldn't be caught dead in nightgowns these days. Pyjamas are all the rage."

"That's fer sure," Angie agreed. She indicated boxes of nightgowns piled on the counter. "Those just came in. I haven't even put the prices on yet." She opened up the top box and took out a sea green gown made of the sheerest fabric Carmel had ever seen — so sheer it seemed positively shameless.

Angie held the garment up to her own outsized body and sashayed up and down the narrow walkway behind the counter. "Lord have mercy. If my Paddy had seen me in anything like this on my wedding night, he'd have been some terror." She giggled saucily. "Bad enough as he was."

Carmel wished she were back out on the street. She could feel the heat rising up the back of her neck. Soon, she knew, her whole face would be beet red. The other clerk noticed her discomfort and good-naturedly reproved Angie.

"Yer a terror yerself, Angie, and 'tis a good thing no one pays any attention to what you sez. If they did we'd have no customers."

Carmel dropped the packaged sea green nightgown into the garment bag which held her suit and left the store, vowing never to go back, even if it meant foregoing buying beautiful lingerie.

The weekend after she purchased her trousseau, she made a special trip to the Cove to see Sister Rita. Besides her teaching duties, Sister Rita looked after the flowers for the church, and as a special favour she sometimes made wedding bouquets.

"Of course, dear, I'd be delighted to make a bouquet for your missal, but I thought . . . I mean, I was told . . ."

"I know. I know," Carmel interjected. "You heard right. I'm not getting married with a Mass, but I still would like to carry a missal." She began to stammer, embarrassed. "I wanted . . . I always thought . . . And even if Ed isn't Catholic . . . I just thought the missal would be a nice keepsake." In the austere visitors' parlour, her romantic notions seemed almost lewd. She added, flustered, "Maybe it's just a silly notion of mine."

Sister Rita hurried to put Carmel at ease. "It isn't silly at all, Carmel. I think it's a lovely notion to want a lasting remembrance of such an important day." She withdrew her hands from the cavern of her large sleeves and pointed to the sun porch that had flower pots placed in each inch of sunlight.

"We have the most exquisite miniature mums. Some yellow. Some white." She made a small circle with her thumb and index finger. "Those tiny ones should be perfect on your missal."

Just as Carmel was leaving the convent, Sister Rita placed a gentle restraining hand on her arm and asked her how her mother felt about the upcoming wedding. "Your mother? Is she happy about your choice of husband?"

Carmel hedged. "Well, she's glad I'm happy. She worries of course. He's a little older than I am and . . ." She let the sentence trail off.

Sister Rita smiled understandingly. "All mothers worry, Carmel dear. When I entered the convent, my mother never slept for months. She was sure I was discontented and that I didn't have the nerve to leave. It took me years to convince her I was doing exactly what I wanted to do." She gave Carmel a penetrating look, and her tone was so concerned it was more like a mother's than a teacher's. "You *are* happy, aren't you Carmel? You *are* doing what you want to do? Because if you are, everything else will fall into place."

Ed and Carmel were married on a Sunday afternoon, and after having supper at Bertha's, they went directly to their own apartment. Ed had rented a place just outside the base, near Vivian and Dusty. It was only two rooms and a bathroom that had to be shared with the owner of the house. One of the two rooms had been converted into a makeshift kitchen, and the other one doubled as a bedroom-sitting room. The place had an impermanent air. The furniture, which even in its heyday had never been of good quality, now had rips and spots and gouges from the rapid turnover of tenants en route to better places.

But as far as Carmel was concerned, it was a crystal palace. She shined the rickety tables and hung curtains and waxed the chewed-up linoleum floor. Her mother had given her odds and ends — tablecloths, doilies, pictures — and these helped to cover up the shabbiness. But even without these things, Carmel would have been sublimely happy. Having Ed beside her at night was enough to make the place seem like a mansion.

She never completely believed she deserved Ed, and she couldn't fully understand why he had chosen her out of the hundreds of women who must have been available. At night after he fell asleep, she would lie awake absorbing him, remembering the smell of his bare flesh, fresh from the bath, and the taste of his neck, salty from lovemaking. She asked nothing more of life than to be allowed to share Ed's bed for as long as she lived and to fall asleep caught up in the ebb and flow of his breathing.

Some mornings Ed had to go to work much earlier than she did, and on these occasions when she was alone, she would stand in front of the mirror and repeat her name over and over again. *Carmel Strominski. Carmel Strominski.* She would let her hands roam over her hips, her stomach, her breasts — now seeing in her body a beauty she hadn't known was there. Ed's love confirmed her as a woman to be desired.

There were times when she could almost convince herself that Carmel Corrigan never existed — that Carmel Strominski had been created whole and complete, full-blown from the love of Ed Strominski. The woman who looked back at her from the bureau mirror bore little resemblance to the woman who worked in the bank back in the Cove. The new woman was beautiful indeed. She had shining hair, glowing skin, sparkling eyes, a dazzling smile and a proud tilt to her head — a tilt that was no longer a defence.

The morning she looked in the mirror and saw — or imagined she saw — the bulge in her stomach, she distanced herself even further from Carmel Corrigan. She smoothed her hands across her belly, caressing the life that was only weeks old.

As she stroked the soft flesh and thought about the child

growing within her, the sparkle left her eyes. How would she tell Ed? He had made it plain he didn't want children right away. He had even said *probably never*, but she was certain that had only been his way of making it clear to her she should take precautions to prevent conception. And of course she had. She had checked the calendar. Took her temperature. Plotted charts for safe and unsafe times. But something had gone wrong.

She couldn't bear to have Ed accuse her of being negligent and careless, or tell her she was stupid to trust the rhythm method. She decided she would keep her secret to herself for a little while. With every passing day there was the hope Ed would change his thinking. She would cling to that hope until her body forced her to do otherwise.

———⊰•⊱———

In the five months of marriage, Carmel never had to spend a night without Ed lying beside her in the lumpy, sway-backed davenport. One morning after she had settled in to her day's work at the payroll office, she got a call from him saying he had to leave to go stateside immediately. He sounded agitated and on edge. Almost distraught.

"How come? Why?" Panic rose in Carmel at the thought of his being shipped to some other base where she wouldn't be allowed to follow him.

"I'm not sure what's going on," he said evasively. "Something about a transfer."

Carmel began to cry. "You're keeping something from me, Ed. I know it. I can feel it."

"Don't be ridiculous, Carm," he snapped. "Stop being melodramatic. If I had anything to tell you, I would. But you know as much as I do about this trip."

His sure, offhand manner mollified her slightly, and she asked, "When will you be back?"

There was a long pause. Ed let out his breath, and she could hear the sigh coming along the wires. "I don't know, Carm." Every word was as heavy as the rocks he bulldozed out of the hillsides on the base. "I honest to God don't know."

"Can't you find out?" She was pressing more than she would ordinarily have done. He didn't like to be pressed. "Can't you ask your supervisor? If it comes to that, tell them you have a wife here. They just can't ship you off somewhere without telling me where."

"You know I can't mention you. We've been all over that before. There's no way I can get more information for you. I don't have any more myself."

"Then I'll call your supervisor. I'll pretend we're just friends . . . I'll . . ."

He cut her off with a short retort. "You'll do nothing of the sort. Stay out of my affairs, Carm. It's my job, and I'll go where I'm sent."

She quickly withdrew her threat. "I don't mean to interfere. It's just that I love you. I need to know where you are."

Ed didn't answer, and Carmel broke the silence by offering to leave work and go home to help him pack.

"I've been there already," he confessed. "I took what I needed." He talked as though someone was listening to his conversation.

Carmel detected the strain in his voice, "Are you at work, Ed? Is anyone there with you?"

Ed didn't answer. The perspiration from Carmel's hand made the receiver slippery. She clutched it tighter. "Ed, where are you? Who's with you?" She almost shrieked into the mouthpiece.

"I'm at take-off, Carm," he said flatly. "The plane is leaving any minute." Just before he hung up, his tone gentled. "Take care, Carm. Take care of yourself."

Hearing the softness in his voice, Carmel wished they were home together with the davenport pulled out. "Phone me," she whispered into the dead receiver. "Phone me the minute you land and tell me where you are."

Even after she was certain the connection was broken, she still clung to the receiver as though to put it down would forever separate them. She trembled from the anxiety of not knowing his destination, nor the date of his return. She tried to hate the war, but then remembered that without the war she would never have met Ed.

———⇒◆⇐———

A week went by, and there was no phone call from Ed. She made logical and illogical excuses. He had been shipped to some remote construction job and there weren't any phones. He had phoned her at work, but she was already on her way home. He had phoned her at home, but because the telephone was in the landlady's part of the house and she was hard of hearing, the call had come but the phone was never answered.

She begrudged the time it took to go and come from work. It meant a half hour in the morning and again at night when she wasn't able to be reached. At work she never took a coffee break. At home she never went outside the door, not even to get groceries. She kept one ear always alert to the phone, and she was determined that if the landlady didn't answer it on the second ring, she would have no qualms about knocking on her door.

She waited for a letter, knowing he wasn't gone long enough for a letter to arrive. She toyed with the idea of calling

Dusty. Perhaps he would know more about Ed's whereabouts. She picked up the phone a dozen times a day to call him but then replaced the receiver. She knew Ed would be furious if he learned she was keeping tabs on him by calling his friends. Each day she told herself to wait one more day and then call someone, Ed's supervisor if necessary.

—✦—

She felt the presence of Father Myrick and Padre Kriepel seconds before she actually saw them. She had been so intent on getting the overtime worked out for the payroll that was due the next morning that she hadn't heard them come in. Afterwards she was to remember with total recall the most minute details of that moment. She was calculating the overtime of John Hendricks — a plumber's helper — and it had amounted to eighty-three dollars and seventy-five cents. There was ink on her index finger from her leaky pen.

When she saw the two clergymen standing before her, sombre and official looking, she must have blanched because Father Myrick said quickly, "Everyone's all right, Carmel. No one's hurt."

They closed her office door and searched for painless words to tell her Ed wouldn't be coming back. He had been called stateside on charges of bigamy. They told her that officials on the base would be in touch with her in a day or two. There was still information to be gathered, but the facts seemed to be clear and unmistakable. They spoke in low, mournful tones, aware that they had no consolation to offer. No hope to give. No comfort to extend.

They took her home. She sat alone in the back seat of Father Myrick's car. The army chaplain sat up front, but he might as well have sat with her because he reached over the seat and held her hands as though otherwise she would jump out and splatter herself over the road. He needn't have worried. Jumping would have taken energy. It would have required movement. She sat like stone.

Padre Kriepel talked softly as he would to an injured animal.

"We'll get the ins and outs of everything for you. We'll get to the bottom of this mess."

But she didn't want the bottom of a mess. She wanted Ed. When they first told her she had screamed that a mistake had been made. "No! No! No! You don't understand." Remembering the picture she came upon in his wallet — a smiling woman and four children — she said, "He has a sister. He doesn't have a wife other than me."

Even when they told her it was his other wife — his legitimate wife — who had pressed the bigamy charges, she whipped right past their logic, their common sense, their evidence. "He has a sister, and she has four children," she kept stating, trying to get them to understand why the mix-up had come about.

They looked at her pityingly. But she brushed the pity aside. She would make them see it was really his sister. The day she came upon the picture, she also thought it was his wife. She had been trying to bring order to his bureau drawers because they were always a mess — handkerchiefs mixed in with undershorts and undershorts with socks. The photograph was in the top drawer underneath some papers.

An illogical but total fear drained the use of her legs, and she had to sit on the edge of the bed to keep from falling. Ed found her there, her eyes boring into the faces of the woman and four children who looked back at her accusingly.

"Oh I forgot to mention to you," he said easily. "I got a letter from Miriam yesterday. She sent along a picture of her brood." His face didn't show a trace of guilt or deception.

"Miriam?" she questioned. "Who is Miriam?"

He shot her an impatient look, the look he reserved for those times when she fell exceedingly short of his expectations. "My sister. Remember? I told you about her. She lives in Oregon. In Portland." He came and looked over her shoulder, scanning the photo.

"And that's Christopher there and Jan and Alex." His voice warmed. "And that one there is Molly. She's almost nine. The baby."

She was certain he had never mentioned a sister, but she was so relieved that she smiled apologetically. "I guess I forgot. I have so much to learn about you."

He sat beside her, and she nuzzled close against him. "It's not fair," she said, half-joking. "You even know when I cut my first tooth and how Millie was the one to discover it, and I know so little about you. All I know is your home address in Oregon and that I had to get from your mail."

He gave a quick dismissing hug as though whoever they each were before they met was of no account to the present. "I'll have a load of pictures sent in," he joked. "You can see what I looked like with curly hair and short pants." He took the picture from her and without even a second glance, tossed it back into the drawer as if it were of no importance.

But even though she believed his explanation, the next day, propelled by some urgency, she freely looked in the bureau. The picture had been moved. She never mentioned this to him, although she continued to check every day to see if he had put it back. She even sneaked a look in his wallet. It wasn't there either.

She tried to put the incident out of her mind, but it always hovered just in the background and just present enough to cause her uneasiness. There was something disquieting about Molly's smile. She looked like a little girl who was having her picture taken to send to her daddy.

One evening, forcing casualness, she brought up Miriam's

name. The had been sitting at the kitchen table having their after-supper coffee. She reached across the table and cupped her hand over his. "I was thinking this afternoon that I would like to meet your family. Particularly Miriam. I always wanted an older sister. I think we would like each other."

Ed brushed aside her chatter with an abrupt statement that he wanted a beer instead of coffee. He went to the refrigerator and took out a bottle of beer and snapped the cap off. He tipped his head back and let the liquid run down his throat. When the bottle was empty, he tossed it aside and returned to the table.

"You'd hate each other," he said ungraciously. "You're nothing alike at all. Like night and day." He reached across the table and pulled her around to sit on his lap. "Enough talk about family. Let's change the subject to something more interesting." He began unbuttoning her blouse, nuzzling the hollow of her neck as he did so. "Your skin is so soft," he murmured. "As smooth as silk."

<hr />

She had been so immersed in her thoughts that she didn't realize they were near her apartment. Father Myrick said they should bypass it and drive on to her mother's house because Carmel shouldn't be alone and they, themselves, couldn't stay with her for any length of time.

"Please take me to my own place, Father," she said, her voice determined. "I want to go to my own apartment." She was certain there would be a message waiting for her from Ed. Indeed, he was probably trying to contact her at work and frantic because he couldn't find her either at home or at work. And if he had heard the vicious rumour that was being spread about him, he would definitely want her to hear the truth from his own lips. She wondered if someone on the job who had been jealous of his upcoming promotion or because he had been singled out for the trip stateside had started the terrible lie.

"We'll stay with you for a little while." Father Myrick looked to the chaplain for his consent as it wouldn't look right being alone with a woman in an apartment.

"Please, Father," Carmel said in an even voice to show she wasn't on the verge of collapse. "I'd really like to be by myself. I'd like to be alone."

"We'll take you to your apartment," Father Myrick told her, "but we're going to try and get Martin to come for you or at least stay with you until you get your bearings." His voice was soft with concern. "You've had an awful blow, my dear. An awful blow."

There was no message at home for her. The landlady said the phone hadn't rung all day, and she assured Carmel she had never left the house, not even to go to the clothesline.

For the first time, Carmel noticed the shabbiness of her apartment. She saw the sway-backed davenport and the gouges in the linoleum. She saw the overstuffed chairs with their oozing insides. She could finally understand why Martin said it didn't resemble Buckingham Palace.

The two priests talked back and forth to one another just as if she weren't present. They talked about Ed as if he were some foreign devil and not the husband she loved with her whole being. She wished she could summon enough strength to tell them to go away and leave her alone.

"A bigamist!" The word drained all charity from Father Myrick's heart. "Jail is too good for him. I hope he rots there." He wiped his hand across his brow to wipe away his guilt for having performed the marriage without doing sufficient checking on Ed's background. "I'm glad they caught up with him now. Before there were children."

From where Carmel was sitting she could see into the only

clothes closet in the apartment. She stared at Ed's parka and noticed that it was wedged in between her dresses. She imagined Ed pressing up against her, loins rubbing against loins.

"Don't worry, girl," Father Myrick said softly. "We'll get everything straightened out. I'll get in touch with the Bishop. A civil case like this won't take any time for an annulment."

"No time at all," Padre Kriepel echoed. "A cut and dried case. I don't think you'll even have to petition Rome."

Father Myrick ran his finger around the inside of his clerical collar. The trauma of the afternoon was making him perspire. "I really don't know what's required, Jim," he said, shaking his head in bewilderment. "I really don't know. I've never had to deal with anything like this. I imagine I'll have to work through His Grace."

Carmel stopped listening. She stared so intently at Ed's parka that she could see through the rainproof outer covering to the grey fur lining. She wished she could remove all of her clothes right then and wrap herself in that parka. She would probably feel warm then. It would be like having Ed's arms around her. She began to shiver. She touched her arms, and they were icy cold. She place a hand tenderly on her stomach and after a few moments felt the only spark of life left in her body. She gave a low moan and toppled to the floor.

Both priests rushed to her side.

"She's fainted, the poor thing," Father Myrick said, and he ran to get water from the kitchen.

Padre Kriepel looked at Carmel's bleached white face and her trembling body. "My God, Peter, she's going into shock. Call a doctor!" He rushed to the closet and got Ed's parka. "I'll cover her with this. She's like a block of ice."

—⟫⟪—

Carmel returned to her old room at her mother's house. Martin and Bertha cleaned every trace of Ed Strominski from the apartment. They packed up his belongings and sent them to the base. Carmel stayed in the house. She never went anywhere — not even to church. Martin often tried to coax her out of her stupor by offering to take her along on some of his taxi fares.

"I'm goin' up the shore today. Takin' Jim McGrath home for the weekend. Why don't ye come along," he would urge. "Come on. Jim won't mind."

She always refused.

Sometimes he lost patience with her, and he'd bark that she was ruining everyone's life but mostly her own. "Jest because some asshole Yank made a fool out of ye is no reason to go around the house looking like the Mother of Sorrows."

He would survey her unkempt hair and the slip that straggled into sight no matter the length of her dress. "Jest look at yerself. Ye looks like something that got washed ashore off Cape St. Mary's."

Sometimes Bertha lost patience with her as well.

"Sure ye've had a hard knock," she would say. "No one's disputin' that. But that's no reason to bury yerself." She would point to Carmel's protruding stomach. "Ye've the child to think about if nothin' else."

Carmel sank lower and lower into her depression. Bertha was terrified she would end up like Ned. She talked about the impending birth of the child in a vain attempt to give Carmel something to live for. "All pain lessens in time, girl," she would say honestly, "even if it never goes away entirely. It mightn't become that much better, but it will become bearable. I can vouch for that much."

One day, desperate to ease Carmel's ever-increasing despair, Bertha confessed about her rape. She hoped that by telling her this, she would convince her it was indeed possible to rise above even the most terrible misfortunes. She told about her pregnancy and how she had been left on her own during the worst ordeal of her life. She spoke haltingly, her eyes not meeting Carmel's, as though Vince's shame was her shame. When she was finished she forced herself to look up to see if the secret she had revealed had had any impact upon Carmel's emotions. The eyes she looked into showed not the slightest change. Bertha turned away, defeated.

She stood up, her failure to help Carmel evident in her heavy intake of breath. She reached for her apron that she had thrown over the back of her chair and began tying it around her waist so she could start supper. Just as she turned towards the stove, Carmel spoke.

"I think I've always known that Father wasn't my father." Her voice held no emotion, as if it didn't matter one way or the other who her father was. "I don't know how I knew. Or when I knew. But I had the feeling it was Uncle Vince." She rubbed her hand across her stomach, a bond of compassion joining her to her child. "But I didn't know he forced you."

"That he did," Bertha answered quickly, hoping to keep the conversation going. "And how I hated him." Even after all the intervening years, her tone still held traces of vehemence. She even confessed about her thoughts on suicide.

"Now, I'm some glad I didn't have the nerve to do away with meself." Her face fell into soft folds. "Ye were worth every minute of the trouble. And ye'll feel the same way when yer child comes. And ye'll even start goin' back to church. Jest like I did."

"But he was drunk," Carmel said, her voice still far away, as if her mind was still hearing the early part of Bertha's conversation. "You said you smelled the beer."

Bertha's heart fluttered. Carmel cared about something! She wanted to believe her father wouldn't knowingly rape a woman. And if that was important to Carmel, it was important to her as well.

"Of course he was drunk, girl. He'd never have done such a thing sober," she lied. "Never!"

Father Myrick came often. Each time he gently rebuked Carmel for not going to Mass and for turning her back on God when she needed Him the most. He kept her abreast of what the Tribunal was doing about her annulment. He quoted from Canon Law and recited the thirteen matrimonial impediments.

As if she cared. As if it mattered to her how a marriage could be dissolved. As if she were interested in the ramifications of matrimonial Canon Law. He used Latin terms and phrases and legal talk, but they were just as pain filled as common language.

He allowed it was possible that the child could be legitimized because, as far as he could determine, Carmel's marriage fell into the category of a *putative* marriage — a marriage contracted in good faith on the part of at least one party.

"The way I read it," he said tentatively, "children conceived of, or born of, a putative marriage are considered legitimate." He explained that there was one hitch: it all depended upon Carmel's ability to prove she had had no awareness of her husband's prior marriage. Such proof, he said, would have to be unassailable insofar as the Tribunal was concerned.

Carmel straightened up in her chair and smoothed her dress. "If I were to present that unassailable proof, Father, would the child still have to be called Strominski?" Her voice held a hint of her old determination. It was the most response she had shown to anything going on around her since the day

Bertha had told her about the rape. "The child is going to be called Corrigan no matter what the Tribunal says."

"I really don't know how to answer that, my dear," Father Myrick replied, disappointed with himself for his lack of knowledge on this issue. "It's a legal matter as well." He looked at her sympathetically.

"Strominski is not a name that would fit in here in the Cove. It would probably be a burden to the poor little thing." He shrugged. "It's up to you, I suppose. If I were you I'd put whatever name I wanted on the forms. I'd just send them to the government." He justified his advice to do something not according to the book by stating, "It's for the benefit of the child. What does the government know about the people in the Cove and how they react to things?"

—————◆—————

A short while before Carmel's confinement — the baby had already dropped and was so low Carmel had difficulty walking — Father Myrick made another visit. He had great news. "The annulment has come through. In record time." His voice jubilant, he said, "I've never heard of one to go through so fast."

The Latin terms, which had become commonplace to all of them, rolled off his tongue with ease. "*Void ab initio*," he stated and pulled a formal-looking paper from his inside coat pocket. He slapped it with his knuckles. "*Void ab initio*." He gave a satisfied sigh as he handed the paper over to Carmel. "It's all behind us now. All behind us. And thanks be to God for that."

After the priest left, Carmel went upstairs and sat on her bed. Her marriage had been wiped away. Canon Law said so. She whispered the phrase over and over again. *Void ab initio.*

Void ab initio. Void ab initio. From the beginning it never was.

Her eyes rested on the old-fashioned white bureau that had belonged to her Grandmother Selena. Once it had held the hopes and treasures of a sea captain's young bride. Now it held every remaining tangible thing from her own marriage. The top was strewn with the personal items her mother had brought back from the apartment and had left for her to sort out: lipsticks, creams, jars of lotions. Amongst the clutter her eyes sought and found a perfume bottle, its midnight blue glass standing out starkly against the white painted bureau. Ed had given the perfume to her shortly before their wedding.

She reached over her bloated stomach and clumsily retrieved the bottle. The night Ed gave it to her she had held it up to the light and stared into the indigo glass, envisioning the mysteries that lay ahead for her when she married the only man she had ever loved or could ever love. She wore the perfume that same night when they went to the American Civilian Club. Ed had danced with no one but her.

She heaved herself off the bed and stood in front of the bureau, staring at herself in the hazy mirror that had lost much of its quicksilver. Although the bottle had long ago been emptied, she pretended to dab perfume on herself: in the hollow of her throat, on her ear lobes, around her hairline. She tried even behind her knees. But her ungainly body wouldn't permit her to reach her knees as she had done on that other night, and she had to settle for further up her thighs. The scent took her back to the most enchanting moments of her life — moments that were more beautiful than her wedding night.

She rummaged through the bureau drawer and located the special picture of Ed she had stored away and which she never had had the courage to destroy. He was wearing khaki trousers and a green plaid shirt and was leaning against the cab of his steam shovel, squinting into the camera. Even now, his exquisite maleness made her catch her breath.

Still holding the picture and perfume bottle, she wrapped her arms around her stomach and moved to the music that filled her head. Ed's lips touched her hair as he whispered a kiss across the top of her head. She began to sing softly.

I'm going to buy a paper doll that I can call my own,
A doll that other fellows cannot steal.

She circled the room, her stomach no longer misshapen.

"Carmel!" Bertha shouted from the kitchen. "Supper's ready. Come and get it while 'tis hot."

The music stopped abruptly, and Carmel dropped down on the bed, puffing from the exertion of whirling across the dance floor.

"Carmel!"

"I'll be down when I'm ready!" she snapped. "I'm straightening things out."

She began to dump the clutter from her bureau top. The perfume bottle landed with a clink into the tin wastebasket. When the top was clear, she picked up the picture of Ed that she had dropped on the bedspread when her mother called to her. She intended to tear it into shreds and let it go out with the rest of the rubbish. She started to rip it in half, but it was like ripping her heart apart. Tenderly she placed it in an envelope and buried it in a bottom drawer. It lay next to her nuptial missal and the dried yellow and white mums.

Just before leaving the room, she surveyed her bulging stomach. For her child's sake she would have to get on with her life. She picked up the wastebasket and headed downstairs. She would ask her mother and Martin to never mention Ed's name in the house again. She would think of him as being dead, or even deader than dead. He never was. He would be like her marriage. *Void ab initio. He never was from the beginning.* She didn't know what she would tell the child when it came time for questions about its father. She certainly couldn't say, "My dear, your father was a bigamist." Perhaps if no mention was every made of him, no question would ever be asked.

———⊳◦⊲———

When her child was born, a girl, Carmel christened her Theresa Elizabeth — Elizabeth after her Aunt Bessie and Theresa because it was a solid name. Although the name quickly became shortened to Tessie, Carmel still felt it had character and substance, not like the frivolous, flighty names some mothers in the Cove were beginning to call their children — movie star names from the movies they had seen on the base.

As Bertha had predicted, Carmel returned to church once the child was old enough to be left in the care of someone else. But she would only go to early Mass, and she would only sit in a back pew so she could get away before the crowd congregated in the vestibule, forcing her to carry on a conversation.

———⊳◦⊲———

When Tessie was two, Martin had another of his "setbacks." This one was worse than the others, and he had to give up driving his taxi for another six months. Carmel was forced to go to work. She took a job in the bank, but one that was lower ranking than the job she left at the base. Even though jobs were scarce in the Cove, she couldn't bear to go back to work at the base. She kept the job even after Martin got well, telling herself it was insurance against another setback.

One dreary, rainy evening, three years after her return to work, she thought about the emptiness of her life as she walked towards her house. The years stretched ahead, dark and vacant. She never wanted to marry again, but even if she did, there was no chance of doing so in the Cove. Her annulment notwithstanding, she was always thought of as a grass widow or as "the unfortunate woman who married the Yank who turned out to be married." The people didn't mean to be unkind. It was just that what had happened to her was so horrendous it couldn't easily be forgotten, especially with the child as a reminder.

As she walked along the wet gravel road, Carmel worried about what would become of Tessie if she had to stay in the Cove. Would she always be known as the child of the woman who married the Yank?

Yet, taking her away from the Cove meant taking her away from Martin. Martin and Tessie had grown so attached to one another that Carmel felt it would be cruel to separate them. It was clear Tessie idolized Martin, and he, in turn, lost all his sharpness when he was with the child.

But Carmel knew that no matter how much it might hurt him, Martin would want what was best for Tessie — and for her as well. He would understand that the best opportunities for the both of them were in the United States.

By the time she arrived at the house, she had made up her mind she was going to get her immigration papers underway again. This time, though, she would have to fill them out for Tessie as well.

Martin had arrived home ahead of her and was in the parlour with the phonograph going full blast. He had brought home a couple of friends, and the three of them were helping empty a bottle of rum.

"Come on in, Carmel," Martin shouted, when he heard her voice in the kitchen. "Jest Bill and Fitz here. Damn car is in the garage, so we're celebrating Fitz's birthday."

"Go on in and join them," Bertha persuaded. "I can look after supper. Tessie's in there in her glory."

When Carmel went in, someone had already turned off the phonograph, and Martin was tuning up his mouth organ.

"Come on, Tessie," Bill and Fitz urged. "Give us a song."

Tessie hung back behind Martin's shoulder. "I don't want to," she said, shy in the presence of her mother.

Martin sat her on his knee and coaxed her to sing just one more song. "Come on, Tess, old girl, give us jest one more. Show them what a great voice ye have for a five-year-old." He whispered in her ear. "Jest one more. 'Like a Swallow.'" Martin began to play softly, and Tessie started to sing.

> *She's like a swallow that soars on high,*
> *She's like a river that never runs dry,*
> *She's like the sun shining on the shore,*
> *My love, my love. My love is no more.*

Everyone applauded, and Tessie shyly slunk back behind Martin's shoulder.

"Ye should see her step-dance," Martin bragged. He began to play another tune. "Watch this." He played "Haste to the Wedding," and Tessie, without any further encouragement, threw back the scatter rugs and began to dance.

After Martin's friends left and supper was cleared away, Carmel told them of her intention to go to Boston and to take Tessie with her. Bertha said it was a splendid idea for both of them. Martin at first looked stricken, but then he quickly recovered and grabbed Tessie up and swayed her back and forth, making believe she was on a boat going to Boston.

The more Martin dipped and swayed, the more Tessie

giggled. Once, Martin almost lost his balance, and Carmel had to grab Tessie to keep her from falling.

"Lunatic!" Carmel shouted. "One of these days you're going to drop that child!"

"Do it again, Martin!" Tessie shrieked, but Martin made no attempt to pick her up.

"My name's not Martin. Didn't ye hear yer mother? My name's Lunatic."

"Do it again, Lunatic!" Tessie lay on the floor laughing at her own joke. "Lunatic," she giggled. "What kind of name is Lunatic?"

———◈———

Aunt Bessie's reply to Carmel's letter about revising her immigration papers was disappointing. She said she was still more than willing to have Carmel come, but she couldn't take the responsibility for Tessie. She explained her husband wasn't well, and besides it was unlikely under those conditions the immigration people would let the child enter. Aunt Bessie suggested that Carmel come anyway, and after she got her citizenship, she herself could sponsor Tessie.

Bertha agreed with her sister. "That's exactly what ye'll do. Ye get in first and then get Tessie in."

When Carmel hesitated, not wanting to leave the child, Bertha persuaded her that it was the best move for both of them. "What's here for ye? And what will be here for Tessie when she grows up? Better for both of ye to make new lives up there."

Carmel agonized over whether to stay or go. Her indecision finally got on Martin's nerves. "Go or stay, Carmel," he told her. "'Tis yer choice. But for the lovin' honour of God, shit or get off the pot." He took a quarter from his pocket and tossed it in the air.

"Heads ye goes. Tails ye stays."

When the quarter landed on the floor, King George's head stared up at them.

Carmel took it as an omen that she should go. "Well, that's it," she said, heaving a heavy sigh. "I'll go, but I'll come home every summer until I get my citizenship. When I get Tessie in, the two of you will come visit us every year." She hesitated momentarily before adding, "I don't know of any rule that says you can't visit the States if you've had TB. I don't think you even have to have an X-ray just for a short visit."

Going to Boston was a mistake for Carmel and one almost of the magnitude of marrying Ed Strominski. She realized this the first day she went to work in the boot factory. She had scoured all of Boston looking for work, but the better jobs had been taken up by the returning servicemen. The ones that were left were low paying — too low paying for Carmel to save enough money to come back to the Cove every summer and at the same time save money for Tessie's immigration. After three weeks of daily searching, she settled for the factory job because it paid more. It was piece work, and she sat on a bench and pressed a lever that pressed a lever that stapled a steel eyelet into the jowl of a brown workboot.

Even with the saving in apartment cost by boarding with her Aunt Bessie and with scrimping and cutting corners whenever possible, Carmel realized she had to make a choice: go home to see the family in the summer or save to sponsor Tessie into the States. She was far too lonesome for the child to wait five years without seeing her, so the choice was really no choice. With a heavy heart she resigned herself to the smell of dyed leather and of going to the Cove for two weeks every summer.

Tessie's Story

Every May, Monsignor Myrick came to Assumption School to hear the catechism of the first communicants. They were grouped like timid sheep at one end of Sister Rita's classroom and separated by an aisle from the older and more seasoned third-graders. The "hearing of catechism" had gone on for years — long before Monsignor's time. He never liked the practice, and he couldn't understand why he continued observing it. He had broached the subject to the convent on a couple of occasions, but he had received no encouragement. He believed it was a torturous occasion for the young children, and he was certain they lived in dread of his coming.

The nuns viewed things differently. They said it was an honour for the children and a carrot for the teachers — one that could be held out to get more learning out of the students. He surmised this day of inquisition was used by the nuns as a prod rather than a carrot. In his younger days, he had been intimidated by the Mother Superior, but those days had long since disappeared, and now his only excuse for not doing away with the practice was his unwillingness to upset the apple cart. He hated fuss and disruption almost as much as he hated the onerous grilling of the youngsters.

On this May morning, his intention was to get the session over with as quickly as possible so he could go back to the rectory and rest his legs that were riddled with varicose veins. The pain of them made him short-tempered. He stopped at the desk of a little girl who had hair as black as a bucket of tar and eyes the colour of wild blueberries. He opened the pink-covered Baltimore Catechism and began his questioning.

"Who made you?"

The child made no move to answer. She sat and stared, her eyes fixed on some point beyond her desk.

Each year Sister Rita was convinced that the current year's crop of youngsters was harder to teach than those of any other previous year. She had no doubt that this group now being tested outranked in obtuseness all the others who had gone before them, and she had thirty-five years of faces from which to select. She had spent three weeks trying to get them to spread their tongue to receive the Host. "No! No! No!" she had shrilled, flinging her veil threateningly back over her shoulders as though she were preparing to take a leap right into their brains. "Not like a cat yawning, tongue stretched half-way across the room. See! Like a petal." She demonstrated by delicately opening her mouth and letting her tongue loll on her lower lip.

But despite her efforts, they were acting like yawning cats again. At least most of them were. The rest were like lizards, tongues flicking in and out so fast it was a wonder Monsignor came away with his fingers intact. Worst of all was this Tessie Corrigan, who didn't know enough to stand up when she was being addressed by the Monsignor.

Sister Rita's memory went back to Tessie's mother. Carmel would never sit there like a lump of cow dung. Carmel had possessed fine qualities, but these didn't appear to have been passed on to this child.

Tessie sat in her seat as if calcified. She had heard Monsignor. And she knew the answer to his question. She knew the answers to all the questions in the book. Martin had drilled her every night until she could recite them backwards and forwards. But Monsignor had skipped a couple of first-graders, and she hadn't expected him to ask her so soon. The fright of it paralyzed her, and all she could do was stare straight ahead at the priest's shiny shoes and at the way his soutane jibbed out over his big stomach.

Out of the corner of her eye, she caught sight of Sister Rita. She was standing slightly behind Monsignor and making frantic levitation motions. Her lips were pursed into a rapid succession of voiceless *ups*. Up! Up! Up! she commanded fiercely. She pumped the air with her upturned palms and conveyed to Tessie her rage and her shame. Tessie saw Sister Rita rub her index finger around the edge of her wimple, sweeping her forehead and her ears before letting it rest in the hollow of her throat. There the heavily starched cloth held the sweat and kept it from dripping into her bosom.

Monsignor glanced again at the catechism.

"Who made you?" he repeated, his irritation growing.

Tessie willed herself out of the seat. She stood up demurely, feet close together, hands cupped loosely at her waist in the hope it would make amends to Sister Rita.

"God made me, Monsignor." Her voice was a mere squeak.

"And Who is God?"

"God is a Supreme Being Who always was and always will be, Monsignor."

"And why did God make you?"

"God made me to know and serve Him here on earth and afterwards to love and enjoy Him in heaven, Monsignor."

Monsignor recovered from his irritation. This one knew every question without a hitch. If they were all like her, he wouldn't have to spend much time at all at the school. He wondered who she was. Impulsively, he reached out and touched the child's shiny black hair.

"And who are you?"

Flustered by his unexpected touch, Tessie answered, "I'm Carmel's Tessie." The instant the words left her tongue, she realized she had misunderstood his question. She should have said, "I'm a child of God and heir to the kingdom of heaven." Worst of all, she had forgotten to add *Monsignor* to the end of her answer.

Monsignor's mouth twitched into the beginning of a smile.

"Carmel who?" he asked, not catching the last name and pretending she hadn't misinterpreted his question.

"Carmel's —" she began, but Sister Rita's quick, bird-like movement to Monsignor's side interrupted her.

"Theresa Corrigan, Monsignor. Carmel Corrigan's daughter."

Monsignor looked puzzled. *Carmel Corrigan!* The name rang a bell, but he couldn't quite place it. There were so many new families in the Cove these days on account of everyone in the bays getting the notion to move to bigger centres that he no longer knew who was who in his parish.

"Carmel Corrigan went to the States, Monsignor. Shortly after the war. Bertha Corrigan's daughter." Her eyes bored the information into his, hoping to trigger recollections that couldn't be discussed in the classroom. She had no intention of publicly airing poor Carmel's deception.

Monsignor stared at the high ceiling of the convent school as though the clue to the child's identity could be found on the brown wooden beams. "Of course! Of course! Of course!" he said. "Carmel's daughter." He wondered how he could ever have forgotten that name. Sometimes it concerned him that his memory was beginning to go like Father Flannigan's did.

How could he have forgotten Carmel Corrigan? Or any of the Corrigan family for that matter. A star-crossed family if ever there was such a thing. Poor Ned. Done away with himself. And poor Carmel. Got fooled by a Yank.

Carmel's face came fully into his view. A pretty thing. Red hair half-way down her back and eyes the colour of blueberries. The child standing beside him had eyes the same colour. He could still see the look in Carmel's eyes the day he had gone to tell her that the blood of a bitch was already married back in the States. He hadn't slept for weeks afterwards. He lived with one consoling thought: none of the others got away with a trick like that. He made certain he had all of their records. And proof from their home town as well. He even telephoned the parents. Right down to Arizona once. Some of them were such devils they even lied on their military records.

Tessie couldn't wait to tell Martin about Monsignor's visit and about her saying she was Carmel's Tessie. She knew he would split his sides laughing. She waited until the three of them were at the supper table.

"Carmel's Tessie!" Martin almost shouted the words, and there was no humour in his voice. "Fer the lovin' honour of Christ, Maw, what have ye done to her? Ye've given her a damn label."

"Watch yer language, young man! In front of the child. Watch yer language!" His mother's eyes snapped with anger. "I'll thank ye to watch yer language."

"Watch *my* language! Ye means watch *yer* language!" He scathingly repeated Tessie's label. *"Carmel's Tessie!"*

"'Tis somethin' ye'd find on a can of molasses or a tin of beans. Yer always callin' her Carmel's Tessie." He jogged her memory, replaying a conversation that morning with Mrs. Flaherty.

"Oh Mrs. Flaherty, I won't be able to serve on the tables at the garden party this summer. Martin's on the road a lot with the taxi and I have Carmel's Tessie to look after."

He laid his fork carefully on the side of his plate so the gravy wouldn't drip on the clean, flour-sack tablecloth, and then he set about admonishing Tessie.

"Don't ye ever again call yerself Carmel's Tessie. Yer Tessie. Not Carmel's Tessie. And if anyone calls ye that," he nodded towards his mother's place at the table, "present company not excepted, speak right up and say, 'I'm Tessie. I'm not Carmel's Tessie.'"

Tessie pouted. She had expected laughter and instead she was being scolded. Just in case Martin had had any say in choosing her name, she wanted him to know she didn't think very much of his choice. "I'm not going to let anyone call me Tessie either. I hate Tessie. And I hate Elizabeth. *Tessie Bessie*. Cows' names. That's what they are."

Her grandmother started to protest, saying Elizabeth was the name of Tessie's great-aunt and the name of the Blessed Virgin's mother, but Martin quickly agreed with Tessie that if she didn't like her name, she had the right to change it. After all, he said, she was the one who had to live with it. "What name would ye like?" he said. "Jest say so and we'll re-christen ye. Jest toss over the name."

Tessie hesitated for only a moment. "I like Grandmother's last name. The one she had before she got married."

"Don't be foolish, child," Bertha chastised. "Ye can't jest go out and pick up any name ye likes. It has to be christened on ye, and it should be a saint's name. There was never a Saint Ryan."

"That's a minor worry, Maw," Martin said. "If we canonize Tessie, she'll be Saint Ryan and that will make it all right for her to be called Ryan then." He picked up his water glass and threw a few drops of water across the table in the direction of Tessie's face. "There now. She's canonized."

He tested the name, linking it with other saints to see how

it would sound in litanies and such. "Saint Francis of Assisi, Saint Theresa of Avila, Saint Ryan of the Cove."

Bertha rolled her eyes heavenwards. "What's to be done? What's to be done? He's a heretic. A sacrilegious heretic."

Martin ignored his mother's agitation and told Tessie she would have to become the patron of some cause. "All saints are patrons of something. They jest don't sit around pokin' their fingers through the clouds all day." He explained the different patronages — the ones that were already taken. "Patron saint of the sick is gone. And of lost articles. That's Anthony, or maybe 'tis Jude." He turned to his mother for confirmation, but she only held her face in horror. "I've got it," he said, grinning mischievously. "Ye've got to be good at whatever it is yer the patron of. So how about good humour? Tessie's always in good humour. She's never sulky or surly, is she Maw? I've never seen her stomp away in a snit or get fightin' mad."

Tessie caught on to what Martin was doing. "Stop it, Martin!" she ordered. "You're making fun of me. I'll never again tell you anything that happens at school." Without even asking to be excused, she stormed away from the table, muttering that her grandmother was right, Martin had no sense.

Carmel sent Tessie a new outfit for her First Communion: white organdy dress, white stockings and white shoes in leather so soft they could be twisted so the toe could touch the heel. The most beautiful part of the outfit was the veil. To Tessie, it looked as wispy as a spider's web.

Her friend Sarah Walsh was furious when she saw that Tessie's First Communion dress far outshone hers. Sarah was usually the best dressed in school because her maiden aunts in the States sent her the latest fashions.

On the Saturday following First Communion Sunday,

Sarah and another friend, Marcella, called at Tessie's house and invited her to play skipping rope with them. Tessie was delirious with happiness. Usually she had to coax them to let her spend the day, and whether she was allowed to be with them depended upon Sarah's mood at the time.

She was no sooner twirling the skipping rope when she sensed something was wrong. They wouldn't let her take a turn skipping but kept her turning the rope. She made up her mind not to let them know she noticed what they were doing and pretended to enjoy twirling the rope.

When Sarah saw she wasn't making any progress in her efforts to taunt Tessie, she dropped the rope and called Marcella into a conference. They giggled and gave sly glances at Tessie, and then they came back and picked up the rope.

"'Tis your turn, Tessie," Sarah announced. "You start to skip, and we'll sing the song."

Tessie jumped in eagerly and waited for them to begin the skipping rope song. In a few seconds they began to chant.

> *Tessie Corrigan is no good,*
> *Cut her up for firewood.*

Tessie's feet never even grazed the rope, and she skipped better than she ever had. But all of a sudden the words to the song changed, and Tessie heard them chanting their new version.

> *Spoons, forks, cups and knives,*
> *Her Yankee father had two wives.*

Tessie's feet stopped moving so suddenly it was if an engine inside them had shut down. She felt the rope kiss the back of her ankles and then snake loosely on the ground.

"Yer *out,* Tessie," Sarah said innocently. Both girls broke into giggles. They dropped the rope and ran towards Sarah's house, looking back over their shoulders, laughing as they ran.

Tessie ran into her kitchen, a sharp pain in her stomach. Bertha was in the pantry making buttermilk biscuits. She came out when she heard the door bang shut, followed by Tessie's loud wailing.

"What is it this time?" she asked crossly, wiping the flour from her hands on her apron. "More fightin' with Sarah Walsh?"

Tessie stood against the door and pulled her sweater sleeve down into her palm so she could swipe the cuff across her eyes.

"They're singing songs about me. Bad songs."

Tessie went and sat on the couch. Her legs barely touched the floor. She looked so forlorn and dejected Bertha's heart ached for her. The biscuits, she decided, could wait. She pulled out the rocking chair and motioned Tessie to come sit beside her.

"Come to Gram and sit a spell," she invited. Bertha smoothed Tessie's hair as she rocked back and forth. She tried to ease her hurt feelings.

"Remember what I told ye, child. Sticks and stones can break yer bones, but names can never hurt ye." She kissed Tessie's cheek. "I spose they're callin' ye Tessie Bessie again?"

Tessie shook her head and gulped back sobs, but Bertha was sure the row had to do with name calling. She launched into an account of the name calling that went on when she was growing up.

"One fellow," she said, recalling the incident with twinkling eyes, "was named Charlie. We used to call him Charlie Barley because his father used to sell hop beer. Charlie would get furious and pelt us with rocks. But we jest got a bigger kick out of that." She began to chant.

> *Jump up, Charlie,*
> *You got barley*
> *Up in the leg of yer drawers.*

She explained how the song had come about. "They said when the constable came to search the house, his father hid the booze in Charlie's trousers. But how true that was I don't know."

Bertha remained silent for a few seconds and then added in a remorseful voice, "But we meant nothin' by it. Nothin' at all. In fact, we didn't know what it meant. Jest somethin' we heard." She wiped Tessie's eyes with her apron. "And ye knows somethin'," she said softly in an attempt to vindicate her youthful lack of charity, "that Charlie went on to become a doctor and I spose made more money in a year than the rest of us did in a lifetime." She twigged Tessie's ear. "So ye sees, me little rabbit, names can't hurt ye."

Tessie's anger rose until it spread throughout her body. Her grandmother was always accusing her of making a fuss out of nothing. "Mountains out of molehills, that's what ye makes, child," she had accused over and over again. But this time she wasn't crying over any molehills. There was no way her song could be compared with "Jump up, Charlie." She would show her grandmother how wrong she was. Tessie began to chant.

> *Tessie Corrigan is no good,*
> *Cut her up for fire wood.*
> *Spoons, forks, cups and knives,*
> *HER YANKEE FATHER HAD TWO WIVES.*

She stressed the last line and dragged it out so her grandmother couldn't miss hearing it.

Bertha sprang from the chair so violently it rocked back against the wall, making Tessie lurch forward, and she almost fell on the floor.

"*That's* the song they sang? They sang *that* song to ye?"

Tessie nodded and began to cry again. She huddled in the chair.

"Get me sweater, Tessie!" Bertha ordered. "And where did I leave me outdoor shoes?" She pranced around the floor in a frenzy. "I'm goin' to get this cleared up right now. I'm not goin' to wait another minute!" As she searched for her shoes and threatened what she was going to do when she went to Eileen Tobin's, she whipped off her apron and flung it on the couch. She grabbed her sweater from Tessie and told her not to go near the stove and to keep out of mischief until she got back.

"Where are you going, Gram?" Tessie wailed. "Tell me where you're going."

"I'm goin' to give Eileen Walsh a piece of me mind." Every soft line in Bertha's face had disappeared. "The likes of her," she hissed. "Gnawing the stations of the cross on Sunday and teaching her youngsters scandalous stuff on Monday. I knows plenty of dirt, too. And I won't be afraid to use it if it comes to that. I'm not the mealy-mouthed thing I was when Carmel was growin' up." Her resolve turned to guilty sadness. "I should have protected Carmel more. I should have hauled the head off those who tormented her about Ned."

Bertha was back in less than an hour. She went immediately to put fresh wood in the stove and tossed the sticks in furiously, her anger still not exhausted.

"There'll be no more songs," she said, her voice hard. "'Tis finished and over with." But she didn't act as if it were over with. She sat on the couch, all thought of the biscuits banished from her mind.

Tessie needed her mind taken off the morning's upset and in the afternoon Bertha decided to air out the parlour, although she usually didn't do that job until mid-June. She forced enthusiasm into her voice. "I needs yer help, Tessie. To air out the parlour. For when yer mother comes." She began gathering up the cleaning equipment and gave Tessie the job of tying a cloth over the broom to reach the cobwebs on the ceiling.

Tessie loved airing the parlour. It was a time for asking

about the people with high collars who looked out at her from their oval frames. Her grandmother was always eager to tell her about the relatives who had come and gone before her. "That's yer Great-Aunt Bessie," she would say, pointing to a sober-looking woman with a cameo brooch. "She went to the States when she was fifteen and earned her own livin' ever since."

On this particular airing out, Tessie was interested only in one relative. In the midst of her grandmother's explanation about the little boy in the short pants being Martin, Tessie interrupted to ask, "Did he really have two wives?" She knew it was a subject she wasn't supposed to discuss. It was not that she had been told to keep silent about her father. It was just a feeling she had that the subject was off limits.

Her grandmother was cleaning the windows with vinegar water. She stopped the cloth in mid-swipe. After a few seconds she said, "I didn't know much about him." Her discomfort was visible in the way she began concentrating on cleaning the panes of glass, grumbling over the soot and the dampness that made everything a mess.

Tessie continued to probe. "My father," she faltered. "They said he was married before he married Mummy. Is that true?"

"Here, help me with this window," her grandmother said with forced crossness. "Can never get these things to open in the spring."

Tessie persisted. "Is he dead?"

Bertha strained at the window still trying to push it open. "Help, Tessie! Don't jest natter."

Tessie pushed at the sill, but she wouldn't allow her grandmother to sidetrack her. "Just tell me. Is he alive or dead?"

"He's dead as far as I'm concerned." Bertha grunted and pushed on the swollen window frame with all her strength. Her evasiveness infuriated Tessie. She threw the cleaning cloth on the floor and screamed.

"You've never talked about him! Mummy has never once mentioned his name. And Martin says I should be told but he's not the one to do it." She made like she was going to leave the room. "I'll find out from Sarah Walsh. *Her* mother didn't keep it a secret."

"Wait!" Her grandmother's commanding voice cut through the stillness of the parlour. Tessie stopped, one foot on either side of the door ledge, her stance determined.

"I don't know whether he's alive or dead, and that's the God's truth, Tessie. I really don't know what was the end of him. Yer mother never said — if she knew. And we never asked."

That answer wasn't good enough for Tessie. It seemed that everyone but her knew about her father. She hated all the people who kept secrets from her and those who knew secrets about her. She especially hated Sarah Walsh. She began to run out of the room, and as she did so she bumped into the red velvet parlour chair her grandmother had pulled out into the hall. Suddenly a wild idea hit her. The previous summer, Sister Francis had come home to the Cove to celebrate her getting the black veil. She held audiences in her mother's front parlour. Everyone in the Cove visited her, and she gave each person a holy memento — a picture of the Blessed Virgin, a medal of the Sacred Heart and on and on. Very special adults got a black or brown rosary. Very special children got a red or blue one. Tessie hadn't been one of the special children, but she had been fascinated by the pile of glass beads on the table beside Sister Francis's flowing sleeves. The variety of the sacramentals appeared to be boundless, and Tessie had stared in awe as Sister Francis passed them out with a smile and a flick of a white wrist and a flash of shiny silver ring.

The vision of Sister Francis faded, and Tessie saw herself seated in the red velvet chair, shrouded in her new black veil. She had an angelic smile on her face as she parcelled out the sacramentals. And she had had her revenge on Sarah Walsh. She had offered her nothing when she came to pay her respects, not even a glimpse of her new silver Bride of Christ ring.

She broke out of her reverie and came back into the parlour her mood exultant. "Guess what, Gram!"

"What?" Bertha answered absently, puffing against the sill of another water-swollen window. "Muggiest day of the year, and I have to start cleanin' the parlour."

"I'm going to be a nun when I grow up. Just like Sister Francis."

"Likely! Likely!" Bertha grunted, pushing the window open far enough to swipe her cloth over the outside sill. With a swish of the cloth she tossed out Tessie's vocation to the convent as easily as she tossed out the wintered-over flies.

"When the divil likes holy water, that's when ye'll be a nun. Yer too spoiled for the convent. Far too spoiled. And thanks to Martin, too quick with the tongue."

"Yes, I will be a nun," Tessie stated, a stubborn set to her chin. "I will so be a nun. And I'll sit right here in this parlour. In that chair out there. And I might or might not give you some of the holy things I'll bring home with me."

———◆———

It was 1948, and everyone in the Cove was caught up in the Confederation issue. There were those — and they were in the majority — who believed that Newfoundland should not become Canada's tenth province. Joining Canada was, according to their thinking, tantamount to selling the country. Even worse, it was selling the country to a godless nation that would do away with the parochial schools on the island. And with the parochial schools disbanded, religion would soon disappear.

There were also those, a very small number — Martin one

of them — who believed Confederation was the route for Newfoundland's future and prosperity. Martin devoted every spare moment to this cause, even neglecting his taxi business to do so.

Martin's cause was Tessie's cause, and she was constantly getting into fights defending it. The child's constant squabbles were getting on Bertha's nerves, and she felt she had reached her limit when Tessie came home with a note from Sister Rita complaining about Tessie's behaviour.

"Tessie Corrigan! Tessie Corrigan! What am I goin' to do with ye," she scolded as Tessie stood in the middle of the kitchen with a hangdog look on her face. "Never in me life before have I received a complaint from a teacher for a child of mine fightin'. Not even for Martin." As she spoke, she brandished the note from Sister Rita. She shouted into the dining room to Martin, who was working on election posters.

"Get out here, Martin, and see this!"

Martin didn't dare smile at Tessie when he came out to the kitchen nor joke with her by asking who won the fight. He felt to blame for what had happened. He was sure it was about Confederation again.

"What happened this time, Tessie?" he asked easily. "What did Sarah Walsh say about me now."

"It wasn't Sarah. It was Bill Rowe."

Bertha slapped the note on the table. "*Bill Rowe*! What were ye doin' in the boys' school?"

"I wasn't in the boys' school," Tessie snapped. "It was on the way to school."

"What were ye fightin' about?" Bertha asked crossly. "Not Confederation again." The weariness in her voice was evident even to Tessie, and she skirted the question.

"It was over nothing. I forget what it was about. I won't fight anymore, Gram. I won't even listen when they call Martin names."

Martin interrupted the conversation to say he had to get posters ready because Joey Smallwood was going to be speaking in the Cove at the end of the week. He hoped his interruption would stop his mother's scolding and she'd let Tessie alone.

After Bertha's tirade was over and she had extracted Tessie's promise not to get into any more fights, she told her to run out and play before supper. Instead, though, Tessie went and sat beside Martin. He picked up a large poster of Peter Cashin, the leader of the Responsible Government movement. He began cutting it up.

"What are you doing?" Tessie asked, still subdued from the confrontation with her grandmother. "I thought you were making posters for Smallwood's speech."

Martin grinned and whispered conspiratorially, "Don't let yer grandmother know. I'm goin' to put a herring's head on Peter Cashin's body and send it to Sarah's father."

Tessie looked aghast. "He'll be mad. I'm not delivering *that*! You can take that to him yourself."

Martin shrugged offhandedly. "Naw, he won't be mad. 'Tis jest a bit of fun. Jest gettin' back at him." He explained how Tom Walsh had sent some trout over to him the day before, and he had deliberately wrapped them in the Confederation paper with a note saying at least the paper was good for something.

As he carefully decapitated Peter Cashin's cardboard head, he asked her about the fight.

"Bill Rowe said I was a traitor, didn't he?"

"Even worse," Tessie said ominously. "He said you were as bad as Joey Smallwood and *he* was Judas Iscariot."

Martin concentrated on wiring the herring's head to the cardboard.

"Are you?" Tessie prompted, not taking her eyes from the poster.

"Naw!" Martin said lightly. "Judas got thirty pieces of silver. I'm not getting a damn cent."

The attempt at frivolity was lost on Tessie, and Martin could sense her impatience. He laid the poster aside and placed his arm across her shoulder. "'Tis all bullshit, Tessie, about me being Judas. Confederation will be good for Newfoundland. I've told ye that before. And if that's the only reason I'll go to hell, ye won't need to send me off in an asbestos suit."

He gave her shoulder a squeeze. "I'm glad ye got into that fight. It shows ye have some spunk." He picked up the poster and began working on it again, talking to her as he worked.

"If yer not willin' to fight fer what ye believe in, ye might as well be a cow. But don't let them get to ye. Pretend ye've gone deaf when they starts gettin' to ye."

Later, after the posters were delivered and Tessie was outside playing, Bertha upbraided Martin for getting Tessie involved in politics.

"'Tis bad enough yer goin' to work yerself into a setback over this Confederation thing. Now ye got that child tangled up in it as well."

"Maw," Martin said patiently, "how many times do I have to tell ye that Tessie should know about what's goin' on. She's livin' in one of the most excitin' times in our history. And Confederation is the best thing that will ever happen to her." He told her how Tessie would be able to travel the length and breadth of Canada without having to immigrate. He added, "She wouldn't have to have an X-ray to do so either. And she won't have to live on the dole if she stays here — a lousy six cents a day while the merchants in St. John's gets rich."

When he finished talking, he had to sit down, the breath gone out of him.

"See what I means!" Bertha scolded, even as she rested her hand compassionately on his shoulder. "Yer wearin' yerself out, and Confederation won't do ye much good if yer six feet under."

But Martin paid no heed to her warning. He continued working for Confederation and devoted every spare minute to it. When he wasn't ferrying speakers around from one place to another, he was cajoling his mother into putting them up in the spare room when they had to stay overnight. He preached Confederation so much that one night some of his friends sneaked into the carriage house and changed the sign on his taxi from "Corrigan's Cab" to "Confederation Cab."

In 1949, Carmel made the journey to the Cove earlier than usual. She came because Bertha wrote that Martin had had another setback, and this one seemed to be worse than any of the others. By the time Carmel arrived, the green dishes were in use again, and the dining room had once more been converted to a hospital room.

Martin's appearance horrified Carmel. He was thin and gaunt, looking worse than he had at the height of his first attack of tuberculosis. She knew his only hope was to get into a sanatorium. She told this to her mother the first chance she got to speak to her alone.

"There are new drugs out that they won't give you outside a hospital. If he doesn't get them, he's not going to make it."

Up until that moment, Bertha thought she was giving Martin the best care available, and she hadn't minded him not being able to get into the sanatorium. But if there were new drugs that could help, she intended to see that he got them.

"If that's the case," she said resolutely, "I'll get him into the san, waiting list or no waiting list." She related how hard Martin had worked for Confederation and if getting him in the sanatorium meant going to see Joey Smallwood, that's exactly what she would do.

"I'll go in to St. John's tomorrow and don't look for me back until I have a bed fer him. If it means sleepin' on the steps of Government House, that's what I'll do."

Tessie came in from playing at that moment, and Bertha didn't want to dwell on Martin's condition in her presence.

"Tessie, tell yer mother about that morning in April when we got Confederation."

Tessie needed no further encouragement, and she eagerly related how she and Martin had made a flag out of bleached flour sacks and then painted a green maple leaf on it. She giggled as she talked, shooting glances at her grandmother, who had been angry at Martin for taking her up on the house to nail up the flag.

"It was still dark," Tessie said, whispering as she must have done that morning when they crept downstairs before dawn. "We climbed up on the house. Gram heard us and shouted through the window, 'Don't be such a fool, Martin, taking a child up on the house at this hour of day. She'll fall and kill herself.'" Tessie's voice parodied her grandmother's angry tone.

"'And she'll get her death of cold. And ye will too.'" She pointed towards the dining room door, which was closed to let Martin sleep. She spoke in a deep voice, Martin's voice. "'History is being made, Maw.' That's what Martin said. 'Tessie should be part of it.'"

"That's the truth," Bertha confirmed, no long angry at Martin's antics. "The two of them were like lumps of ice when they came in, but that flag flew for days until the wind ripped it to ribbons. It made Tom Walsh some mad."

⟫◆⟪

The emptiness of the dining room after Martin left for the sanatorium lay like a cold potato in Tessie's stomach. Even when the dining room table had been moved back into place, she could still see Martin lying in bed, propped up on pillows and drinking tea from the sickly green cup. She could hear him scolding her to go wash her hands with lye soap because she had touched something in his room that was sure to be full of germs.

Every three months they went to see him. At least her grandmother got to see him. Because Tessie was underage, she had to wait in the visitor's lounge until her grandmother returned from Martin's ward.

When Martin had been in the sanatorium a full year, they made the trip after a wait of only two months. Millie came with them, and she sat with Tessie in the waiting room while Bertha visited Martin.

When Bertha returned, she didn't speak but sat with her head bowed and her hands shading her eyes. After a while she looked up, and her lips began to tremble.

"I thinks he's done fer," she said, wringing her hands to keep from crying. "I hardly recognized him. He looks that bad." She straddled her face with one hand to show the hollowness of Martin's cheeks. She looked sadly at Millie. "Oh God Almighty, he's sunk right in. So thin he is."

She related how she didn't know him and passed by his bed. She smiled, a bittersweet smile. "And he knew I didn't, the divil. He said, 'I bet ye've seen better lookin' fellows with the sheet pulled all the way up.' I fairly gasped I was that surprised, and I said, 'Oh my God, boy, ye've faded somethin' terrible. What are they doing to ye?'"

Bertha took a handkerchief from her purse and daubed at her eyes. "I asked him if they gave him any pills, and he said they brought them around in a coal bucket three times a day, and they ladled them out with a coal scuttle, and I said, 'Boy, ye should have a priest. Maybe God would help ye if ye'd see a priest.' And he said, 'Saints don't need priests, Ma.'"

Her lips trembled again, and she had to rub her mouth with

the handkerchief to get control. "'Some saint,' I said. 'Haven't darkened the door of a church in ten years.'" She brightened. "But he told me a Father Kelley visits him all the time. Says he was fer Confederation although it almost got him defrocked." She shook her head sadly. "I told him it was his soul, not his country, he should be concerned about now."

Having related all there was to relate, she wiped her eyes and put the handkerchief back in her purse. She suddenly remembered she was supposed to tell Tessie that Martin was waiting to see her.

"Oh my heavens, Tessie girl. I almost fergot. He's waitin' fer ye. He said fer ye to go outside towards the back of the building. He's on the ground floor, and he'll go to the window. 'Tis open sky high like all the rest."

Tessie started to rush outside, but Bertha halted her. "Here!" She dug into her purse and came out with a small bottle of St. Anne's oil. "Take this with ye. I got it from the shrine this week. He'll take it from ye." She admonished Tessie's retreating back. "Don't stay long. He's hardly strong enough to stand up, let alone go to the window, and the nurses will have his head if they catches him out of bed talkin' to outsiders like that."

Tessie clutched the bottle of oil, warm from her grand-mother's purse, and raced towards the back of the sanatorium. The windows were open so wide she could easily have walked through either one of them without stooping. She saw a man in the distance leaning out through a window, and she ran until she came abreast of him. When she got up close, she realized it wasn't Martin, and she started to rush past.

"Forgot me already," Martin hollered. "Gone a year, and ye forgets me in that little time."

When she realized it was Martin, she gave a delighted giggle and ran towards him. He put his hands up as a brake. "Whoa there! No closer," he warned. "Germs in here are bigger than the rats on the wharves in St. John's."

"I got something for you," she panted. "Something Gram said to give you." She held out the bottle of St. Anne's oil, and he reached out his arm full-length, careful not to brush his fingers against hers.

"What's this?" He read the label but pretended not to understand. "A shot of whiskey, is it?"

"No, stupid," she giggled. "It's St. Anne's oil."

He scrutinized the bottle and asked with feigned ignorance, "When did Maw render out St. Anne?"

Tessie could hear laughter coming from behind Martin. She lowered her voice. "She got it from the Shrine of Ste. Anne de Beaupré in Quebec. She sent away for it for you. To cure you." She demonstrated how he was to put the oil on his thumb and then make the sign of the cross on his chest with his thumb.

"That's all there's to it?" He looked at her in amazement. "If jest one thumbful will do the job, I'll have this ward cleared out in no time. We'll be able to turn this place into a dance hall before the week's out."

Again Tessie heard the laughter in the background. This time it made her angry. "Don't be sacrilegious, Martin!" she snapped, using her grandmother's tone and her mother's words. "All you do is mock. Like Mummy says. How can God cure you if all you do is mock?"

"I'm not mockin', girl," he said soberly. "At least I don't mean to. 'Tis jest a bit of fun." He took the cap off the bottle and placed his thumb over the opening to catch a few drops of oil. He opened his pyjama top and made the sign of the cross on his chest.

"Wrong hand, stupid," Tessie admonished. "You have to use the right hand. Put the oil on with the *right* thumb."

Two weeks from the time of the visit, Bertha got word that Martin was dead. He hemorrhaged one night just before the lights were turned out on the ward. Nothing could have been done to save him.

Bertha insisted on going in to accompany the body back to the Cove even though Millie tried to convince her otherwise.

"Ye stay here, Bertha. Let me and Eileen Walsh go with Aloysius."

Bertha brushed her suggestion aside. "I'm goin' in, Millie. I have to go. For me own mind's sake. There's things I wants to get cleared up. And don't worry. I'm up to it." She nodded towards Tessie's sweater hanging on a chair. "'Tis herself I'm worried about. I'm happy the poor boy is out of his sufferin', but she's not takin' it too well."

"They were close, so close," Millie said. "He was like a father."

"Oh, more so, girl. He was mother and brother and father all in one. It used to hurt poor Carmel's feelin's. She'd save her money to come home to see Tessie, and the child would pay her no mind at all. Jest wanted to be around Martin all the time."

It was Millie's turn to nod towards the sweater. "What did she say when ye told her?"

"Nothin' at all. Not a blessed word. Never shed a tear. Jest went out and sat on the wall of rocks in the meadow — the one Martin always sat on and played the mouth organ when I couldn't stand his playin' in the house anymore."

Bertha went into the dining room and beckoned Millie to follow. She went to the window. "See her! Still there. Singin' to the top of her voice when I went out." She pushed open the window. "Listen! Still at it."

Tessie's plaintive voice filled the room.

> *She's like a swallow that soars on high,*
> *She's like a river that never runs dry . . .*

Millie wiped her eyes with the back of her hand. "She's an odd little duck, ent she. In some ways she's like a weed, nearly everything is above ground. But in other ways, she's as deep as the ocean. No fathomin' her."

———⊰⊱———

The things Bertha wanted to get cleared up at the sanatorium had to do with Martin's lapse from the church.

"Was there a priest on hand when me son died?" she asked the nurse who had been on duty that night. "I wants to know if he got a chance to receive the Last Rites. I needs to know that."

"Father Kelley was with him. Right till the end," the nurse said compassionately. "I know that much." She added. "They were real good friends. But of course the screen was around the bed, so I can't say for sure. We were rushed off our feet that night."

"Did he ask for the priest?"

"I'm sorry, Mrs. Corrigan," she said, her tone sympathetic. "I really can't recall. There were other nurses on duty. And I could get Father Kelley for you on the phone. He'd be the one to talk to. He might even be right here in the san now. He did say he wanted to see you when you came in."

Bertha was afraid of hearing what she didn't want to hear. She shook her head hurriedly. "No. No. No need to bother him now. I'll come to see him when I feels better. I jest wanted to know if he was on hand that night and if there was time for the Rites."

Martin was buried in the plot that would have been his father's if Ned hadn't been placed in the piece of ground out by the fence. Martin's grave was adjacent to Mrs. Selena's, and there was still room left for Bertha and Carmel and Tessie.

—————◆—————

Two weeks after Tessie lost Martin, she found her father. Not in the flesh. On paper. Her mother had brought pictures of her Aunt Bessie to show the family, and when she went back to Boston after the funeral, she forgot to take them with her. Tessie found them when Bertha sent her to her mother's bedroom to get the bedsheets to put in the wash. Tessie picked up the envelope from the bureau top and rifled through the dozen or more pictures inside, and as she did so, she came upon another envelope, this one yellowed with age. It wasn't sealed, so she looked inside and came upon the photograph of a handsome, smiling man leaning against a piece of earth-moving equipment. Along with the picture there was a postcard. A red rose covered its glossy front, and at the top of the card in gold letters were the words, FOR YOU A ROSE IN PORTLAND GROWS. There was no message on the back.

Tessie knew the picture was of her father. And she also knew she shouldn't have found it. Her heart pounded so hard from her contraband find she could barely catch her breath. She trembled with the terrible realization that her father wasn't dead. She didn't know how she knew this just by looking at the picture and the postcard, but she was certain it was so.

She put the postcard back in the envelope but stuffed the picture down the front of her school uniform and smuggled it to her bedroom and hid it underneath her pillow. For almost two weeks she kept sneaking it from her bedroom to her school-bag. Every morning she would make sure it was in her school-bag just in case her grandmother would find it while she was at school. Finally, the burden of this toing and froing got too much, and she placed the picture back where she found it. She tried to pretend that the envelope that lay on the bureau in wait for her mother's next visit was just any envelope. But the bureau top drew her into the room over and over again. With each look she tingled with fear, fascination and anger.

———◆———

The year Tessie turned sixteen, her last year in school — and what was supposed to be her last year in the Cove because her mother was working on her immigration papers — the bishop decided in the interest of economy to amalgamate the boys' and girls' schools into one building to be operated by the convent.

One morning, early in October, Tessie looked across the classroom and locked eyes with Sarah Walsh's brother, Dennis. Dennis was a year older than her, but on account of a bout of rheumatic fever, he had lost a year of school.

Tessie had never particularly liked Dennis, any more than she had liked the rest of Sarah's relatives, and for that reason — they were Sarah's relatives. But that fall morning when her eyes bolted with his, Tessie forgot her feud with Sarah. The coming together of their glances gave off vibrations that were so forceful she was certain they could change the direction of the wind.

"Let X equal the speed of the train," Sister Clarence announced, writing on the board with her special wooden con-traption that kept the chalk from messing up her habit.

Tessie heard but paid scant attention. Who cared about the speed of a train when currents passing between her and Dennis were faster than the speed of light? *White hot currents!* She could feel the heat centreing in her loins and moving upward and downward from that point.

Sister Clarence must have felt the heat, too, because she reached deep underneath her veil and wimple and unhitched her wide, flowing sleeves to expose arms tightly sheathed in black serge. The students called her serge arms, crow's legs.

When Tessie was a child, she had asked Martin how the nuns hitched on their big sleeves. She had seen them run their hands under their wimples and detach the over-sleeves in a matter of seconds. Martin said they had a couple of cup hooks screwed into their neck glands. He had dug his fingers into each side of his neck, winced, and then said, "It hurts like hell, but they offer it up for the sins of the world."

Usually Sister Clarence took time to fold her sleeves neatly before placing them on her desk so that they would be ready to be rehitched if a knock came on the door. On this particular day, she merely threw them across the back of her chair.

"Let X equal the speed of the train," she repeated, more insistent this time to sever the connection between Dennis and Tessie and to recapture the attention of the class that had now focussed on the electric currents shooting across the room.

"Tessie Corrigan!" she bellowed. "Pay attention and stop mooning over Dennis!" She gave the desk a sharp whip crack with her chalk holder.

The circuit broke immediately, and Tessie turned crimson.

"Sorryster," she mumbled, sliding the words together in the manner of all convent students.

"Do you want to fail your year?" It was a rhetorical question but with enough bite behind it to make Tessie reply, "Noster."

Dennis had not been castigated. The injustice of this rankled Tessie, but she understood why he had not been. Dennis's Uncle Pat was a Jesuit in Ontario. And Dennis himself was going to be a priest. He was planning on going to St. Bonaventure's College in St. John's for one year and then on to a seminary in Ireland.

After that first encounter, Tessie and Dennis walked together every day to and from school, holding hands when they were sure no one was looking. On a few occasions, when they were certain her grandmother wasn't home, they stopped in at Tessie's and swapped a few hesitant kisses. Once, Dennis fumbled with her uniform, trying to get it unbuttoned at the neck, but the heavy serge was like a coat of mail, and the neck opening was only big enough to let him run a couple of fingers down the base of her throat.

"Oh Tessie! Oh Tessie! Oh Tessie!" he panted as he fumbled and failed to get access.

Mostly, though, they just talked. Dennis was always trying to find a solution to his unsolvable problem: how could he be a priest and marry Tessie as well? If he could find that solution, he would be the happiest person in the world.

The simplicity of his life irritated Tessie. She could not detail anything that would make her the happiest person in the world. There were some things, like Dennis's presence, that made her happier than she would be otherwise, but nothing, absolutely nothing she could think of would give her total happiness.

That spring, on an occasion when they were lying on a strip of beach in a secluded cove watching the clouds scudding out of the path of the wind, she asked him if he sometimes felt he had no centre. He hadn't had any idea what she was talking about.

"I mean," she explained, rubbing her fingers on the soft down of his jaw, "do you have this longing inside you for something, but you don't know what it is?"

He shook his head lazily, delighting in the brush of her fingers against his face. "My trouble is," he replied huskily, "I have two centres, and if I have one of them, I can't have the other."

As they talked, a water spider crawled near her, and Dennis reached to squash it with a beach rock.

Tessie grabbed his hand. "Don't do that," she admonished and picked the spider up with a piece of driftwood and moved it out of the way. "Martin always told me never to kill a harmless spider." She related how he had sat her down and told her that creatures had as much right to live as she did. When she argued that creatures didn't have souls and therefore they couldn't be murdered, he had asked how she could be so sure they didn't have souls. Besides, he said, if she believed they didn't have souls, then they had only a very short life span. He had asked how she could be so selfish as to deny a spider a few weeks of life when she had years and years in this world and forever in the next.

When she had finished telling Dennis about the spider incident, he had reached over and cupped her hand with his. "Martin was real important to you, wasn't he?" His voice was soft. "After all this time, you still remember so much about him." His tone held wonderment.

She loved Dennis at that moment, not because he sent currents coursing through her veins, but because he understood about Martin.

"Sometimes," she confessed, "I wonder how much of my memories are hand-me-down ones from Gram." She shyly confided to him that she was convinced Martin was still around and told him of how one day the previous summer she had passed by the rose tree in her front garden. A bumblebee was working its way from bloom to bloom. She said she stared at the bee, and then, for no apparent reason, a terrible loneliness came over her, a longing. It was then, she said, that she had felt Martin's presence. "It was as though he were standing right beside me, assuring me that everything was going to be all right."

Confiding to Dennis things she had never shared with anyone else made Tessie realize he was becoming very important to her.

"You won't leave me, will you, Dennis?" She asked plaintively. "You won't go away to the seminary in Ireland?"

"I won't go unless you come with me," he said lightly. "I promise."

"Then you won't be going," she replied, surely.

When Bertha learned about the courtship of Tessie and Dennis, she tried to nip it in the bud by telling Tessie she was almost through school and not even the King of Siam should get in the way of her leaving the Cove. She quickly pointed out that Dennis, although a nice enough boy, was a far cry from the King of Siam. And to further discourage the relationship, she pointed out that his mother was grooming Dennis to be the next Pope and that in itself should be sufficient reason for Tessie to give him a wide berth.

When Eileen learned about the courtship, she commanded Dennis to put a stop to it immediately.

"Tessie Corrigan!" she said, wrinkling her nose like she had gotten a whiff of mildew. She outlined the flaws in the Corrigan family. "For all anyone knows," she said, "her father may have been a German spy or a highwayman. Or even a lunatic — the type of lunacy that is passed on." She delved into the Corrigans' blemished tree, covering Vince and Ned and ending with Martin. "A fine fellow in most ways," she allowed. "But he was a lapsed even though his mother said he received the Last Rites." She felt, too, that Martin's tuberculosis was a weakness that could also be passed on.

Eileen made it very clear, though, that she wasn't opposed to the courtship solely because it involved Tessie Corrigan. Overriding the failings of the Corrigan family was the matter of Holy Orders. Wasn't Dennis going to follow in the footsteps of his Uncle Pat? Or partially in the footsteps? She had long ago given up the dream of Dennis's becoming a Jesuit. Intellectual endeavours were not Dennis's strong suit. However, her brother Pat had comforted her by saying that most lay people don't know the difference between one order and the next, and that being a secular priest wasn't all that bad. And from a practical standpoint, he told her, a secular priest might be better because the bishop would probably foot the bills if Dennis consented to come back to the diocese.

⋙•◆•⋘

Before school finished in June, Dennis broke the news to Tessie that he had made up his mind to be a priest, and therefore he wouldn't be dating her anymore.

"I'm going back with Father Pat for the summer, and in the fall I'm going to St. Bonaventure's and from there to the seminary."

Tessie reacted even worse than he had expected. She begged him not to leave her and accused him of letting his mother run his life. The more he protested to the contrary, the more Tessie cried.

"But you promised you'd stay with me forever," she sobbed. "You lied to me."

"I wish I could have you and the priesthood. But I can't." He looked forlorn. "If I have to make a choice, it has to be the priesthood. And it's my choice — not Mother's."

Pictures flashed before Tessie's eyes that had nothing to do with Dennis. She saw her mother getting into Martin's car to go away to the States. She could see the way her brown suit coat strained over her waist as she reached to put the suitcase in the back seat. And she saw the emptiness of the dining room after Martin went to the sanatorium.

"Ye've got to stop this foolish brooding." Bertha scolded Tessie for falling into a depression. "Get out with yer girlfriends and take yer mind off Dennis Walsh." She bustled around Tessie's bedroom, opening windows to let in the light. "Don't think fer a minute he's in his bedroom up in Ontario brooding over ye."

Sometimes, though, she stopped her scoffing at Tessie's overreaction to her jilting and sympathized. "Tessie, child," she would say, speaking softly, "If he's goin' to devote hisself to the Lord, even if he was nudged along by Eileen, I don't think it would be right fer ye to stand in his way." Then she would add matter-of-factly, "Besides, yer mother will be down in August, and ye'll likely be goin' to live with her soon after."

Tessie hadn't the slightest interest in mixing with her friends. Nor did she want to go to the States. She spent her days in her room. She read constantly, mostly material she could lay her hands on without having to go looking outside the house. Her grandmother had subscriptions to most of the major religious magazines, and Tessie read these from cover to cover.

A short story in one of them intrigued her because the plot almost paralleled her situation with Dennis. The young man in the story had left his girlfriend to join the priesthood. His leaving had devastated her. Some time afterwards, the heroine entered a convent, but the young man was unaware of this. After many years had passed, someone from the priest's parish came to call at the heroine's convent. When the caller was taking his leave, the heroine said, "Tell Father Brennan that Sister Matthew — Rose Nolan — was asking about him."

Tessie substituted her own ending. "Tell Father Walsh that Sister Martin — Tessie Corrigan . . ." She reworked the ending several times until finally she had it to her liking. "Tell Father Walsh that Mother Martin — Tessie Corrigan — was asking about him."

The story stayed with Tessie long after she had read it, and over the next few weeks she was convinced she had a genuine vocation to the convent. Her enthusiasm mounted as she thought of the life of service that lay ahead of her. She would go to the far reaches of the world and save souls. Her good works would give her the centre she always lacked.

Even though Tessie was convinced her vocation was a true one, there was some voice within her telling her it needed enlivening — possibly even bolstering. She prayed to St. Gabriel of Our Lady of Sorrows — the patron saint of young religious — to strengthen her resolve. As her fervour increased, the pain of Dennis faded until it disappeared entirely.

"Ye've got to be clear off yer head," Bertha snorted when Tessie told her she intended to enter a convent. "I told ye once ye wouldn't last in a convent longer than a snowball in hell." She waved her hand to encompass the house. "Ye've had this place to yerself fer too long. The whole run of things. Ye won't be willing to put up and shut up like ye'll have to do in a convent."

Carmel, thinking of the years she spent walking to the subway on winter mornings, being practically pushed aboard it and then jostled all the way to her factory job, where the stench of leather almost turned her stomach, was delighted with Tessie's vocation. She wrote enthusiastically about the benefits of convent life. "You'll have peace and happiness. They'll educate you so you won't have to spend your days perched on a bench punching eyelets."

She, however, suggested that Tessie still enter the United States and join an order there. She pointed out that there were more orders to choose from in Boston.

Tessie considered this advice, then rejected it. She didn't want to leave her grandmother, and she really didn't want to go so far away from the Cove. Her missionary work would have to be confined to Newfoundland.

She met with the Mother General in mid-August. It was a soft day, and the wind was still. The windows in the visitors' parlour were discreetly ajar, but open enough to let in the scent of the double roses that were growing on all sides of the grey stone building. The Mother General sat opposite Tessie in a cane-bottomed chair. Her back, arrow straight, rested against a petit point cushion. She spoke in a whisper as if the parlour couldn't stand a loud voice.

"There's a lot of investigation that must be carried out. Lots of letters we must write before we can give you an answer." She went on to describe the life that awaited Tessie if the investigation was positive.

"Our day begins at six." Her hands fluttered lightly on the arm of the chair. A shaft of sunlight angled in through the open window and lit on her silver Bride of Christ ring. Tessie thought of doves alighting from missionary spires, of chants on early morning hillsides, of sunrises on green meadows. She thought of peace and harmony, of devotion and fulfillment, of dedication and purpose. Never once did she think about a brass bell clanging in a damp dawn to rouse her from sleep. Nor did she think about regimentation and rules and stifling togetherness. And above all else, unquestioning obedience, especially to the postulant mistress.

———⊰•◦⊱———

"Lights out means *just that*, Miss Corrigan!" The postulant mistress's sharp voice snapped across the Common Room as the postulants were leaving to go back to their cubicles. "We leave our selfishness and our defiance out in the world when we enter these walls."

"Yes, Mistress," Tessie answered, her selfishness and defiance barely in check. She was seething. Why did she have to put the lights out at a certain time? If she weren't sleepy, why couldn't she read? Why was she expected to be like Agnes O'Reilly, who always began snoring seconds after the lights were turned out? And the biggest why of all: why didn't someone besides herself complain about ridiculous and outdated rules?

But no one ever did. From the day that she asked about the censoring of the mail onwards, she told herself firmly that she would be like the rest of the sheep and just go along with whatever was asked of her.

"We don't *censor* mail, Miss Corrigan. Slitting open letters is only symbolic of our humility." Sister Jerome peered over her glasses, her eyes as cold as a day in January. "Now has anyone got some *sensible* questions to ask?"

For two and a half months Tessie kept her promise and acquiesced to all rules and regulations. Then an incident occurred that tested her forbearance. They were in the Common Room for mail call. Sister Jerome, as usual, was present. The postulant who was sorting the mail passed a package to Tessie. In her excitement at getting the unexpected parcel, she forgot about Sister Jerome and the rules regarding gifts. She tore off the brown paper and pulled out a black cashmere sweater. The wool was so soft that she ran her hands over it and nuzzled her face on the sleeve. All of the material she had touched since coming into the convent was hard and coarse. Even the towels were rough. One of the postulants surmised they washed the towels in spar varnish just to get them that rough. Tessie kneaded her fingers, kitten-like, deep in the softness of the sweater, making purring sounds as she did so. Then she pulled off the heavy cardigan she was wearing and started to slip on the new one.

She felt the piercing stare of Sister Jerome and looked up to see her outstretched hand, fingers beckoning. Too late, Tessie remembered she had broken another rule. Gifts belonged to the community of sisters. There were no personal possessions. Although the receiver of the gift was usually permitted to keep it, it first had to be relinquished to symbolically support the vows of chastity, poverty and obedience.

Tessie passed the sweater to Sister Jerome, who took it, tight-lipped, and anchored it under one of her buttocks, letting the sleeves dangle obscenely so they brushed the floor and sucked up any dust left behind by the postulant on cleanup duty that morning.

Tessie bristled and barely managed to keep her temper in check. She was helped by the dismissal bell that rang just as her fury was beginning to blaze.

⊰•⊱

A few days later she stumbled to the washroom after being summoned awake by the morning bell. Agnes O'Reilly was already there and was stooped over the washbasin, splashing water over herself like a hen scratching in loose earth. Stretched over her oversize nightgown and riding halfway up her broad back was Tessie's black cashmere sweater.

Tessie forced herself to wait until after morning Mass, when Sister Jerome would be out in the sunroom reading her Office. No one was supposed to interrupt her when she was there, and for that reason Tessie knew she would be alone, and she could get her full attention. She ran over the hardwood floors, un-mindful of the rule never to run in the convent and unmindful of the clattering noise of her heavy brogue shoes.

Sister Jerome was seated by a table. She was holding her prayer book in one hand and fingering her beads with the other. Tessie didn't even wait to knock. The sight of the mistress looking so serene when she herself was in absolute turmoil heightened her fury.

"You gave my sweater — my mother's present — to that fat slob Agnes!"

Sister Jerome coolly smoothed the pages of her prayer book, making sure there were no wrinkled leaves before splaying it open, spine up on the table. "You are quite right, Miss Corrigan. I did give a sweater to a postulant yesterday. She needed it."

Tessie fumed. "You didn't give *a* sweater. You gave *my* sweater. And you gave it to that fat slob Agnes. In a week it will be so dirty you'll have to parboil it to get it clean." She ran over to a flower pot, and, pretending it was a wash basin, demonstrated Agnes' method of washing her hands. The dirty soapy water ran down her wrists and over the cuffs of the sweater.

Sister Jerome drew her mouth into a sharp, thin line and reached for her book. "You may go now, Miss Corrigan," she said, her tone dismissing. "Come back to talk when you have a little less anger and a little more charity."

Humiliated, Tessie started to leave but stopped in the doorway and flung words at Sister Jerome that surprised even herself. "Oh I'll go," she said, deliberately leaving off *Mistress*. "But I won't be back. I'm leaving this place forever."

She stormed up the stairs, the clumsy shoes spread out before her. She would find Mother Superior and get the key to the pantry closet where her "walk-in" clothes were kept in her grandmother's suitcase. And she would get the "walk-out" money her mother had given her for the required deposit. The clothes were always kept for a year, the money also. They were kept to take care of cases such as hers.

Halfway up the stairs she met Sister Margaret, who looked after the office work for the convent.

"Oh my dear, I'm so sorry to hear about your poor grandmother."

Tessie stopped so suddenly she almost fell forward. She clutched the banister for support.

"What about Gram? What's wrong with her?"

Sister Margaret's hand flew to her mouth. "Oh my dear, I'm so sorry. I thought you had heard. I thought that's why you were running." She wrung her hands, flustered at what she considered to be overstepping her bounds.

"The call came just a little while ago. I thought Mother Superior had found you."

Mother Edward hurried down the stairs, her beads and cross flailing out before her. "That's all right, Sister Margaret. I'll take over now." She laid a consoling hand on Tessie's shoulder. "We just had a call from a Mrs. Morrissey. Your poor Grandmother. It was a blood clot in her leg that broke loose. She's gone, poor soul."

Tessie sat down on the steps. Her grandmother couldn't be dead. In all the years she could remember, Tessie couldn't recall her grandmother ever being sick enough to even lie down.

Mother Edward squeezed down beside her on the steps, her composure softening. "Mrs. Morrissey said how close you were to your grandmother. So we'll make an exception. We'll treat it as if she were your mother, so you can go home for the funeral." Her voice gentled even further. "God granted her a lovely death, dear. No suffering."

Tessie left the convent forever that morning. Mother Edward and even Sister Jerome tried to convince her to stay and not to give up her vocation. Sister Jerome said that some girls found it tougher than others to adjust to the regimentation, but when they did, they usually made the best sisters. She had added, "They usually end up being the pathfinders for the order."

Tessie assured them her leaving had nothing to do with her

grandmother's death. And it didn't even have anything to do with the cashmere sweater. It had to do with her own lack of vocation.

She left after breakfast, and as she had promised, she said nothing to the other postulants about leaving permanently. As Mother Edward pointed out, "It might cause unrest." She didn't even let any of the others see her in her walk-in clothes and stayed in the kitchen until the taxi drove up to the back door.

As the taxi pulled away from the iron gates, Tessie looked behind her at the lilac trees and the rose bushes stripped bare from the raw November wind. The sky looked as grey as the convent walls. She folded her arms around herself for warmth, grateful for the heavy sweater Sister Jerome had insisted she pull on over her white cotton blouse. She thought wryly, "I stayed longer than a snowball in hell, Gram. But not much!" She wished she had left one day earlier.

———⊱◆⊰———

The summer visits hadn't been sufficient nourishment to preserve the strength of the bond between Carmel and Tessie, and Bertha, aware of the tenuousness of this bond, had striven to keep it from breaking apart. It was she who had criss-crossed their letters, transmitting their lives, one to the other, and it was she who had provided a crossroads for the yearly reunion. Although no mention of it was made, both Carmel and Tessie understood the impact Bertha's death would have on the continuance of their relationship.

After the funeral, Carmel stayed an extra day in the Cove to help sort out what remained of Bertha's life. They began in her bedroom, arranging her belongings into piles: to be saved, to be given away, to be thrown out. They piled and sorted in silence, and the tension in the room was as overpowering as the smell of camphor wafting out of the old wooden trunk.

From time to time, just to break the stillness of the bedroom, each of them would hold up some article and inquire as to which pile it should be relegated to.

Carmel, having been separated from her family for all those years, was more conscious of the bonds being severed, and she was, therefore, more anxious to hold them together.

"I can renege on renting the house if you want to stay here until you get your bearings," she offered agreeably. "No need for you to rush into anything."

"I'm not rushing into anything," Tessie responded politely. "I figure if I can work for a year in St. John's — store clerk or something — I can get enough money to go to Montreal."

"Then you've given up all thought of coming to the States."

"My mind is set on Montreal," Tessie answered evenly.

As they talked, they flung things into the various piles. Carmel ignored Tessie's cool civility and made another attempt to establish some rapport with her.

"I could spare a little cash. I have a little saved. Enough to tide you over until you get on your feet."

Tessie's tone remained civil. "No need. But thanks anyway. I have the walk-out money. And I know people I can stay with in St. John's until I line up a job."

Once more they lapsed into silence. After some minutes, Tessie — aware that she had halted the conversation — attempted to open it again. She picked up a cigar box that held Bertha's jewellery. It contained a few inexpensive brooches her sister Bessie had sent her from time to time and other odds and ends of costume jewellery. Tessie rummaged through the box and pulled out a string of imitation pearls and held them up for Carmel to see.

"This was Gram's favourite. She said Martin gave it to her, but she couldn't remember when."

"For my wedding." The words left Carmel's lips suddenly and without warning. Flustered, she tossed one of Bertha's skirts into the wrong pile.

"Well, that would explain her forgetfulness." Tessie's voice dripped with sarcasm. "Nothing having to do with your wedding could ever be remembered. Everyone had amnesia when it came to that." She dropped the pearls back in the box.

"It wasn't that way at all," Carmel said for lack of anything better to say, yet she knew something had to be said or the conversation would disappear entirely. "We just thought it best not to bring it up." She looked absently at the separate mounds of clothes, and when she spoke again it was in a solemn, regretful voice. "Perhaps there was a better way. But if there was, we didn't know any." She avoided Tessie's eyes and concentrated on a scorch mark on the cuff of one of Bertha's sweaters. She hesitated momentarily before tossing it into the throw-out pile.

"Some best way," Tessie replied cuttingly. "I was almost nine for God's sake, before I even knew his name. I had to coax it out of Martin." The years of betrayal and deceit burned in her eyes.

"What was I supposed to think? That I grew under a rock?" She pitched an old hat of Bertha's in the direction of the piles, not caring which one it landed in. "And I had to figure out on my own he wasn't dead, like you led me to believe. And the way I found out he was divorced was from a song Sarah Walsh taunted me with." She added bitterly, "Did being divorced make him a renegade or something? And couldn't you understand how he felt? If he had told you, you wouldn't have married him, would you? What choice did he have but to hide the truth from you?"

Carmel sat down on the bed as though the blouse she was holding had suddenly turned to lead. Divorced, is that what Tessie thought? She lowered her head and shut her eyes to squeeze back the tears. At least it was better than knowing her father was a bigamist.

Tessie could see she had wounded Carmel, and she hated herself for broaching the taboo subject, on this day of all days. After all the years that had passed, this was not the time for recriminations, and Bertha's bedroom was not the place for them either. She tried to make amends.

"She sure didn't have much, did she?" She flicked an old apron into the throw-out pile. "Just three miserable little piles. That's all that's left of her."

"In the way of things, that's all." Carmel understood what Tessie was trying to do, and she, too, made an effort to steer the conversation to a less stormy subject. "But she didn't measure in things. She had us. This house. And the Cove. She wanted us to get out of here and better ourselves, but the Cove was home to her."

Tessie smiled, remembering Bertha's stories about how much she hated the place when she had first arrived. "Did she ever tell you about the first spring she came, and the sea flooded the flats? She went to the store, and Mr. Murphy said it was too bad the Cove wasn't two more feet above sea level . . ."

Carmel interjected, "And she was thinking it was too bad it wasn't two more feet *below* sea level."

Mother and daughter laughed, but the sound was hollow, and it wasn't enough to bridge the years of separation.

Carmel and Tessie left the Cove together the next day. They drove in the same taxi to St. John's. Carmel went to the airport to catch her flight back to Boston, and Tessie went to her friend's house on the outskirts of the city. When they said goodbye, they smoothed over the awkwardness by making vague plans to meet again. In the few minutes left to them, they tried to say something to confirm that the summer connection would still continue, but neither one could bring to mind the right words.

———⊰•⊱———

When Tessie moved to Montreal and was hired on with the Sperry Travel Agency as a clerk typist, she made a pact with herself that she would learn the ropes of running the company from the ground up so that one day she would own her own company. By the time she was twenty-six, she intended to be assistant manager of Sperry. Twenty-six was just an inside figure she picked to give herself a little leeway, because thirty was the outside limit for becoming her own boss.

She had no illusions that her rise to administrative heights would come without a price, but she was willing to pay it. From that first day when she was directed to her office — a cubicle containing a desk and a rubber plant that was stunted from lack of sunlight — she never missed an opportunity to learn someone else's job, especially if that job was higher up the scale than hers. If anyone was out sick or if the workload piled up, Tessie was the first to volunteer her help. She took night courses from whatever institution offered specific courses in travel agency work, and barring the availability of these, she took general courses in administration.

Her social life was a wasteland. Because marriage was not a priority (she had no desire to repeat the heartache of her mother and, for that matter, her grandmother), she had no need to waste time on female predation tactics. Some summers, when her mother came back to the Cove to see about the house and to visit with Millie, she would take time off to go back too, but never for longer than a few days. In fact, a year earlier, when her mother retired and returned to live in the Cove, she hadn't managed to get back home at all. All of her energies had gone into promoting herself on the job.

She miscalculated her rise to assistant manager by one year. She was twenty-seven when the agency took an early closing one afternoon and brought out the champagne to celebrate her promotion.

Because of the party, she was late getting home that evening, and as she was opening her apartment door, she heard the telephone ringing. Thinking it was probably a customer stranded somewhere, she sprinted across the living room to answer it.

"Hello," she said, out of breath from rushing. She shucked her coat and gloves even as she spoke.

"Is that Tessie Corrigan?"

"Yes," she answered tentatively. "Speaking." She could tell it was a long-distance call by the hum on the line, and she wondered what customer had gotten stuck and where and what strings she would have to pull to straighten things out.

Millie Morrissey's hands had trembled as she waited for the operator to connect her to Tessie's number. She had never made a call outside of Newfoundland. She expected to have to go through a long rigmarole of operators to make the connection. When Tessie answered so quickly it startled her, and everything she had planned to say to gently break the bad news evaporated.

"Tessie, girl. This is Millie Morrissey. From home." Her voice quivered, and she had to swallow several times to keep it under control. "I don't have very good news for ye. Not very good news at all. Yer poor mother. She's dead."

Tessie lowered herself down on the couch and clutched the phone so hard the skin stretched white over her knuckles.

"Tessie?" Millie asked anxiously. "Are ye all right, Tessie?"

"I'm all right, Millie. I'm all right," she replied, her voice a whisper.

"God help us, girl, she's gone." Millie's keening voice supplied the hour and the minute of death, but Tessie was barely listening. Carmel couldn't be dead. She was barely in her fifties. Besides, hadn't she taken early retirement so she would have time to take things easy?

"The heart, girl," Millie informed. "Went jest like that." Tessie could almost hear the snap of Millie's dry fingers. "Jest about died on the phone. Called me and said she wasn't feelin' good. I went right over and wasn't there more than a few minutes when she went." Millie sighed gratefully. "At least she didn't go all by herself. All alone. Thank God I could be with her."

The not-going-all-alone hadn't been intended as a rebuke, but Tessie took it as such. She now wished she had gone home last July or August. And she wished she had not missed so many summers in between. But she had always let other things, mostly her work, take priority.

Millie said that Carmel's death should not have come as a shock to either of them. They should have known, no matter what Carmel had told them about being tired of being pushed on and off subways, that she would never have quit her job in Boston and returned to the Cove if sickness hadn't forced her into it.

"I'm as certain of that as I am of standing here holding this phone." The need to convey the full message to Tessie had forced Millie to get her voice under control. "It was too expensive to die up there. That's why she came back."

Millie changed the subject abruptly, becoming conscious of nattering away on a long-distance call. These things could be said later when Tessie came for the funeral.

"About the arrangements?" Millie asked, rushing her words

to make up for the time she had wasted. "There's a funeral home here now. About two months ago. So you won't have to face *all that*."

Tessie was well aware of what facing *all that* meant. She had faced it on two other occasions. It meant turning the parlour into a makeshift wake room. Worst of all, it meant coming back from the cemetery and putting the parlour to rights. It meant returning the couch to the space that had been given over to the kitchen chairs to hold the casket. It meant saving candle stubs for the next time, but on the pretext they were for when the lights went out, everyone knowing full well you didn't use blessed candles for secular use. It meant prying open the windows and letting in the northeast wind in the hope it would remove death from the parlour, where it clung like damp cobwebs to the wallpaper.

⸺◆⸺

Tessie arrived in the Cove the next day, just as dark was closing in. Millie had insisted that she stay with her instead of going home because, without a fire, the place would be like an icehouse. Millie said it was the coldest and stormiest February she had ever witnessed.

After the supper dishes were cleared away, Millie and Tessie pulled chairs close to the kitchen fire and talked across the stove. Millie had been to the funeral home that afternoon, and she catalogued for Tessie the visitors who were there. "Eileen Walsh was there," she said, running her hands down her body. "All decked out in sealskin. Head to toe." Tessie could imagine Eileen dressing up in her best for the occasion. Beside her Bertha had always looked dishevelled, as though her slip were hanging or her sweater was buttoned wrong.

"And Sadie Collier came. But you wouldn't know her.

Moved here after you left. Her husband killed himself last year. Jumped over a cliff on the downs." Millie shivered compassionately. "Poor divil. His mind was tormented over something. They buried him *inside* the fence." She wrinkled her mouth. "All that stuff is done away with now. And for the best. Not like in poor Ned's time." She gave Tessie a querying look. "You did know he was moved inside the fence, Ned was? More exact probably, the fence was moved outside him." She hrrumphed a dry humourless sound. "A lot of good it does now. Them it mattered to are all gone."

———✦———

Millie had prepared her spare room for Tessie. Her best room. Just before she left the kitchen to go to bed, Millie rushed to the stove and manoeuvred a hot beach rock out of the oven and into an old sweater sleeve knotted at the bottom.

"Here, take this with ye." Millie jounced the sack up and down like Tessie remembered her grandmother doing to make sure the knot would hold. "It'll keep yer bed hot most of the night." A whiff of scorched wool filled the kitchen, making Tessie pine to be nine years old again and back home living with Bertha and Martin.

She stayed awake most of the night, partly on account of the storm. The room backed on the ocean, and all night long the northeast wind battered across the beach and made the old house seesaw on its rafters. Tessie was certain that at any moment the flat roof was going to go sailing across the meadow, and they would have to run for shelter. But memories were the real reason she wasn't able to sleep. Hour after hour she flipped through the past like pages in a scrapbook, resting her gaze on this memory, passing quickly over that one. When daylight broke, she gave up all thought of sleep and lay searching the room with her eyes, one ear cocked for sounds of Millie getting up.

The room was so much like her bedroom at her grand-mother's that it was as though the years had been peeled away and she was a child again. The homemade quilts and pillows were a dead weight. Martin once complained that the quilts on his bed could be used for ballast in a boat. The hooked rug in the middle of Millie's floor had a white rooster straddling its centre. Her bedroom rug at her grandmother's had a skinny yellow cat squatting slightly off-centre. Exactness had never been one of Bertha's strengths. Tessie recalled when the rug had been hooked. She had helped make it by cutting up strips of cloth. The cat's whiskers were made out of the legs of an old pair of cotton stockings of hers. There had been enough strips left over to make a border at the very edge of the burlap.

Even the wallpaper in Millie's room was similar, if not identical, to the wallpaper in her childhood bedroom. Big, overblown roses climbed to the ceiling in trellised rows. And Millie's room was every bit as cold as she remembered her own to have been. The nails that had popped through the paper during the night still had frost on their heads, a dull silvery film that she used to lick off. Afterwards, she would go crying to her grandmother because little pieces of skin would have pulled away from her tongue and remained on the nail heads.

"Glory be to God, girl," her grandmother would say crossly, wiping her eyes with the tail of her flour sack apron. "Haven't ye any better sense than that?" She would nod her head rapidly, mumbling between sobs that, yes, she had more sense than that.

"Well, for pity's sake, use it then," her grandmother would snap. If Martin was awake, he'd holler from his makeshift hospital bed in the dining room, tormenting her as usual.

"Maw, tell her about that young one who tried to lick the frost off the railway spikes. Left her whole tongue on a goddamn spike. Dried up in the summer as hard as a piece of kelp." Martin's voice would hold a shudder, as though he had seen the kelp-like tongue himself. She would shudder too, as her mind saw the curled-up seaweed parched brittle by the sun. But her horror never lasted, and the next morning she would be back licking again, savouring the delicious fear that maybe this was the time more than snippets of skin would remain on the frosty nail.

———✦———

Although Millie had admonished her to stay in bed until she had warmed up the kitchen, Tessie got up as soon as she heard her moving about downstairs. She counted to three and then jumped out on the rug like a swimmer plunging into icy water. She dressed rapidly, pulling her clothes from the bedpost where she had placed them before going to bed because she couldn't find any hangers in the room. She pulled on a black turtleneck sweater and a black skirt she had borrowed from a neighbour in her apartment building. Millie had contributed the black stockings.

Just before she left the room, she took a quick glance in the spider-tracked mirror over the bureau. In the half light and in the unfamiliar clothes, she was startled to see so much of her mother and grandmother staring back at her. There were the same small-boned features. The same deep-set blue eyes. The same high cheekbones. Only the hair was different. Her mother's and grandmother's red hair had come from the Ryan side of the family. Hers, jet black, was a legacy of her annulled American begetter, a man in a photograph.

The cold linoleum cramped the calves of her legs as she ran down the stairs to the kitchen. Millie was hunched over the stove, trying to coax more heat out of the shovelful of coal she had just dumped in. She prodded and poked as funnels of black smoke escaped and rose in the draft to the ceiling.

"Thought I told ye to stay in," she said crossly, snapping the soot between her hands. "Didn't do much good to tell ye to stay in until the place warmed up." She reached into the oven and pulled out a warmed-up cushion.

"Sit down and take a load off yer feet, girl. Ye looks like death warmed over."

"I didn't sleep," Tessie confessed. "The storm."

"And everything else as well," Millie added, sitting heavily in the rocking chair on the opposite side of the stove from Tessie. She began finger-combing her yellow grey hair, trying to tuck the straggling ends into the bun she had hurriedly knotted on top of her head.

"If the bloody kettle ever boils, we'll have a nice cup of tea. And that should help." She scowled and pushed the kettle around on the stove trying to bully it into boiling. She sat back and sighed wearily. "Oh my. Oh my. Oh my. The way life is."

She began talking about Carmel again, saying mostly the same things she had said the night before.

"Like a daughter to me she was." Millie looked across the kitchen and beyond the table of potted plants that were still covered with towels to keep off the night's frost. Her gaze stretched back over the years when Carmel was a child.

"I spose it was because I didn't have chick or child of me own. That's why." She paused, silently recalling why she had made someone else's child so important in her life. She turned to Tessie to explain. "Yer grandmother was so busy with her problems. Sometimes I'd take yer mother for the day jest to give poor Bertha one less person to worry about." Her eyes connected with Tessie's over the stove, trying to join her together with threads of other lives.

"Yer grandmother and me were as close as sisters." Thinking about her own sisters, all of them married in the Cove with families of their own and not enough time to visit for morning tea, as Bertha had managed to do, she added, "More so, in fact. Jest because yer family doesn't mean yer close."

Millie had filled the kettle so full that when it boiled the water bubbled out through the spout and scattered across the hot stove like frenzied marbles.

"Well, 'tis about time ye boiled," she acknowledged grudgingly and reached into the oven and pulled out the toast she had kept warming there.

In the time it took them to eat breakfast, the kitchen had heated up enough to melt the frost on the windows, and little rivulets of cloudy water and thin splinters of ice ran down the panes and puddled on the sills. Millie heaved herself out of the chair and went to get a dishcloth to sop up the water.

"Jest look at that," she grumbled, her mouth puckering in distaste as she wiped off one of the panes and then dried it with her sweatered elbow. "No wonder everything rots or mildews."

She peered out through the cleaned window. "God help us, girl. Jest look at that! Can't see yer hand before ye when the squall comes. 'Tis a good thing Tom Walsh promised to shovel us out." She explained. "He's got the government plough. Does the roads. Sez he'd do the cemetery road too." She added. "And me brother-in-law, Joe, is going to get a couple of young fellows to dig out the grave if 'tis filled in." She prophesied dourly, "And filled in 'twill be. That's fer sure."

Tessie crossed the kitchen and stood beside Millie. Together they looked out at the storm that had winnowed drifts up against the paling fence that separated Millie's yard from the pasture land that once belonged to the Corrigans. Just beyond the pasture, Bertha's house, later Carmel's house and now Tessie's house, squatted in a meadow, forlorn and dejected, like a car left behind by its owners. Snow had matted against the clapboards, and icicles hung unevenly from the window ledges.

Millie saw what Tessie saw, but neither one spoke. They

continued to stare out, Millie's blue-veined hands worrying the wet dishcloth into a ball. A sudden squall battered more snow up against the window, and both women jumped back as though the drifts had hit them in the face.

"Glory be to God," Millie gasped, her breath almost taken from her. "What a day 'tis goin' to be. What a day on the hill!" She threw the dishcloth on the table and crossed the room to put more coal in the stove. She glanced into the mirror hanging on the wall near the covered flowers. As she did so, she caught sight of her flannel nightgown poking out underneath the sleeves of her husband's sweater.

"I must look a fright," she apologized. "Aloysius's old sweater, the Lord have mercy on him. But I'll be dolled up fer the funeral. Couldn't shame poor Carmel. She always looked like a stick of chewing gum, so neat she was."

When she finished banking the fire, she glanced at the clock. "We still got two hours before Mass. If ye don't mind, I think I'll have a lie down. I didn't sleep very good either."

She started to leave the room, and her hand flew to her mouth. "Mercy sakes! I almost forgot! The envelope! Of course Carmel knew she didn't have long. Why else would she have given me that envelope? She asked to make sure ye got it. I said at the time, 'What's all this nonsense? Why can't ye give it to her yerself, since she's coming home this summer?'"

Flustered by her forgetfulness, she hurried upstairs and returned with a manila envelope, unsealed. She passed it to Tessie, repeating Carmel's request. "Said to make sure ye got it. And now I'm off fer me nap."

Tessie knew that Millie and Carmel had no secrets from one another, so she was sure Millie knew what the envelope contained. Still, she was glad that she was alone in the kitchen when she dumped the contents into her lap. There were two rings, and these shone brightly against her black skirt. She recognized one of the rings — a wide, worn band. It was her grandmother's, and it had once belonged to poor Mrs. Selena, as Bertha used to call the old woman, time having worn smooth the sharp corners of her memories.

The second ring was a narrow, white gold band. It was barely worn. She surmised this was her mother's wedding ring. The last article the envelope contained was a missal. It had an ivory-coloured cover — the type of missal a bride would carry for her nuptial Mass.

Tessie opened the missal, and just inside the cover, next to the page that contained all the statistics on her mother's marriage, was a wallet-sized photograph of a handsome man about forty years old. He was leaning against a tractor, and he was smiling into the camera.

Tessie knew the picture well. But when she had first seen it, the back had been blank; now in her mother's precise handwriting there was an address in Portland, Oregon. In the same section as the picture, and folded neatly so that it fit the dimensions of the missal, was a letter. Tessie unfolded the pages carefully, knowing before she even began reading that she was unfolding the mystery of Ed Strominski.

⟫⟩◆⟨⟪

"A bigamist, for the love of God! A lousy bigamist! And I thought the hush-hush was because he was divorced!" She spoke out loud, and her voice was a hollow echo in the empty room. She began to sob. "If only I had known. If only I had known. I wouldn't have blamed her for going to the States without me. I wouldn't have blamed her for never mentioning him."

In the letter Carmel also had related the truth about her own father and about Bertha's rape. She had closed by saying that she didn't want tears shed over what was now in the past and that, despite her sorrow, she had known magic with Ed. A fleeting magic, to be sure, she said, but magic nevertheless.

The letter was almost poetic. Tessie would never have believed that her mother was capable of experiencing magic. Her feet had always seemed to be anchored to the ground. It suddenly came to Tessie that she knew very little about the woman called Carmel. To her she had always been a summer visitor who came and stayed for two weeks every August. She wore neatly pressed blouses and spent her vacation getting her daughter's clothes ready for the coming school year. Her grandmother had never put much store in fashion, and if Tessie's uniforms were too long, she would say they would keep her knees warm in winter. If they were too short, she would tell her to brag about how tall she had grown over the holidays. But Carmel, not wanting her daughter to be different from the others, had always made sure the uniforms were neither too long nor too short.

There were other things Tessie remembered about her mother. Mostly inconsequential things. She like the bedclothes to smell fresh and clean, so she would sprinkle toilet water on the pillow when she tucked her into bed.

"Those feathers!" she'd say, sniffing the mustiness, "they smell so damp."

Tessie remembered that night she had asked her about Ed Strominski. It had been the summer after Sarah Walsh had sung the song. Carmel had been tucking the flannelette blanket around her shoulders before saying good night. The question had just popped out of her mouth as though it had been waiting there for the right time to escape.

"Is my father alive or dead?"

Carmel had jumped back as if she had just touched a hot stove. After a few seconds, she answered, her voice low, holding the shame of her lie. "For all intents and purposes, he's dead."

Tessie folded the letter and carefully placed it back in the missal. She knew she now couldn't wait until after the funeral to go to the house. And she had to go alone. She hurriedly pulled on her coat and boots in case Millie would wake up and insist on going with her. She found the extra key to her house that was always kept over Millie's kitchen window and then quietly eased herself out the back door.

Although the house had been rented for several years before her mother returned from the States, the inside still looked the way Tessie remembered it. Carmel had kept one room for storage, and when she returned, she had put everything back it its usual place.

The patchwork quilt in the kitchen — the couch quilt — was neatly folded, ready for use. On winter evenings Tessie remembered how her grandmother would get a big fire going and put potatoes in the oven to bake for their nighttime snack.

As they waited out the baking time, her grandmother would connect her to her mother and to Martin through the quilt.

"See that square right there." She would point to a piece of pewter-coloured cotton. "That was a shepherd's robe I made for Martin when he was in a Christmas play. And no other colour would do." She would chortle recalling the impish Martin. "A lot I knew about shepherds, and anyway, he would never stand still long enough for me to measure him right."

She would point to another square. "See that reddish square there. That was a couple of yards yer Great-Aunt Bessie sent home. I made it into a dress fer yer mother. She wore it fer the first time for King George's coronation. We had a big splash here. A dance and everything."

Tessie left the kitchen and wandered into the parlour. Even the doilies were back on the tables, and the pictures were rehung in the same spots as before. Tessie could hear her own childish voice asking her grandmother about the people who looked out from the frames.

"Gram, who's that?" She would have pointed to a little boy in short pants.

"That's Martin," her grandmother would answer, her voice love soft. "Yer Aunt Bessie snapped it the summer she came. It was that same summer Martin threw the rock at Eileen Tobin and hit Carmel instead. Almost clove her skull. Left a permanent white streak."

All the while Bertha talked she swiped the ceiling and walls with a threadbare towel. Sometimes she would pause and stare fallen-faced across the room, recalling some sorrow the pictures would evoke.

"And Gram, who are those two army men?" She would be pointing to two men in khaki uniforms, standing side by side in an oval frame.

Bertha's voice would take on a irascible tone, and she'd pretend to be annoyed with Tessie's constant interruptions.

"Why is it, child, that every time I starts to clean the parlour, you asks the same questions. And ye waits till I'm stretchin' for the ceilin'."

"But who are they?" she would persist petulantly. "I forget."

"One's yer great-uncle and one's yer grandfather. And don't ask me which is which because I'm not getting' down off this chair to sort them out."

Tessie remembered how she always hung onto the subject like a dog with a bone. "Is my grandfather on the left or the right?"

"Up here, child," Bertha would retort in exasperation, "I can't tell me left from me right. And what does it matter anyway which is which. They're both deep in the sod."

Tessie turned to leave the parlour to go up to the bedrooms. As she did, she caught sight of Martin's harmonica lying on the three-legged mahogany table beside the hall door. She remembered how her mother had burnt or destroyed Martin's belongings after his death, but she couldn't bear to part with his harmonica. Instead she had washed off its silver covering with disinfectant and charged Tessie never to play it. "Don't ever play that mouth organ, Tessie! It's full of germs."

Now Tessie ignored that warning. The intervening years were sufficient to kill even the hardiest TB germ. She began to play the song Martin had taught her.

> *She's like a swallow that soars on high,*
> *She's like a river that never runs dry,*
> *She's like the sun shining on the shore,*
> *My love, my love. My love is no more.*

The tears spilled down her face. She let them fall until she was finished playing, then she put the harmonica back in its place and wiped her eyes with the back of her hand. She rejected the notion of going upstairs. The remnants of herself were not up there. They were within her.

On the way back to Millie's, she kicked the snowdrifts before her and considered what she would do with the house. She had come home with the intention of selling it, but now she wasn't so sure. In her letter, Carmel had suggested she keep the house because, as she put it, "everyone needs a place to come back to." Perhaps her mother was right. Perhaps one summer day she would want to return to the Cove to pry open the parlour windows and let in the damp, salty air. Those who would carry her forward would be helping her dust the oval frames. As she reached to get at the cobwebs clinging to the ceiling, she would tell them about Bertha and Carmel and Martin and the rest of the short-tailed Corrigan family that had withered down to her, Carmel's Tessie — and to them — the children of Carmel's Tessie. She pulled her coat tighter around her, shivering from the biting wind, thinking Millie's prophecy was probably correct. It was going to be some day up on that hill.